DECEIVED III

By

The Phantom

RJ Publications, LLC

Newark, New Jersey

The characters and events in this book are fictitious. Any resemblance to actual persons, living or dead is purely coincidental.

RJ Publications

Thephantom_8182@yahoo.com

www.rjpublications.com

Copyright © 2012 by RJ Publications

All Rights Reserved

ISBN 0-9819998-9-1

978-0-9819998-9-0

Printed in the United States

September 2012

1 2 3 4 5 6 7 8 9 10

Chapter One

Stink had been questioning his choice to return to the United States ever since he arrived at the airport. And even now as he listened and gathered his things at the sound of the female's voice chiming over the P.A. system, he couldn't stop himself from heading toward the boarding area.

"Come on, pops," Rah-Rah said, his excitement apparent in his smile and hurried steps. "America awaits and I'm ready to get there."

Close on his son's heels as they boarded the large plane, Stink couldn't help but think that Rah-Rah's rush to get to America was what worried him the most. He was already too wild for the Dominican Republic and with all the drama that could be found back home, Stink wondered if maybe he was taking him to a place where he would be better off or worst. Shaking his head at the thought as they took their seats, the trip began to make less sense to him every passing moment. What he found even crazier was the fact that with the exception of Rah-Rah, everyone else in their immediate circle had made a perfect transition into their new lives in the Dominican Republic. Bonni had become the perfect wife. She and the girls loved the country wholeheartedly. Cross was in his element, living the life that he always dreamed of. With money, fast cars and even faster women who were the epitome of perfection, he acted as though he had never lived anywhere else in his lifetime. Though Rah-Rah was the reason and the cause of the majority of drama Stink faced, he was still his favorite of the three children that shared his name. And although he favored him in actions as well as feature, he wasn't even his biological son. As he glanced over at the mirror image of himself, Stink figured that maybe there was truth to the theory that, 'if you around someone long enough they really did begin to look like you after all.'

Hearing the slight chuckle that erupted from his father, Rah-Rah turned from the windows and scenery beyond and asked, "What you laughing at, pop?"

Biting down on his lip as he smiled at his son, Stink said, "Nothing, son, I was just thinking… that's all."

Switching gears as he clapped his hands together, Rah-Rah said, "Pop, I can't wait to see my grandma, aunts and the rest of the family. It's been so long, and I wonder how it's going to feel?" He rambled on more to himself than his father.

Though he gave no response, Stink nodded his head agreeably as Rah-Rah spoke. Listening to the one-sided conversation as he stared off into the clouds, Stink wanted Rah-Rah to be reunited with his real family. After all the problems that they had been forced to contend with in the Dominican Republic, due to his son's vicious temper and constant run-ins with the authorities, a part of Stink's sub-conscience could see nothing good coming out of their return to America and the city of "Bad News."

Stink and Rah-Rah's arrival back into the United States was received with no fanfare or grandeur. There were no limousines, Mercedes Benz or excited friends and family there to welcome them back, and that's exactly how Stink planned it, when he decided to notify no one that they were coming. He wanted to remain under the radar and as he and Rah-Rah hailed a cab and hopped in, it was clear that his plan had gone perfectly. Rah-Rah couldn't believe that after all the stories he had heard about his father and Uncle Cross' reign in Newport News, Virginia, there was nothing extra about his arrival to Newport News, Virginia. His father was a damn Kingpin, and back in the Dominican Republic their family was treated like royalty. The look of disappointment all but contented his features was too overwhelming for Rah-Rah to hide as he turned away from his father and stared at the passing traffic.

Stink saw the look that his son had attempted to conceal and instantly understood what caused it. He had been raised in a flamboyant manner and wasn't accustomed to anything short of being showered with attention. If nothing else, just maybe coming back home for a while would bring him down to earth, somewhat. Nevertheless, Stink couldn't let the look pass without at least making an attempt to question him about it.

"What's wrong, son?"

"Nada. I'm good," Rah-Rah replied flatly.

Stink knew how his son would quickly revert to Spanish when he was dealing with issues, and he was well aware that this was one of these times. Grasping Rah-Rah's shoulder, Stink said, "Brighten up, man, you're about to see your grandmother and aunts."

"Yeah, but where are they?" Rah-Rah questioned, stretching his arms out wide.

"Maybe they're not trying to be seen."

"Nah, man, that's not what it is," Stink smiled, thinking that he had pegged his son's thoughts accurately. "Nobody knew we were coming, Rahsaan."

"You mean our trip here is a surprise?" Rah-Rah asked, instantly pepping up.

"Yeah, I guess it is," Stink replied, thinking that maybe he should have notified someone of his intentions after all.

Rah-Rah's bright and excited demeanor immediately returned, overshadowing his black attitude from moments earlier after Stink's revelation. He now understood fully why there was no one there to meet them, and he was cool with it now that his father had explained things, but as he shifted positions in search of some comfort, there was still one thing that Rah-Rah needed some clarity on.

"Aye, pop, I understood why you kept our arrival a secret, but uh, couldn't you have at least gotten us a car?" Rah-Rah held his father with a questioning look.

Smiling at his son's serious face, Stink replied, "Maybe later."

Their trip through the city caused an array of emotions to rush the two passengers. While Rah-Rah's excitement increased with each block that they covered, due to the new and different sights that his eyes feasted upon, Stink's mind was troubled by what he encountered. Although the city had undergone a mass transformation, which was evident by the newly erected buildings, the negative past that he shared with Newport News, Virginia, still loomed heavily and there was no covering up the pain and anguish that Stink had suffered in the city. The farther they traveled into the city and the bright structures turned into a crumbling reminiscence, the inequality seemed to grow even stronger.

"We're here, 2701 Oak Avenue," the stated as they pulled up to Rah-Rah's grandmoth in the city's east end, returning Stinks thought ... the present.

"Thanks," Stink stated as he tossed the man a crisp hundred dollar bill and helped Rah-Rah gather their things. Exiting the cab, to Stink's dismay, the driveway was filled with cars as they approached the residence, which meant that they were about to be met by a house full of people who more than likely still hated his guts. Even though over 13 years had elapsed since their departure, Stink doubted that Rah-Rah's family had forgiven him for Trina's death, which they had never believed he wasn't responsible for in one way or another. Just the thought of what Rah-Rah's grandparents had put him through after their daughter's untimely death, made Stink want to stop the cab and forget his prior plans, yet, he felt that he owed this visit to his son after depriving him of his family for so long.

Leading the way to the familiar residence, Stink stared at his son realizing that they now stood the same height and Rah-Rah was no longer the little boy that he whisked away over a decade earlier, but a man who now matched his own stature. There were even times that Stink actually found himself questioning the paternity test results from long ago. Though Rah-Rah didn't share his light complexion there were so many other ways that their resemblance was uncanny.

Knocking on the door and taking a slight breath, he noted the look of nervousness that Rah-Rah suddenly wore like a second skin. Stink braced himself for the inevitable encounter when he heard the sound of footsteps approaching from the other side of the door. As the door slowly began to open and Rah-Rah's grandmother came into view, the menacing scowl that was once menacing to him no longer existed. Upon recognition of the two men standing before her, she was shocked and tears openly poured down her smooth cheek were proof of her joy as she folded her long-lost grandchild in her arms and thanked Stink for his safe return with nothing more than the beautiful smile that radiated from her face at that very moment.

Stink spoke softly into the phone, giving Bonni an update on their trip, while he watched Rah-Rah in the next room engrossed in his family and their reunion of sorts. Though for the most part everyone had been respectful to him, he had still picked up on a level of hostility from a couple of Rah-Rah's uncles. Like himself, they too had been heavy in the streets of bad News at one time or another. Only with the exception of Trina's brother, Swoop, who Stink had never had the pleasure of bumping heads with, due to the fact that he had been locked-up on a 15-year sentence throughout his relationship with Trina. The dilemma that occurred after her death, the rest of her family understood, because he was a headbuster. However, as he listened to Bonni rambling and watched Swoop who had been glaring at him ever since he arrived, from the other room, Stink knew that the big man didn't share his family's forgive and forget mentality. He didn't want any problems and he hoped that Swoop was in the same mindset as himself, but as they held one another with unblinking stares, Stink decided that he would cut out when he finished his call and let Rah-Rah and his family get reacquainted in his absence.

"…and can you believe that Rahsaanique didn't even answer her phone, bay? Then on top of that, Tauia had the nerve to come in the house last night at two on the morning?" Bonni argued. "Rahsaan, are you even listening to me?" she snapped, raising her voice an octave.

"Mmmm Hmm," Stink replied, breaking eye-contact with Swoop.

"Mmmm Hmm! What does that mean, Rahsaan? Do you agree with your daughter's carrying on this way? Is that fine with you?" Bonni was aghast.

"Baby! Hold on," Stink announced, cutting Bonni off in mid sentence. "That's not what I'm saying. I was only responding to what you were saying. It's just that the stress of being back here is taking its toll on my thought process," he added, looking back in the other room and finding Swoop still in the same spot ice-grilling him.

"I'm sorry, baby. I can imagine that it's probably strange being back there," Bonni said, immediately reverting back to wifey mode.

"Yeah, it's real strange, and to be honest with you, I'm not sure whether I'm going to leave Rahsaan here or not," he announced, watching Rah-Rah being swarmed by the house full of relatives that seemed to be arriving by the moment.

"What do you think is best?"

"I'm not quite sure, but I'm going to visit Jose tomorrow and by the time I return, I'll know what my next move will be. Regardless of my decision, I'll be home in a few days."

"Okay, baby. Look, still tell Rah-Rah I love him, and I can't wait to see you."

The sincerity in Bonni's voice made Stink long to be with her.

"I can't wait to see you as well, and I'll give Rah-Rah your message. Oh, and Bonni, get in contact with Cross and have him hit me up at the Ommi Hotel in room 971. Also, I wouldn't want any mishaps to occur at this point, so tell him to use a safe line, okay?"

"I will," Bonni said, adding, "and, Baby, I love you," before ending the call.

Stink returned the phone to his pocket and headed into the living room to see Rah-Rah before he made his exit. Though he tried his best to ignore Swoop's heated stare, it was beginning to anger him that after thirteen years he was still unable to shake the drama that seemed to plague him every time he set foot in the city. Lasting the battle with himself and letting any pretense of trying to avoid whatever situation that Swoop was trying to get into, he turned and mean-mugged the bigger man letting it be known that he was now on whatever as well. Swoop gave Stink a sinister smile and walked off. Watching him go and continuing on his son, Stink realized that the less time that he spent in Bad News, the better his chance would be of making it home.

Chapter Two

The last two days were like a world wind for Rah-Rah. Being surrounded by the family that he didn't even know existed was proving to be exhilarating and he looked forward to being around them. However, at the moment he was more interested in exploring the new and different environment that he had been granted access to. He quickly rushed out to venture a little in the neighborhood. As he walked through the neighborhood, Rah-Rah could sense the excitement that seemed to linger in the air. Never had he seen so much action taking place around him. Although he was unaware of how drugs were responsible for the festive mood that resonated with the young men who severed their wares around him, by the money that was exchanged for the miniscule packages that were given in return, he understood that something big was taking place. If not for the street tutelage that he had received from his Uncle Cross, Rah-Rah would have been completely in the blind. Nevertheless, from the moment that he had gotten old enough to understand the teachings of the street, Cross, the self-proclaimed street scholar, had taken Rah-Rah under his wing and given him the many lessons that he felt Rah-Rah would need for survival if he were ever to find himself in the urban jungle.

Rah-Rah was thinking of the weapons training, hand to hand combat and many other things that Cross had forced him to endure as he made his way through the crowd that milled in front of the store when a voice off to his left called out to him, slowing his steps.

"Aye, young-blood, slow your roll and let me holler at you," the old man said, staggering towards Rah-Rah.

After seeing who had called him, then witnessing his unkempt appearance, Rah-Rah was about to keep it moving, until he heard the disrespectful comments that the younger men who waited around the store tossed at the stranger who seemed to be down on his luck. His father and Bonni had taught him to respect his elders and just because the man who was headed towards him was down on his luck, it didn't mean that he too wasn't deserving of that same respect.

"Yeah, what can I do for you?" Rah-Rah asked no sooner as the man approached him.

Openly scrutinizing Rah-Rah, the man cupped his chin within the confines of his thumb and forefingers. "You're not from around here, are you, young man?" Not even awaiting an answer he said, "I can tell that you're foreign to these parts. Well, allow me to introduce myself, young-blood." The old man removed the torn and raggedy glove that was on his right hand, even though it was mid-summer and he had absolutely no need for it, then announced, "My name is Leon Richardson, but my friends call me Bulldog, and you are?" he asked leveling his hand in Rah-Rah's direction.

Staring from the man's face to his hand, then back again, Rah-Rah found humor in the whole situation but thought it only right that he returned the courtesy that had been offered. Shaking the man's hand Rah-Rah said, "They call me Rah-Rah, but my real name is Rahsaan and it's a pleasure to meet you, Bulldog." The smile that the man gave in response to the introduction was well worth the time that Rah-Rah had taken to give him.

"Rahsaan, huh?" the man said drifting off in thought, and then quickly snapping out of it. "I don't know why that name rings bells in old Bulldog's mind but anyway, do you think that you could lend ole Bulldog a dollar?" he asked.

Rah-Rah smiled, thinking that Bulldog had to be the most articulate and cunning bum in Newport News. Even though he had no problem giving the man a few dollars, he decided to toy with him for a moment first. "Why should I give you my dollar, man? I just met you, plus, I don't know if you're good for the loan," Rah-Rah said, folding his arms across his chest.

"Why?" Bulldog blurted, a sour look now resting on his face. "I'm hungry for one, Rahsaan. Secondly, Bulldog never reneges on a bet or loan I'll be dammed if he starts today."

"Is that right?" Rah-Rah questioned, continuing the laugh that threatened to erupt at any moment.

"It sure is, unless everything I was taught my whole life was wrong," Bulldog argued.

"Okay, you win, but instead of giving you a dollar come on in the store with me so we can buy you something to eat." Seeing the slight but evident frown that appeared when he withheld the dollar, Rah-Rah added, "Then I'll buy you a pint of your favorite wine."

Bulldog's smile stretched the contours of his mouth when he said, "That's why I fuck with you, young-blood, and if you even need anything from ole Bulldog, you can always find me out back in the alleyway behind the store.

Remember that, Rahsaan, there's nothing that goes on around here that ole Bulldog don't know about."

"Yeah, I hear you," was Rah-Rah's response as he headed inside the store with Bulldog hot on his trail.

Rah-Rah skipped on a bottle of spring water as he walked back to his grandmother's house, thinking about Bulldog as well as all the things he had seen during his lone excursion through the hood. Though the lifestyle that he had witnessed thus far was new to him, Rah-Rah was fascinated by what had been revealed. It would definitely take some getting used to, but Rah-Rah was up to the task of finding himself a spot in the mix.

"Ummm!" Rah-Rah stated, searching out the sweet aroma that he hadn't had the pleasure of smelling since his arrival into the United States. The air around him was thick with the scent of marijuana, and the closer he got to the area where it originated from, the more he found himself longing for the euphoric feeling that the herb brought him when he consumed it.

Walking further up the block, when Rah-Rah was only a few houses away from his family's dwelling, he observed the source of his investigation sitting on a porch with a cigar wedged in between his lips. Though Rah-Rah quickly turned his head in an attempt to give the young man who looked to be around his age some privacy, he couldn't help the awkward glance that he tossed in the man's direction as he took a number of deep takes from the cigar.

"What's poppin' blood?" The young man questioned in a raspy, smoke-filled voice. "You smoke?"

Rah-Rah stopped and turned around at the unspoken initiation, but found it add that the young man's reference to him as blood was totally different from how Bulldog had used the term.

After receiving no response to either of his questions, the man stood and slowly began to descend the porch steps, releasing a gust of weed smoke. "Yo, what's good, blood?"

"What's up?" Rah-Rah answered, watching the man closely as he closed the distance between them for any signs of an impending threat. Though he detected none, he quickly ascertained that the shorter man possessed a cocky demeanor that up to now Rah-Rah had never encountered in anyone besides his father and Cross.

Handing the cigar to Rah-Rah, the short, skinny man gave Rah-Rah a pound and asked, "You from around here, Damu?"

"Nah," Rah-Rah said, letting a stream of weed smoke drift from the corner of his mouth before taking another take and passing the cigar back. "I'm from the Dominican Republic."

"Word? You from Dominican?" the man's eyes widened with surprise.

Smiling at the man's lack of intelligence, Rah-Rah said, "Nah man, it's called the Dominican Republic."

"Oh, okay," the man said, drawing heavily on the cigar. "Then you must be out here doing your thing then?"

Shaking his head in agreement and reaching for the cigar, Rah-Rah wasn't quite sure of what his 'thing' consisted of, he was certain that if he continued to make acquaintances with the types of individual like the skinny man who now stood before him, there was no doubt in his mind that he would find out.

Chapter Three

Stink couldn't quite understand why he felt the way he now did, but as the elevator whisked him up to Jose's residence, his stomach was doing a series of summersaults. The sweat from his brow as the elevator came to a stop and the doors slowly began to open, gave an even greater indication of his nervousness. However, as he stepped through the doors and was met by Juan and Hernando, who grasped his hand in greeting, he felt foolish for feeling anything besides elation at the overdue reunion between himself and the only real father figure that he had ever known.

"Jose awaits you out on the balcony," Hernando announced, opening the door to the cavernous penthouse and leading Rahsaan to his boss as he had been directed.

Reaching the door that led to the balcony, Rahsaan accepted Hernando's graciousness, allowing him to open the patio door and usher him inside where Jose sat reading a Wall Street Journal. "Thanks, Hernando." Receiving a head nod and smile in response to his show of gratitude, Rahsaan watched the bodyguard make his exit then walked across the vast terrace and locked eyes with the man who had given him the life he now lived.

"Stink, how are you?" Jose questioned standing and hugging the younger man who returned his greeting with the same zest that was given. Releasing Stink and pointing to the chair beside him, Jose said, "Rest yourself and let us talk, my friend. It has been a long time since we last spoke."

Rahsaan took the offered seat and noted that although Jose had aged well since their last meeting, but the sprinkling of gray hair had begun pepper his once proud black curls. Time had started to work its magic on Jose in the same manner that it had affected him. They had been friends for over twenty years and they had gone through so much in that time that Stink found it hard to believe that they had actually made it to this point.

"So Stink, how are things in the Dominican Republic?" Jose asked, drawing Rahsaan out of his brief contemplation.

"Everything's good." Stinks reply was flat as he turned away from Jose's piercing stare and adjusted his position in the high-back chair that he sat in.

"My friend, what is it that's bothering you?" Jose moved to the edge of his seat with a questioning look in his eyes.

Though it wouldn't have surprised him if Jose was already aware of his dilemma, after momentarily contemplating the situation, Stink blurted, "I've been forced to bring my son to the United States because he's been causing somewhat of a raucous on the island."

Jose allowed Stink to vent without interference as he listened intently.

"I mean I could have sent him here by himself but I wanted to be sure that nothing I may have done in the past could come back to haunt him in my absence," Stink explained.

Placing his index finger against his temple before responding, Jose asked, "Is there something you may have done that I'm unaware of, my friend?"

Without having to think on it, Stink blurted, "Of course not."

"There's nothing to worry yourself about then," Jose said, extending his arms wide. "Your son is safe. Believe me!"

Hearing Jose's unspoken meaning, Rahsaan understood fully that Jose had just given him the guarantee that any enemy that he once had, had since been annihilated, thus his devious past deeds had been laid to rest.

"So it would be safe for me to leave him here?" Stink asked.

Jose laughed, then seriously informed, "Unless he creates new enemies, while he's here he won't live in any danger."

"I think that may happen before the week is out." Stink shook his head in disgust.

"Sounds like someone I know," Jose grinned.

Pointing to himself, Stink said, "I know that you're not talking about me."

"My friend, if your son is anything like you were in your younger days, then it may not matter where you send him. If there's trouble to find, it will attract him like a magnet."

"Jose, that's exactly what I'm scared of," Stink announced sadly.

In the short span of a day, Rah-Rah and the skinny boy who he had shared the weed-filled cigar with had become friends. It seemed that Brian who had acquired the name B-rock by some way or another had turned out to be Rah-Rah's type of guy. Though he carried himself like a young thug and seemed to be scared of nothing, the only thing that Rah-Rah didn't like about him was the fact that he praised some nigga named K.B. that he couldn't seem to stop blabbering about.

Turning down the music as they cruised in B-rocks older model Cutlass, B-rock bragged, "Rah-Rah, I'm telling you, yo… you gotta meet my nigga K.B. The nigga has got all the juice in the city and he's the fuckin' truth, man. All the Dames bow down to the five-star general, my dude."

Rah-Rah smacked his lips dismissingly. He was tired of hearing about the faceless nigga that B-rock continued to big up. If B-rock wanted to ride the nuts of a true gangster, Rah-Rah would have loved to introduce him to his Uncle Cross. "So what, is this K.B. nigga, a fuckin' soldier in the army or something?" Rah-Rah joked.

B-rock gave Rah-Rah a sharp look of displeasure, then said, "Nah man, that's his rank in the Bloods, yo."

"What's up with this Blood stuff you keep talking about?" Rah-Rah's interest had suddenly been piqued after hearing B-rock speak about rank and a group of individuals who were willing to bow down to another man because of it.

B-rock was beyond disbelief as he frowned at Rah-Rah. "Man, I know that you've been stuck in the Dominican Republic for the majority of your life and shit, but there's no way that you haven't heard about the Bloods." Pausing to gauge Rah-Rah's reaction, he boasted, "We're the worst gang that the U.S. has ever seen, nigga!"

Rah-Rah concealed his interest well, but still asked, "Well, how did your man K.B become a five-star general?" His words dripped with sarcasm. "Did he go to school for that shit?"

B-rock was slowly beginning to lose his composure due to Rah-Rah's ill-mannered humor. "Look Rah, this shit is real over here, my nigga… and on the real, you can either get with this shit or get rolled over by it."

Nodding his head up and down in response to what just been revealed to him, there were still some things that didn't make sense to him about the Bloods, but Rah-Rah could sense the sincerity in B-rock's tone. Suddenly serious, as Rah-Rah turned to face his new partner, he only wanted to know one more thing. "If I wanted to become a five-star general, what would I have to do?"

B-rock took a moment to mull over Rah-Rah's question before giving the answer that he knew would deter Rah-Rah from any further questions on K.B.'s status and why he held reign over the whole city's Blood populace. "You got to put in lots of work, yo! And in case you don't know what work means, it's Red-Rum spelled backwards!" B-rock's laughter resounded through the car after misreading the look of excitement Rah-Rah wore as fright.

However, as Rah-Rah leaned into the upholstered seat and closed his eyes, he had already decided that he would become the next five-star general and K.B. was now on borrowed time. He also decided to put an end to B-rocks laughter as well. "Aight, I see where you're coming from now, man. Now that I've got a better understanding of what it takes, I'm ready to set this Blood shit in motion as soon as possible. So check it, holler at your man K.B. and see who he wants murdered first, then we'll deal with the others later."

B-rock's jaw and mouth hung slack at the completion of Rah-Rah's words. The joke was suddenly on him, but instead of laughter Rah-Rah turned the music back up and began to bounce his head and shoulders to the sounds, excited that he would soon get the chance to put Cross' vast training to the test.

Chapter Four

"Stink, have you lost your damn mind?" Cross blared through the phone. "What are you thinking, son?"

Moving around the hotel room, packing the suitcase with the phone pressed between his ear and shoulder, Rahsaan smiled at the defined accent that Cross used when angry. Even after spending the last thirteen years in the Dominican Republic Cross was still a New Yorker to the death, and not even his advanced age had calmed the New York swagger that resided within him.

"Relax, bruh, everything is in order...." Stink began only to be cut short by Cross' rapid-five rebuttal.

"In order, are you fuckin' serious, fam? You're killing me right now, Stink." Cross spat. "You and I both know that there's no such thing as order where your son and my nephew is concerned. Rah-Rah is bonkers when he's here with us and you actually expect him to stay out of trouble in Virginia with nothing but that lame ass family of Trina's to hold him down?" Before Rahsaan could respond, Cross yelled, "Hell no, he won't!"

Stink's mind was made up and he realized that his conversation with Cross was going nowhere. He had a few things that he needed to see to before he boarded a late flight back to D.R. and he figured that they could continue their argument when he returned. "Cross, I got to see to some things, man. I'm going to call you when I touch down, fam," Stink said ready to end their call. However, he heard the last thing that Cross said before he beat Stink to the punch and ended their call first.

The words kept playing themselves through Stink's mind as he stood in the middle of the floor with his phone dangling by his side. "You're going to regret this shit before it's over with, Rahsaan! You just watched and see!" At that moment, Stink hoped for his sake and Rah-Rah's that Cross' premonition failed to come true, because he would never survive the guilt if any harm was to come to his son.

"Okay, have I forgotten anything?" Stink rambled on, unable to hold Rah-Rah;s gaze due to the sadness that now gripped him as they hurried through the airport terminal. The closer they got to the gate that would separate them, the more Stink felt his emotions bubbling to the surface.

"Nah, Pop, I think you pretty much covered everything," Rah-Rah said, grasping his father's wide shoulders in a soothing gesture. "I've got the contact information for your man, and I promise to stay out of trouble."

Coming to an abrupt stop as they reached the departure gate and flight that had begun to board, Stink turned to his son and beheld the picture that stood before him. It was clear that Rah-Rah was far from the little boy that he had once nurtured and protected; a man now stared back at him. His heart ached at the reality that whether he and Cross like it or not they had no other choice than to release the hold that they had on Rah-Rah and give him the chance to find his own way in the world as they had done themselves.

"Son, I," Stink began but stopped to clean his throat when he began to choke up. "I want you to know that we love you and you can come home whenever you're ready."

. "I know, Pop."

Quieting him with a wave of the hand, Stink continued, "If there's anything that you need, and I do mean anything, don't hesitate to call me or your uncle Cross and we'll move Heaven and Earth to make it to you." Enfolding his son in a bear hug, Stink released him and slowly began to back peddle towards the gate at the sound of the last boarding call blaring over the P.A. system, but not before Rah-Rah's words reached him.

"I love you, Pops. Tell Bonni and the girls I love them as well, and call me when you touch down," Rah-Rah yelled, waving to the only father he had ever known as a tear slid from his eye, staring down the empty corridor, for the first time since Stink had rescued him over thirteen years earlier, Rah-Rah truly felt alone.

Chapter Six

"K.B., man, you should have been there! I ain't never seen anything like it, Blood." B-rock was beyond excitement as he spoke about Rah-Rah's deed with passion.

K.B. glared at the two Bloods who had gone on the mission with B-rock and Rah-Rah and received affirmative head nods. He too was shocked but happy to hear the account of Chico's death. The M.S. 13 leader had been a thorn in his side for years, stealing Blood territory all over the city. Now, finally, the Honduran troublemaker had been disposed of. The funny thing is when he gave B-rock the instructions for the new recruit to handle the problem, he never expected the lil' nigga to complete the task. What were the chances of him doing the unthinkable when so many men before him had failed at the task?

"So you say, he was throwing knives at them amigos like a fuckin' ninja and shit, huh?" K.B. smiled and rose up out of the high-back chair that he had been sitting in and started walking around the desk.

"Yeah, K.B., dude was real with his gangster. I mean, who the hell uses knives to kill a nigga when they got a damn gun on 'em?" B-rock said what everyone in the room had already been thinking.

The thunderous music that resounded through the office door from out in the strip club area was the only thing that could be heard while K.B. thought about what had been revealed to him. Though he never spoke to or with new recruits for some reason, tonight he chose to break a long-standing rule. He wanted to meet this Rah-Rah nigga.

"You say he's out in the club, right?" K.B. questioned B-rock.

"Yeah, he's in the lounge sweating the hos."

"Send him in on your way out," K.B. said flatly.

The men realized that they had been dismissed, yet they were accustomed to being spoken to in the no-nonsense manner that K.B. used with all his Blood soldiers. Thus, as they exited the office and sent Rah-Rah inside, they thought nothing more of the incident as they each found strippers of their liking and settled in to enjoy the night.

Rah-Rah was ready to meet the mighty K.B. but he hated to leave the company of the voluptuous Pepper who had introduced herself and kept him company while B-rock and their little crew left him behind. Draining his drink and thinking how much he would have loved to hit the chocolate frame that she all but opened to his curious gaze, Rah-Rah knocked at the office door.

"Come on, it's open!" K.B. yelled.

Entering the large office, Rah-Rah scanned the room seeing the plush coach and chairs, 60 inch flat screen and leather pool table, before he gave his complete attention to the man who leaned against a desk in the center of the room.

"What's poppin', Blood?" K.B. questioned, pointing to the coach. "Have a seat."

Doing as he had been told, Rah-Rah watched K.B. closely as he closed the distance between them and took a seat in the chair across from him. Though K.B. couldn't have been older than thirty, he was overweight and his hairline had begun to recede. However, his richly tailored attire spoke of his affluence and influence.

"Well, Blood, my man B-rock speaks highly of you… and it's come to my attention that you put down a viscous show earlier." K.B. gazed Rah-Rah's demeanor as he spoke.

Rah-Rah downplayed his part in the night's events. "They give me too much credit when all I really had on my side was lots of luck and two idiots for my targets."

K.B. laughed at Rah-Rah's show of modesty but knew better than to believe a word of it. However, at that moment he realized that he liked the young killer who sat before him. "Okay, I hear you, young blood, but on the real, those two idiots that you just spoke of were cold-blooded killers. Thanks to you they're no longer a problem to the B.N.B (Bad News Blood) set, and on that note, I'd like to welcome you into our organization." K.B. leaned forward and gave Rah-Rah a pound.

Grinning, Rah-Rah wanted to show K.B. more excitement and gratitude for allowing him entrance into the Blood organization then he actually felt. In all truth, Rah-Rah could care less about being a Blood. Joining the organization only put him in a better position to take it from the unsuspecting fool who called himself running game.

"Now that we got that out the way," K.B. said, standing to his full 6 foot 4 inch height, "while you were in the club, did you see anything that you liked?"

The smile that Rah-Rah now wore at the remembrance of Pepper was genuine. "I sure did, and her name is Pepper."

"Say no more, she's yours for the night," K.B. announced, reaching for the phone and speaking in a hushed tone.

As Rah-Rah replayed K.B.'s response to his saying that he liked Pepper, he concluded that maybe there were a number of perks that went along with being a Blood after all.

"Oh, Rahsaan... sssss," Pepper moaned, slowly watching her hips on the tip of Rah-Rah's length, then allowing him to slam himself all the way into her depths. Breathing harder as she squelched up and bit her lip, the way he sexed her had her body trembling.

Rah-Rah thought that Pepper was pretty, but her array of fuck faces made her beautiful, and he'd been receiving them and many other treats from her all night long. Feeling her muscles milking him as she slowly slid up and down his ebony length, he concluded that if the other strippers who worked for K.B. were as talented as Pepper, he would be spending a lot of time in the establishment.

"Oh, si.... Ohh.....ohhhh," Pepper cried out, bouncing and grinding on Rah-Rah's pole as she fought for her nut.

"Shit!" Rah-Rah exclaimed at the warm tightness that enveloped him, bringing his seed to bursting proportions as well. Pepper was out of control now, and her means were deafening and pleasurable as the orgasm that she had fought so hard to obtain shook her body. She came for what seemed like minutes before she jumped off Rah-Rah and ripped the condom from his length, choosing to complete the task with her mouth. Rah-Rah's eruption, though guilty obtained, was as earth-shattering as Pepper's as he watched her swallow him whole through a pair of wide eyes.

Kissing the head as she grabbed the cup of ice water off the dresser and took a drink, Pepper stroked the steadily softening slab of meat in her hand lovingly and gave Rah-Rah a sly smile. "You good, daddy?"

After the long night that Rahsaan had experienced at the hands of the thick beauty who lay beside him, the only thing that Rah-Rah could do was shake his head up and down.

Chapter Seven

"I see you had another long night, huh nephew?" Swoop asked , appearing out of nowhere and blocking Rah-Rah's path.

"What?" Rah-Rah frowned, tired and not in the mood to be answering any questions.

Wearing a smirk, Swoop leaned against the wall and flexed his huge arms as he folded them across his chest. "No offense, nephew. I just been noticing that you been spending mad time with them Blood niggas, and I'm starting to hear things.'

"Is that so?" Rah-Rah laughed.

"Yo, it's your life, my man. I just thought that I'd pull your coat to the fact that your mens and 'em are bad news, that's all." Swoop smiled, hunching his shoulders in a manner that stated that either way there would be no sweat of his back.

Rah-Rah prided himself with being a good judge of character, and he found nothing that was remotely likeable about his uncle. In a short period of time he had revealed himself to be a snake and Rah-Rah planned to keep a close eye on him.

"Yeah, aiight," Rah-Rah said. "Was there anything else that you needed to warn me about, or can you possibly get out my way so I can get a little shut eye." Rah-Rah's words dripped with sarcasm.

Swoop ice-grilled his nephew, then gave Rah-Rah enough room to pass but not enough that he would be able to go by him comfortably. Thus, receiving a heated glare in return Swoop was unprepared for what happened next.

Rah-Rah smashed his shoulder into his uncle as he walked past, sending the larger man stumbling. He never stopped or slowed his steps as he reached the stairs, but the words that reached his ears as he climbed them took his breath away.

"That's all right, lil' nigga. You got that!" Swoop stop. "But let me leave you with one more word of advice before you bounce... Don't let your little fiasco with Chico and Manuel go to your head. Real gangsters don't die that easy."

Turning to face his uncle, who laughed and gave him a conspiratorial look as he walked out of the house, Rah-Rah read the threat that lied beneath his uncle's statement and didn't like it one bit. Though he hated to admit it, somewhere along the way he made a mistake and he realized that down the line there was a possibility that it would come back to haunt him. As Rah-Rah dropped down on the stairs and placed his head in the palms of his hands, he hated that he had failed one of his Uncle Cross' main rules; Rah-Rah had left a witness to Chico and Manuel's murder alive and he knew that he wouldn't be able to kill his mother's brother.

"Baby, look who's here," Bonni announced, walking down the stairs and sashaying her thick, bikini clad frame across the white sandy beach with her arm entwined in Cross' arm. Her smile was bright and beautiful as she swung her long, dark tresses over her shoulder and leaned forward to place a soft kiss on Stink's lips, before turning to Cross and winking her eye and racing off into the surf.

Watching his wife dive into the clear, blue Ocean, Rahsaan's breath still caught in his chest whenever he laid eyes on his gorgeous wife. It amazed him that in her forties she was still as stunning today as she had been the very first time he had laid eyes on her and her daughter nearly twenty years ago.

"Ungh umm!" Cross loudly cleaned his throat as he sat hunched in the beach chair wearing a mad-face.

Returning his attention back to his reluctant guest, Rahsaan wanted to laugh at Cross' blatant show of immaturity but he didn't want to throw gasoline on the fire that had been brewing between them ever since he had returned from America without Rah-Rah. He had missed his best friend and brother dearly and wanted nothing more than to repair their relationship.

"I'm glad that you finally remembered how to get to the house, man. I was beginning to worry about you," Stink announced, trying to break the ice.

Cross sucked his teeth and picked at his fingernails in response to Stink's attempt at breaking the ice.

"Come on, Cross, Damn! Stop trippin', it ain't that serious," Stink argued. He'd had enough of Cross' attitude.

"Not that serious, huh?" Cross sat up in his seat and locked eyes with Stink. "Well, how about I put you up on game, son. Your boy, Rah-Rah, is no different from you and I at the same age, B. The problem is, somewhere along the way, you seem to have forgotten that."

I ain't forgot shit!" Stink blared, holding Cross' stare, then turning away.

"Just hear me out, high. Aiight?" Cross relaxed. "The boy was raised by a set of killer ass kingpins, and all

- 32 -

he's ever heard his whole life is stories of our exploits. Now that he's been unleashed in that same environment with the tools that we've equipped him with since the age of five, there is no way that Rah-Rah is not going to do him, bruh."

Even though Stink didn't want to believe what Cross was saying, the truth of his words hit closer to home than Cross could ever know, because Stink too had been second guessing his decision ever since his return to the Dominican Republic. To make matters worst, their communication with Rah-Rah had faded lately and that in itself had raised an alarm.

"Okay, Cross, I have to admit that you're making mad sense, and this is what I'm going to do...." Stink began, grabbing his phone and punching in a series of numbers. "Jose. Yeah, it's me. I'm fine and yourself? Umm hmm." Stink laughed. "I need a favor, my friend. Send someone to Virginia and check up on my son. If there's anything of importance going on, hit me back at this number, all right. Thanks Jose."

Stink ended the call and laid the phone back on the table. "If there's a problem Jose will find out. Until then, let's just give Rah-Rah the benefit of the doubt. Shit, it's only been a couple weeks and how much trouble can one man actually cause in such a short period of time.

Chapter Eight

"I'm not going to accept anymore excuses!" K.B. yelled, smashing the ax handle into the young man's ribs who was strapped to the table. "You niggas got me fucked up if you think I'm going to keep taking these motherfuckin' losses. As of this moment, if you give my dope spots up to these MS13 bitches you're gonna pay in blood. Do I make myself clear?" K.B.'s voice loomed throughout the club filled with a sea of Blood faces.

A chorus of, "Yeah, Blood. We hear you, man, and yeses," rang out as K.B. motioned for Rah-Rah to follow him and stormed out of the club. Rah-Rah followed close on his heels and caught the keys to the red Rang Rover that K.B. tossed him before getting in the passenger side. Hopping in the driver's seat and handing his strap over to K.B. for safekeeping in the stash spot, Rah-Rah started the truck and pulled out into traffic.

"Roll the shop and grab this paper from Meesa, yo," K.B. directed still angry.

Rah-Rah said nothing as he u-turned the truck and headed in the direction of K.B.'s girl, Meesa's beauty parlor. They had been rolling together daily since the first night that they had met, and although K.B. was cool to hang out with, as Rah-Rah had expected, he wasn't built anywhere near the reputation that the streets had bestowed upon him. Today's beating of the young Blood was proof, because Rah-Rah would have killed him instead.

"Yo, Rah," K.B. began, drawing Rah-Rah from his thoughts, "If we had more real dudes like yourself in our crew, we could easily wipe those MS13 niggas out, man. Even with Chico dead they have only seemed to become more of a problem."

Pausing to think on the problem, Rah-Rah said, "I think that we have more real soldiers in our ranks than you give the Bad News Bloods' credit for, K.B.

"Word?" K.B. questioned incredulously. "You really think so, Rah?"

"Yea, I do." Rah-Rah knew that if he were their leader their ranks would only be filled with the most vicious killers.

"So you're saying that if I were to give you the heads up you could put together squad of murderers for me?"

"No doubt. Not only would I put them together, but with your blessing I would lead a campaign of death and destruction against the MS13 while regaining our territory in the process." This would benefit Rah-Rah much more than it would K.B. if he were to actually go for it.

"That's a good idea." K.B smiled brightly, slapping Rah-Rah on the shoulder as he pulled the truck in front of the beauty shop. "See, that's why I like you, nigga. Not only can you think, you follow orders good. Now go get my paper from Meesa, my nigga."

Rah-Rah exited the truck thinking that his plans were falling into place much faster than he had thought. However, as he entered the shop that instantly became quiet no sooner than he walked through the door, he was treated to an array of beauties.

"Hey there, handsome," Meesa flirted, drawing giggles from the many women who lounged around them. "Where is my sad excuse of a man?" she added walking towards him.

"K.B. is out front. He asked me to get that," Rah-Rah stated absentmindedly allowing his eyes to tread over her succulent breasts, flared hips, and round behind.

"Don't I wish," Meesa smiled conspiratorially. "Follow me," she winked causing an explosion of laughter from the women and making Rah-Rah blush as he trailed behind her towards the contents of K.B's safety deposit box. She was once one of K.B.'s strippers.

"Close the door, sweatheart." Glancing over her shoulder as she bent at the waist, giving him an unobstructed view of her rounded, heart-shaped behind, Meesa said, "How old are you, baby?" as she began to open the safe.

"Old enough to handle myself, yet young enough to make it seem taboo," Rah-Rah boldly replied, his eyes never leaving her ass.

Meesa stopped what she was doing and scrutinized Rah-Rah closely, seeing the look of pure lust was plastered on his features as he held her in an intense gaze. Laughing in order to lighten the mood, although she found him to be deliciously attractive, he worked for K.B., was at least ten years younger than her and she couldn't imagine him being worth her life.

"Ungh umm, now ain't you something, with your cute ass self." Meesa shook her head and stood with a bag of money in her hand. "Just for the record, what's your name?"

Meesa asked, staring into his dark, glistening eyes once more, finding their depths hypnotizing.

"Rah-Rah, but being as though we're going to soon be good friends, feel free to call me Rahsaan." Grabbing the bag and tossing her an intuitive smile, Rah-Rah left the office. He liked what he saw, and he had decided to alter his original plan somewhat. When he decided to get rid of K.B. for good he would keep Meesa around. There was no doubt in his mind that she would be worth it.

"Grandma, how are you feeling today?" Rah-Rah asked, planting a kiss on her cheek as he took a seat beside her on the couch.

Baby, God is good," she announced, rubbing his head gently. "He bought you back to me, now didn't he?"

"That he did, grandmother... that he did." Rah-Rah allowed his words to linger, enjoying the feel of his grandmother's hands as they massaged his head. He felt a special connection to her that the rest of his dead mother's family were unable to obtain, and being there with her the last few weeks had been a blessed experience.

"You know, Rahsaan, your mother loved you very much," his grandmother said, staring off into space as she spoke. "Even though she made the mistake of cheating on that boy and he turned out not to be your father, she loved Stink also. It's a shame that they went through so much while she was alive, yet God still saw fit to have him raise you as his own anyway." Shaking her head at the way that the Lord worked at times, she added, "Stink has been a father to you in all the ways that matters, and he's a damn good man. Never forget that, son. Okay?"

"I won't, grandmother... I promise," Rah-Rah said, momentarily regretting the path that he had already begun, knowing that his pop would be brokenhearted when his wrongdoings were finally unleashed to the world.

Chapter Nine

"These are the niggas that you've picked, huh?" K.B. questioned, walking tiger, his pit-bull around the pool and the young men who stood around him.

"Yeah, Blood, this is our elite," Rah-Rah lied, meaning that the men who stood around them were his army.

K.B. had never been one to give credit to his underlings, but in less than a month's time Rah-Rah had entered their ranks and blew past the other soldiers. Someone had taught him well. Although K.B. had yet to mention it, he couldn't understand why Rah-Rah never sweat him about money or product but always seemed to stay laced in the best of everything. Deciding that he would question him about it later, K.B. said, "You will each answer to Rah-Rah, and he will report directly to me."

Rah-Rah's face was impassive as he watched K.B. stroll around the pool with tiger on a gold chain like he was Nino Brown or something. After giving him the squad of Bloods, unbeknownst to K.B. he had turned over control of his whole dynasty and his reality would soon collapse upon him like a ton of bricks.

"Rah-Rah, we need to talk in private. You niggas bounce!" K.B. snapped, walking through the patio doors.

Watching him go inside, then giving each of the fifteen men who walked past "Blood" handshakes, Rah-Rah entered K.B.s house and slid the door shut behind him.

"I'm down here," K.B. yelled.

Rah-Rah walked through the exclusively furnished home, in the direction of where the voice had come from. He peeked in every room as he slowly descended the spiral stairs, but stopped in his tracks when he saw something that caused his eyes to bug out of their sockets. Meesa stood in front of a full length mirror, naked, rubbing her beautiful dark skin with baby oil. Rah-Rah was stuck as he watched her fingers sink into her soft skin. Her body was glorious and he wanted to touch it so badly that his fingers were nonchalantly flexing.

"Rah-Rah, come on, Blood!" K.B. followed causing Meesa to turn around and catch Rah-Rah behind her. Walking to the bedroom door, she stood wide-legged with her hands planted on her hips, proudly displaying her body to his hungrily feasting eyes. Meesa than gave him a sneaky grin and slowly closed the door.

"Shit!" Rah-Rah growled, wanting Meesa's pussy so bad that he could taste it. Only as he hurried down the steps and found K.B., he knew that he would get the chance to do just that.

"Damn, Damu, what took you so long?" K.B. questioned pouring two glasses of liquor and passing one to Rah-Rah.

"I was busy watching your bitches pussy, nigga!" was what Rah-Rah wanted to say but what came out was, "I was sweating how tight your crib is, Blood. I've never seen anything like it," he lied, being as though he had been raised in a mansion.

"That's what's up, but you know it goes… only the best for K.B., my dog," he boasted.

"Anyway, now that you got your crew all handpicked and shit, what's the next move?"

"I want to take a few weeks to train them and gather some information on a few of the MS13's operations, and then I plan to cause our Latin friends a lot of problems." Seeing the excitement that K.B. was unable to hide, Rah-Rah figured that there was no better time than the present to ask, "What kind of artillery can you get your hands on?"

"Why?" K.B.'s eye raised. "What type of weapons do you need?"

"Let's see, Rah-Rah did a mental calculation. "I'm gonna need fifteen AR-15's with five spare clips a piece and seventy-five thousand bullets, as well as fifteen sixteen shot Beretta's with the same amount of spare clips and ammunition, a number of concussion grenades, laser scopes for each of the weapons and body amour," Rah-Rah said, watching K.B.'s smile turn into a frown.

"Damn, nigga! You going to war with the MS13 army or the Taliban?"

"I'm going up against the MS13 army and whoever else chooses to stand against the B.N.B, and with all due respect if you want to regain this city, it would be in your best interest to fill this order for me."

"You're going to fuckin' break me, Blood, but if that's what you need then that's what you'll get. Now is that all?" K.B. asked shortly.

Thinking on it, Rah-Rah joked, "You think that you may be able to find a nuclear warhead, nigga!" They burst into laughter.

Meesa listened in on their conversation from her porch on the stairs. What she heard caused her already brewing juices to flow unrestrained down her thick, dark thighs. She loved herself a gangster, and even though she had never cheated on K.B. with any of his workers, Meesa wanted the young nigga who called himself Rah-Rah badly. He possessed a handsome cockiness that was hard to come by alone, much less be found in an individual who personified the characteristics of a killer. Unlike K.B., who Meesa knew firsthand to be a top notch con-man and coward, she knew the real thing when she encountered it. Now, after hearing him use finesse to direct K.B. to do his bidding and give him his own crew of assassins in the process, Meesa knew that Rah-Rah aspired to be the Boss and actually possessed the game to accomplish the feat. She also made up her mind that when the time arrived that K.B. would be toppled from his throne; she would continue to occupy her seat at the top. As she slowly returned her steps and closed the bedroom door behind her, Meesa smiled at the knowledge that her mother didn't raise a fool.

Chapter Ten

"I can't believe you, yo." B-rock argued.

"What can't you believe, man?" Rah-Rah asked, knowing the answer but wanting to hear it out of B-rock's mouth instead of continuing to second-guess why his man had been acting shady the last few weeks.

"Pssst…" B-rock shook his head and looked away.

"Aiight then, nigga, if that's how you feel get at me when you're ready to get whatever is eating at you off your chest." Rah-Rah stood from where he had been sitting on the porch and wiped his jeans down, then turned to walk away.

"Rah, how you going to put a squad together and not give your boy a spot?" B-rock blurted.

Inwardly smiling as he stopped and turned to face B-rock, Rah-Rah saw the hurt in B-rock's face before the smaller man had the chance to look away. Though he had known the reason that B-rock had placed a distance between them, he had his own reasons for making the choices that he had made. Regardless of what B-rock thought, there had been no malice in his decision.

"Damn man, that's what's been bothering you?" Rah-Rah asked cautiously. "Come on, fam, that ain't for us. I would have straightened this weeks ago if you had just come to me with the issue instead of getting all in your feelings and shit." Rah-Rah laughed.

'Oh yeah? Well I guess that means I'm in then, huh?" B-rock gave Rah-Rah a hope-filled glance.

The desperation that Rah-Rah saw before him caused him to look away. There was no way that he could let B-rock down lightly so he just gave it to him straight. "Nah dog, I can't let you in."

"That's fucked up, Rah!" B-rock spat, standing up. "If it wasn't for me, nigga, you would have never got put on, much less found yourself in the position that you are now. This is how you pay me back, huh?" Shaking his head, B-rock was boiling when he said, "You know something, you're a real cold piece of work, man."

Rah-Rah allowed B-rock to vent, holding his own anger in check. "Now that you're finished, let me speak, aiight?" Receiving no response, Rah-Rah continued. "I don't make rash decisions, B-rock. I make calculated ones, and the reality of the situation is that you're not cut out for this part of what I plan to do…"

"What's that supposed to mean, yo? There ain't nothing soft about B-rock, my dude." B-rock argued, banging his chest.

If Rah-Rah didn't like B-rock and respect the fact that he was as real as he claimed to be, he would have slapped the hell out of him, but having him wasn't a part of the scheme that he had planned for B-rock. Even though he didn't trust him enough to share what he proposed to do, Rah-Rah had no other choice than to tell B-rock enough of the truth to put him at ease.

"Look, relax man. Ain't nobody questioning your gangster, because if I felt that you were soft, I wouldn't even be fucking with you," Rah-Rah snapped, calming B-rock somewhat. "Now, I didn't want to say this but you've left me no other choice. The reason why I didn't pick you is because I want to keep you alive to help me get this paper, and at least half the niggas I picked won't make it."

"B-rock's eyes avoided in shock. "They won't make it?"

"Nah. I've spent nearly a month now training them hard for a number of missions that will claim a lot of lives and put us in position to make a whole lot of paper. And that's where you come in," Rah-Rah stated, retrieving the smile that suddenly brightened B-rock's features.

"Well, now that you put it like that, I think I can understand. Now how about you tell me how you and I are supposed to get this paper that you speak of when only K.B. decides who eats and when?" B-rock asked.

"You just let me worry about the details, man. All you need to be thinking about is how you're going to spend your dough," Rah-Rah said, meaning every word.

"Enter," Jose stated, looking up from the computer screen he had been glued to until he heard a tap on the door. Directing the two men who entered the room to take a seat, he shut the computer off and clasped his fingers in front of him as he leaned back in his leather, high-back chair.

"So what have you two brought for me?" Jose asked flatly, seeing the fear that resonated on the faces of both his associates.

Miguel, the larger of the two Spanish men cleared his throat and leaned forward in his chair," Patron," he began addressing Jose as the Boss that he was, "So far no one has turned up in Chino and Manuel's murders. We have our people in Virginia searching high and low for their killers, and although no one is talking we're sure that they will surface soon."

Jose listened to Miguel while holding him in the unblinking gaze, forcing him to lower his eyes upon completion of his speech. Giving Miguel no response, Jose turned his attention to Santiago who he hoped had fared better than his associate and asked, "What about you, my friend?"

"Patron, from what we've been able to find out so far, the young man that you asked us to check on is hanging out with a number of low level Bloods. So far he doesn't seem to be involved in any illegal activities, but he has been in the company of one of our competitors who goes by the name of K.B. on numerous occasions."

What had been revealed to Jose grabbed his attention, but wasn't enough to cause him alarm. Santiago had clearly stated that Rah-Rah didn't seem to be involved in anything illegal, only Jose didn't like the fact that he had attached himself to associates such as K.B. who had been Chino's strongest competitor. Nevertheless, Jose didn't feel that Rah-Rah's actions, thus far, warranted Stink's involvement.

"Keep an eye on him, Santiago, and keep me informed on his movements." Jose turned his eyes back to Miguel, acknowledging Santiago's slight bow and release of breath as he sat back in his chair. Silence permeated the room and Jose noted Miguel's discomfort as the large man began to sweat.

"Miguel, listen to me and hear me good," Jose softly stated. "It has been over a month and a half since Chino's murder and I don't understand why his murderer still lives and breathes. We have an army in that city and there is no excuse for you not to know who killed my nephew. None!" Jose yelled, causing Miguel to flinch. "Now get out there and find whoever is responsible and don't return until his head sits right here!" Jose slammed his fist on the desk and dismissed them with a wave of his hand.

Watching the men leave, Jose made his mind up that if Miguel didn't bring him the head of the man who killed his nephew soon, he would take Miguel's head instead.

Chapter Eleven

Rah-Rah watched K.B. closely while the self-proclaimed five-star general sat beside him in quiet contemplation. His attention was centered on the busy restaurant across the street that Rah-Rah had brought him to see, and what he saw was beyond interesting.

"You really think that they're moving work out of that joint, Rah?" K.B. asked excitedly, turning to speak for the first time since their arrival.

"Yeah, I'm pretty sure of it," Rah-Rah answered shortly.

Cutting his eyes back across the street and saying, "It wouldn't surprise me one damn bit," he added, "Rah, how did you come across this place?"

Rah-Rah smiled. He could hear a trace of suspicion in K.B.'s tone, yet his grin told a different story. "I just played my cards right and patiently waited for their men to lead me here, as well as a number of other places."

"There's more spots than just this one?" K.B. was beyond himself with excitement.

Rah-Rah nodded his head 'yes', seeing the greed that already had K.B. counting what he felt was his money.

"When do you plan to hit 'em up, son? You've been training niggas for a minute now."

"Tonight's the night, Damu," Rah-Rah announced, bringing a huge smile to K.B's face. However, inside he was seething at the realization that K.B. hadn't taken the time to ask him whether the mission would be safe or if he could join them. The cowardice that Rah-Rah saw in him was beyond disgusting, and it took every bit of strength that he possessed for him to draw out his plan until the right moment instead of putting a bullet in K.B.'s dome right then.

K.B. had no idea of the thoughts that ran rampant through Rah-Rah's mind at that moment. As usual, he was too caught up in thinking about himself and what he would soon gain because of the blood and sweat of another. Failing to recognize Rah-Rah for the dog that he really was, and thinking that he would be happy with scraps like the rest of his Blood brethren, K.B. said, "If you pull this shit off and they're really holding paper up in that joint, I'm about to throw you something nice, my nigga."

"That's what's up, big dawg." Rah-Rah forced a smile. Only as he pulled off, listening to K.B. talk incessantly about the night's caper he couldn't stop thinking about the day that he would throw K.B. something as well. He just hoped that K.B. was ready for the hot ones that awaited him.

Rah-Rah gripped the gold-plated pistol and marveled at its beauty, feeling the power that came along with its ownership as he thought about the night that he had taken it from Chino's dead body. No one in his crew knew of its existence, but after tonight, he planned to strike a mighty blow to the MS13 organization while placing fear into the hearts of everyone who encountered him and his new pistol from this point on. Placing it inside the strap that hung beneath his arm and donning his jacket, Rah-Rah stared at his reflection in the mirror. What he saw before him was a combination of his father and uncle, and that was all that he had ever wanted to become. Thus, as he back pedaled towards the door, never losing sight of himself, Rah-Rah winked at the man he saw and said, "This is what you've always wanted, Rah, and there's no turning back now, lil' daddy."

Bursting through the bathroom door and witnessing the preparation taking place around him caused Rah-Rah's heart to swell with pride. He had spent the last few weeks putting his men through the most grueling training possible, and as he looked around him, Rah-Rah knew that it had paid off; they had truly become a real elite unit and he was proud to be leading them into battle.

"You niggas ready to put this work in?" Rah-Rah asked, catching the SK that his little man, Trooper, tossed him. The fifteen responses that rang out around him affirmed what he already knew. "Aiight then. We've been over the plan enough times that each one of you should be able to pull the caper with blindfolds on," he stated, looking around him to make sure that no one had any questions or comments. "Now, before we walk out this door, anyone here want to bail? If so, do it now because I don't want no one with me that really ain't with me."

The ice-grills that contorted the faces around him as they stared throughout the room in search of the weak link in their armor proved once again that he had chosen the right group of men. It also heightened his resolve that these same men would soon help to make him rich and keep him safe. For that alone, Rah-Rah planned to see to it that his men would share in the wealth as well.

"Okay, Bloods, let's go get this paper." Rah-Rah said, grabbing the bag filled with flash grenades, "And don't hesitate to kill anyone who tries to resist!"

Four cars entered the Conquestral restaurant and bar's parking lot from a number of entrances and pulled into the spaces that would give their three man teams the closest access to their prepared entry points. They had gone over their strategic operations numerous times, and to remain inconspicuous to the many Latin's patrons that entered and exited the establishment, a man slipped from each of the cars in intervals until only the drivers remained.

Rah-Rah waited patiently, giving his men time to work their way into their respective spots. Peering down at his G-shock watch and seeing how much time had elapsed since their arrival, he turned to Trooper and said, "Let's get it poppin', baby," feeling the Dodge Charger lurch forward. Trooper whipped the car into the parking lot as Rah-Rah removed the gold plated Colt. 45 and screwed a silencer on the tip, and then placed a set of white contacts in his eyes. He grinned at the thought that he would forever be remembered at that moment as the crazy nigga who ran up in their spot on some 'Bully' shit.

"Oh shit, Blood, where mine at?" Trooper pulled the slide back, jacking a round inside the chamber of his rifle.

"Next time we roll, we'll all rock these joints," Rah-Rah promised as the three men around him exited the car and hurried towards the front door of the restaurant. Swinging the door open and firing his Colt into the Spanish maitre D's face, Rah-Rah wished that he had thought to get the white contacts for his whole crew. The chaos that erupted all around him as his men shot the Latino gangbangers that they knew and others that they didn't in order to bring the fear that was necessary to obtain order, suppressed any other thoughts that Rah-Rah may have had with the exception of getting money.

Moving through the crowd who were now face down on the floor, Rah-Rah ignored the cries and whimpers of the wounded as he flung the door open that led to the kitchen and grabbed a cowering cook who put his hands up in fear.

"Please, no hurt me, senior!" the man cried.

Rah-Rah dragged the man across the floor to where another man laid with his hands above his head, and without asking the man a question he lowered the gold-plated .45 and shot the man in the back of his head. Before he pulled the trigger, he saw the fleeting glance that both men gave one another when they laid eyes on the gun. Rah-Rah had no doubt that they knew who the gun belonged to before him, and now that he possessed it, everyone who knew Chino also knew who killed him.

"Now I'm going to ask you this one time, and if you answer correctly you have my word that I won't do that to you," Rah-Rah said, using the barrel of the gun to point at the man who lay on the floor with a hole in his head. "Comprende?"

"Yes, senior!" The man shook his head furiously.

"Yeah, I thought you would." Rah-Rah heard light laughter behind him. "Now, where is the coca and dinero?" Rah-Rah asked turning the gun on the scared man.

"Si," the man's eyes lit up. "Mucho dinero's! Mucho coca!" he cried, pointing at the wall.

Looking from the man to the wall and back again, Rah-Rah helped him to his feet and gently pushed him forward. "Undalay! Undalay!" he yelled, causing the man to trip as he hurried to the freezer that stood near the spot that he had pointed to and began to punch a series of numbers into a keypad. The group of Blood soldiers that stood near him held their weapons at attention, awaiting any unseen threats that may have arisen.

After completing his task, the Spanish man moved aside. At that moment the wall in front of them slowly began to rise upward, revealing an elevator lift. The man turned to Rah-Rah and pointed to the elevator. "Dinero and coca."

"You three come with me. The rest of you stay here," Rah-Rah instructed, pushing the Spanish man on the lift ahead of him. Placing the .45 back in it's strap and reaching for the SK that hung at his side, Rah-Rah removed the safety and compressed the button that activated the infrared beam. After giving his men time to do the same, he said, "It may be a trap so keep your eyes open, "then he hit the button marked 'down' and felt the lift come alive.

Rah-Rah felt a nervous energy like he had never experienced before as his mind tussled with the unknown possibilities that could await them at any moment. So far they had encountered little to no opposition which he found odd. However, when the lift stopped and they exited with their weapons raised, Rah-Rah couldn't believe that the MS13 organization had been so careless. What he saw as his eyes swept the confines of the basement was neat, plastic wrapped packets of money that measured at least a foot in diameter, a number of money counting machines and at least forty bricks of what he assumed was heroin instead of cocaine because of its dark brown hue. Bags of ecstasy pills and barrels of marijuana were scattered around the room as well.

"I want this shit packed up and out of here as fast possible. Get everyone who we can spare down here now," Rah-Rah ordered the man who stood the closest to him, instantly sending him into action. He then turned to the scared Spanish man and said, "Gracias, mi amigo," bringing a smile of relief to the man's face that quickly resolved when Rah-Rah said, "Trooper push his fuckin' wig back, man!"

"No senior...." Was all the man could plead before the silent slugs from Trooper's weapon ended his life.

"Thugs! Thugs!" glancing down at the wide-eyed Spanish man grinning at his work, Trooper turned and locked eyes with Rah-Rah who held him with a smile. "Yo Raucous," he snapped, giving Rah-Rah a new name that he had no idea would soon stick to the young general who would in time be reknowned for bringing the raucous, "remember to grab me a set of them eyes next time!"

Laughing, Rah-Rah gave the young Blood a pound and left the room. He had done what he came to do, and now he felt like he had finally been able to step into the shoes of his father and Uncle Cross. All of his training had paid off in a big way tonight, and for the first time Rah-Rah really felt like he belonged. With him, it had never been about the money; money was the last of his problems; he had five hundred grand in a safe deposit box in one of the city's largest banks. He wanted the power, and tonight's caper would undoubtedly place him one step closer to his goal.

Chapter Twelve

"We did that shit, Blood! We really did that shit, nigga!" K.B. announced, shocked but excited that their B.N.B set had actually stuck a blow of such magnitude against the massive MS13 army. Embracing Rah-Rah, K.B. drank greedily from the bottle that he grabbed with his free hand and yelled, "You, damu, are the reason that we're here tonight. This nigga here is the truth!" he added, thinking about the immense sum of money that Rah-Rah had delivered to him earlier in the night. Any doubt that he had once harbored against Rah-Rah no longer existed; in his eyes the man who he now hugged and gave props to in front of the club filled with Blood brothers had solidified himself.

Rah-Rah listened closely to K.B.'s drunken banter, inwardly smiling at the elevated position that the head of their set continued to shower him with. In his eyes, the night's events had all been worth it just to see how easily K.B. had bowed to him after receiving the money and work that he would soon take back. Rah-Rah's thoughts disappeared and his attention was instantly consumed by the beautiful female who gracefully moved through the crowd carrying a briefcase. As she headed his way, no one else existed around them; their eyes were locked in a silent dual.

"You all know my baby, Meesa," K.B. said, grabbing the briefcase no sooner as she reached the slightly elevated platform that would normally be crowded with strippers. Opening the metal case and flashing the thickly banded bills, K.B. announced, "This case holds a quarter of a million dollars." A number of surprised "ooh and ooho" erupted around the room at the mention of so much money. He then handed the case over to Rah-Rah and said, "Burn it, 'cause you earned it, son."

The room filled with people looked on in awe when Rah-Rah accepted the briefcase and handed it to Trooper who stood near the platform. "Share that shit up with our people, Blood. We all earned it." Saluting K.B. who had a dumbfounded look on his face as he stood with his mouth aghast, Rah-Rah hopped from the platform and joined in the celebration that his men were now engrossed in.

Meesa couldn't help the gaze that she tossed in her man's direction after the stunt that Rah-Rah pulled. He stood in place, drinking greedily from his bottle, hatred burning beneath the fake smile that he wore. If nothing else, Meesa knew that K.B. hated to be outdone in any way, and he had intended to make a grand statement by presenting Rah-Rah with such a grand sum of money, only to have Rah-Rah steal his shine when he gapped it with his man instead. Meesa liked how Rah-Rah had used K.B.'s show of strength to make an even greater statement of his own. He showed the type of traits that real leaders carry. His swag was on point, and Meesa decided that regardless of how young he was, the next time that the opportunity presented itself, she was going to seduce him.

Rah-Rah never allowed Meesa to escape from his sight. He watched her move through the slowly thinning crowd like a hawk circling its prey, and each time their eyes met, her smile brightened and she seemed to place an extra twist in her hips. He wasn't sure whether it was the alcohol he had consumed or the ecstasy pill that he had taken for the very first time, which was responsible for his heightened urgency to have Meesa, but his pole ached with the yearning to explore her depths.

"Rah, holler at your dude real quick," K.B. said, waving him over. "Check it, I've got some shit to handle but we'll get up tomorrow, aight?" he stated, banging fists with Rah-Rah.

"Aight. Be easy, Blood." Rah-Rah said, watching K.B. and another Blood leave the club. He quickly did a once over of the club, searching for any sight of Meesa. He was ready to give up and find someone else to quench his sexual thirst when he felt a gentle tap on his shoulder. Finding who he was searching for was right behind him, Rah-Rah knew that the best gift of the night had yet to be presented when Meesa hooked her finger in a 'come here' motion and led the way through the club to K.B.'s office.

Momentarily stopping to open the door, before Meesa could finish turning the key Rah-Rah had already pressed his groin into her behind and reached around to grab a hand full of her swollen titties, eliciting a soft moan from her as her body relaxed into his hand. Rah-Rah pushed the door open and Meesa into the office, closing it and locking it behind him. He knew that he was taking a big chance fucking K.B.'s woman in his office, yet he had already crossed the point of no return. As she leaned up against the large desk and pulled the short dress over her head, revealing her chocolate D-cup breasts and phat mound in a lace Victoria Secret panty and bra set, he feasted on her deliciously proportioned thighs and the gap that advertised her round ass cheeks from the front.

"I hope you're up to the task, lil' Rah-Rah," Meesa said, sucking on her bottom lip.

Rah-Rah responded by lifting her up on the desk and sliding between her thick thighs. He then began to kiss her with the intensity that he had held dormant ever since he laid eyes on her earlier in the night. Their lips and tongues found a rhythm, and as their fever grew, their hands too began to explore.

"Rahsaan!" Meesa mumbled at the touch of Rah-Rah's large hands kneading her exposed breasts, softly pinching the extended nipples between his thumbs and forefinger as he nibbled on her neck and ears. Unhooking her bra and removing it, Rah-Rah took his time kissing each of her titties, alternating between the two as Meesa squirmed on the desk, moaning softly and guiding his head from breast to breast.

Meesa raised his head and slid her minty tongue into his mouth as she slowly raised his shirt over his head. She then broke their kiss and unbuckled his belt, loosening his jeans and lowering them and his boxers down over his hips. Her eyes widened at the length and thickness of his dick when it was released from the confines of his boxers. Meesa licked her lips and swallowed the saliva that threatened to drip from the corners of her mouth as she used both hands to stroke it from its head to its base and back, loving the thick veins that pulsated with blood and its hardness.

Rah-Rah's eyes were glued to Meesa as she stroked him. She was so sexy and her body was crazy. Unable to take it any longer, he pried her hands loose and pulled her body to the end of the desk, then spread her legs wider as he ripped her thin panties from her and pushed her down on the desk.

"Shit!" Meesa groaned, loving the way he took control. She knew that Rah-Rah was ready to break her off, and after having to fake it for so long with K.B.'s little dick and lackluster skills, she was excited when felt one of her legs being thrown over his shoulders and he slowly started to push the head of his dick into her tightness. She arched her back and forced him to go in deeper than planned.

"Damn, Meesa!" Rah-Rah groaned, slamming his length inside her, hitting rock bottom.

"Sssss...... oh God, Rahsaan!" She cried out feeling him deep in her stomach. "I can't take you like that, boy."

"Umm hmm," Rah-Rah growled, slowing his pace but still going deep, rotating his hips with every stroke. Meesa no longer had any complaints. Her moans and low whimpers became louder and more insistent as he fingered her clit in concert with his deep strokes. He knew that her orgasm was quickly approaching as her breathing sped up and her legs began to tremble.

"Uuuh, right there, Rahsaan! Don't you dare stop!" Meesa groaned loudly. Her body began to shake violently as Rah-Rah continued his assault on her wet pussy.

Rah-Rah pulled out and lifted her from the desk, leaning her over the desk and changing positions. Grasping her hips, he slid back inside her and began to hit it deep and hard. The sounds of their bodies smacking together, her juices popping and the sensual moans that slid from her parted lips filled the room. This and the effects of the ecstasy caused Rah-Rah's excitement to overflow.

"You think I'm up to the task now, Meesa?" he asked, pounding into her opening.

"Yes.... yesss... yesssss, Rahsaan. Ssss, you feel so good inside me!"

Hitting the pussy harder, her ass jiggled uncontrollably with every stroke. "Throw that shit back then if it feels so good to you," he ordered, feeling her immediate compliance. "Damn!" That's what I'm talking about." Rah-Rah's strokes quickened.

"Come on, Rahsaan," Meesa pleaded on shaky legs as she tossed a pain-filled look over her shoulder. "Let me get that nut baby! Please!"

Tuning out her pleas, Rah-Rah continued to pound into her tightness. Whether Meesa realized it or not, she was in for a long night, and tonight would only be the first of many more to come.

Chapter Thirteen

"Congratulations, Rah, or is it Ruckus because that's what I've been hearing everywhere I go these days?" B-rock laughed.

"Real funny, nigga, but I'm still Rah-Rah to you." Reaching in his pocket as he dropped down on the porch steps besides B-rock, he removed a thick, banded roll of bills from his pocket and tossed it in B-rock's lap.

"Damn, what's this?" B-rock's eyes were wide as he thumbed the roll of cash excitedly.

"It's your cut of last night's caper, yo. I knew that you didn't think that I would forget about you."

B-rock was tongue-tied as he calculated that he had at least fifteen thousand dollars within his grasp. Never had he possessed so much money at once. "Nah, umm, I didn't think you would forget a nigga," B-rock lied. Extending his fist to Rah-Rah he said, "Thanks, man."

"Pssst, that shit ain't nothing!" Rah-Rah blew the compliment off. "We're about to get some real paper, B, so don't even sweat the small shit," he said, thinking about the five keys of heroin he kept.

Although B-rock couldn't imagine that he would be able to come up any more than he just had, he liked the sound of what Rah-Rah was saying. Now he just wondered what Rah-Rah had in mind. Whatever it was, B-rock was interested.

"Whatever you got in mind, count me in," B-rock announced, pocketing his newfound riches.

"So that's your word?" Rah-Rah questioned. He held B-rock with a no-nonsense stare.

"Hell yeah it is!" B-rock exclaimed, returning Rah-Rah's glare.

"Then it's settled, my dude." Standing, Rah-Rah began to walk away then tossed a look back over his shoulder. "I'm going to take over Tidewater Park out in Norfolk tonight, so be ready when the sun goes down because you're going to run it for me."

B-rock's mouth hung slack as he watched Rah-Rah walk away with a smile on his face. He wasn't sure whether his newfound friend had lost his mind or what, but Tidewater Park niggas were renowned for their independences and treachery, and there was no way that they would just stand by and allow a crew of Newport News niggas to come in and take over their projects. When the sun went down he would receive the answer to all of his questions.

"You sure that's him?" Rah-Rah asked his passenger, never taking his eyes off the young man who exited the pearl white Mercedes Benz S500.

"As sure as I am that my mommy had me," Bulldog slurred, scratching his groin and staring out the passenger window. "Duke used to get that dog food money out the Park wit' my nephew before the nigga went and got himself a life sentence," he added. "Yeah, that's Jamil fo' sure."

Rah-Rah continued his observation, noting how niggas converged on his jack no soon as his feet hit the pavement. There was no doubt in his mind that the nigga was the man in his hood; his jewels, his whip and popularity defined his status.

"Hey Bulldog, how does this Jamil nigga get down? I mean, is he bout his or what?"

"Son's a fool," he answered without a second thought. "He came up under a nigga named Benny Reed who had the city under pressure throughout the late 80's and early 90's. Murder is second nature to the lil' nigga, Rah-Rah, so if you have any intentions of going up against him, make sure that you're not bullshittin'!"

Rah-Rah laughed, then put the rented Cadillac CTS in drive and slowly drove past Jamil and the group of hustler that circled him. He drove slowly because he wanted to memorize his victim and the men around him. However, as he turned the corner and lost sight of Jamil in the rearview mirror, Bulldog's words played in his head. 'If you have any intentions of going up against him make sure that you're not bullshittin'. Turning up Rich Boy's anthem, ' Sitting on top of the World' Rah-Rah inwardly smiled at the fact that the ole' nigga that lounged beside him without a care in the World, had no idea who he was in the company of. When the time arrived, the last thing that Rah-Rah planned to do was bullshit with Jamil or anyone else who had what he felt was his.

"You good, B-rock?" Rah-Rah asked, removing his gold plated Colt. 45 and checking his clip. He then connected it to the new contraption that he had designed and had made especially for occasions such as this.

"Yeah, I couldn't be better!" B-rock replied sarcastically. "I can't think of no other place on Earth that I'd rather be at this moment then with you, on my way to get murdered."

Rah-Rah laughed, then checked to make sure that his vest was secured just in case someone happened to get off a lucky shot. He saw humor in their predicament even though he knew that B-rock thought he was crazy.

B-rock glared at Rah-Rah, wondering what he found so humorous. As far as he was concerned, there wasn't a damn thing funny about the two of them rolling up in Tidewater Park dolo, talking about they were taking over something. He wasn't sure how they did things back in the Dominican Republic, but B-rock understood that to pull that shit in Norfolk was the equivalent of asking to be killed.

Seeing the projects up ahead, B-rock decided to make one last attempt at stopping Rah-Rah from committing suicide. "Aye, listen here, family! The shit ain't going to work, man." His heart rate began to beat much faster when he saw how many niggas occupied the block. He had to swallow the vomit that threatened to erupt from his stomach when Rah-Rah pulled the fitted hat that he wore low and put in a pair of all white contact lenses.

"Pull right up beside that white Benz, playboy, and I'll handle the rest," Rah-Rah said feeling a rush of adrenaline that he was beginning to yearn for. Like his Uncle Cross had taught him, there was no other feeling that could compare to knocking a nigga's head off. And ever since he'd killed Chino, Rah-Rah had been chasing the feeling.

"Shit!" B-rock barked, releasing the safety on the Chinese made AK-47 that lay across his lap with a double banana clip taped to it. He was scared as hell, but as he pulled up beside the Benz as directed and heard Rah-Rah say, "I got this nigga," as he exited the passenger door, B-rock was left with no other option then to play his position and hold Rah-Rah down.

Rah-Rah saw Jamil standing up against the side of a building surrounded by a group of hustlers, politicking, and made a straight B-line towards him. He felt the weight of his Colt with every swing of his arm and inwardly smiled as he thought about the fact that he should have at least tested his new apparatus before going into a war zone. However, as he reached the group of men and drew their attention, his last thought before addressing Jamil was 'oh well.'

"You Jamil?" Rah-Rah questioned, walking inside the circle of men and invading Jamil's personal space.

"It depends on who's asking!" Jamil replied, taking a step back and reaching an arm inside his North Face jacket.

Locking eyes, Rah-Rah felt no fear as he held Jamil's stare. He knew that he had the upper-hand so he never thought to look around him at Jamil's people. "They call me Ruckus," Rah-Rah said, using his newly christened nickname, "And I was told that you're the man to see out here, my nigga. You are the one who runs the Park, right, or am I hollering at the wrong nigga?" Sarcasm dripped from Rah-Rah's words.

Jamil flipped the safety on his weapon and ice-grilled Rah-Rah, not liking the way he had approached him. He hated the wicked look that the intruder gave him as he held him hostage in the white-eyed stare. "Yeah, I'm Jamil, and whoever you are they told you right. I run this shit, B. Now what the hell you want?"

Rah-Rah tossed a glance over his shoulder for the first time since his arrival, noting the evil looks that Jamil's crew held him with. Smiling, he then turned back to Jamil and said, "I want the park for one, and I just wanted to make sure that I would be killing the right nigga, unless by chance you would rather keep your life and continue to run this joint for me," Rah-Rah said calmly.

It seemed as if the night became deathly quiet after his announcement. Jamil held Rah-Rah with a momentary look of disbelief, then looked over Rah-Rah's shoulder and searched the darkness for the army that had to be somewhere behind him. Seeing no one, his attention returned to Rah-Rah once more.

"Either I'm being punked or you have a fuckin' death wish, so you think you might want to run that shit by me again, Ruckus or whoever the hell you said you were?" Jamil growled, removing his Desert Eagle and letting it rest against his leg.

Rah-Rah's arm swung upwards so fast that Jamil never saw the Colt .45 slid from the sleeve of his jacket until the bullet excited out the rear of his head. Before the men around him could reach for their weapons a series of sniper rifles barked from a number of positions that Rah-Rah had strategically placed his men earlier. As ordered, his men had left one of the men standing and as Rah-Rah turned his gun on the trembling man who smelled like he had urinated on himself, and he calmly asked, "You want a job, nigga?"

The man's eyes were wide as he vigorously shook his head 'yes'.

Ignoring the people who ran around him, Rah-Rah said, "Good answer. What's your name?"

"Q... my name's, Q," the man stuttered.

"Aight, Q, that's what's up." Back-peddling across the grass in his haste to make it back to the car and B-rock who swept the AK-47 in every direction as he stared down the sights, Rah-Rah pulled a Newport pack sized package out of his pocket and tossed it to Q. "Bubble this and see how they like it. It's a sample, so move it however you see fit. When you finish hit my dude on the jack and we can get rich. The number is inside," Rah-Rah announced getting in the car.

Q released a pent of breath as he watched the Cadillac CTS bend the corner. He couldn't believe what had just happened. As he looked around him, seeing a number of dead homies, his connect, Jamil, was the one who he had always liked the most. However, after witnessing the black blood that formed a puddle beneath his head, then looking at the package he held, Q had no choice in the future course of his life than to get money with the new nigga in the Park. Hearing the sounds of sirens approaching, as Q disappeared into the maze of buildings he concluded that it didn't matter whether he sold dope for Jamil or Ruckus as long as his money stacked.

Chapter Fourteen

"Baby, have you spoken to Rahsaan?" Bonni asked, walking up behind Stink with her arms wrapped around his waist.

Though Bonni couldn't have known it, Stink had been thinking about Rah-Rah as he stood on their balcony peering into the ocean and gently lapping waves. "Nah, I haven't been able to contact him lately," Stink said, turning to embrace his beautiful wife, showing more zest than he actually felt.

"Oh," Bonni stated, shortly. She could see the worry in her husband's face, and even though she too was concerned, Bonni hated to see Stink in this state. Closing her eyes due to the soothing feel of Stink's massaging fingers as he caressed her neck and head, she pulled back and looked upwards into his handsome face. "Baby, I hate to sound so negative, but my gut feeling is telling me that things aren't right with Rah-Rah back home."

Giving her a false smile, Stink said, "Look baby, you don't have to worry. I'm sure that..."

"No, Stink!" Bonni exclaimed, cutting him off. "Listen to me, boo. I know that Rahsaan isn't my biological son, but I raised him from the age of five and love him as if I birthed him myself. That being the case, I have a strong connection with him that only another mother can understand. Therefore, if I tell you something isn't right with him, then you need to take heed, baby."

'Relax, Bonni, Rahsaan is fine," Stink said, trying to convince his wife of something that he himself wasn't so sure of. "If there's nothing else that I'm sure of, I know that our son is more than capable of taking care of himself. Plus, I left him five hundred thousand dollars in a safety deposit box in case he needed anything. The boy is just finding himself and getting reacquainted with his family in America. Not to mention, you and I both remember how exciting life can be when you're eighteen."

"My son will be nineteen in two months," Bonni said sadly.

"Okay, nineteen then," Stink said, opening his arms wide and beckoning Bonni into them with a nod of his head. "He's just fine, baby, and I'm sure that he'll call when he finds the time." Stink held his wife tightly and gently rocked her, hoping that he had succeeded in calming her fears, somewhat. However, as he stared out across the endless expanse of ocean that separated them from Rah-Rah, he too felt uneasy about his inability to contact his son, and he realized that as Bonni said 'something back home wasn't right.'

"I don't know what to tell you, High!" Cross said, using the slang that he had used in the early nineties. Shifting gears as he whipped the Black Ferrari in and out of traffic with ease, Cross cut his eyes at Stink then quickly returned them to the winding road. "What did Jose say?"

Hunching his shoulders, Stink said, "Nothing."

"Nothing? What the fuck you mean nothing!" Cross barked, nearly sideswiping a car while glancing at Stink.

"He ain't never get back at me, son!" Stink said. "I don't know what's up with him these days, man. I guess he has more important shit going on than trying to chase behind Rah-Rah all the way in Newport News."

"That's bullshit, High! After all the money we made that nigga back in the day he can't brush you off like you're a fuckin' peon or something. What the fuck is wrong wit' son!" Cross argued, getting angrier by the moment.

Stink shook his head at his man, truly amazed that Cross was still as wild today as he had been thirteen years earlier. He couldn't help the smile that he wore as he thought about all that they had been through in their time together as well as how Cross had just reacted to Jose not contacting him with the information he had requested. He realized that his Spanish friend was probably one of the biggest drug lords in the United States, but after cultivating their relationship for over two decades he too felt that Jose owed him this small favor.

"Hit that nigga again, High! Apparently he's forgot who the fuck he's dealing wit', and I'd hate to have to pay our old compadre a surprise visit," Cross threatened.

Although normally Rahsaan would have felt that Cross was acting extra and discounted his tirade, after receiving no response from his old friend and mentor for so long, he too was beginning to feel disrespected. He wasn't sure what was going on but he would call Jose again later, in search of some well-deserved answers.

Chapter Fifteen

"I can't stand that little nigga!" Swoop barked, dropping the remainder of his uneaten chicken back in the box that sat in his lap when he caught sight of Rah-Rah and a group of his boys exiting their cars.

Looking up, Dundee had grease and hot sauce smeared all over his lips as he searched for the culprit who his partner spoke of. "Who the hell you talking 'bout?"

"Man, I'm talking about my sister's son… that lil nigga wit' the red sweat-suit and white fitted hat on," Swoop spat, pointing his finger. "If he wasn't family I'd split his fuckin' wig!" he added, showering the steering wheel and dashboard with spittle.

"Damn, I forgot that Trina had a son, man. That nigga done got big as hell too," Dundee said, noticing how big Rah-Rah's chest and shoulders were in comparison to the men that walked inside the chicken shack behind him.

"Pssst, that nigga ain't shit… just like the nigga that raised him!" Swoop argued, glaring at the entrance to the chicken shack.

Dundee and Swoop had been thick as thieves since Juvenile Hall, over twenty years earlier, and like himself, Swoop had done a lot of crud ball shit in his time, but for the life of him he couldn't find any viable reason why his partner should have been so angry at his own nephew.

"Aye, I ain't trying to get all up in your family's business and shit, but what the lil nigga do that got your big ass all in an uproar?" Dundee questioned, stuffing his mouth with mashed potatoes as he awaited an answer.

Swoop tossed his man an evil glare, thinking whatever his reasons may have been for disliking his nephew, it was really none of Dundee's business, but before he had the chance to tell him so, a grey and black Aston Martin pulled into the parking lot and honked the horn. Soon after, Rah-Rah walked out of the restaurant and got inside.

"Oh shit!" Dundee exclaimed after seeing the dark-skinned female lean over and give Rah-Rah a long sensual kiss.

Although Swoop said nothing, his features carried the same sentiment as he watched his nephew swap spit with one of the oldest chicks in the city, not to mention the wifey of one of the most notorious gangsters in Newport News. How Rah-Rah had pulled that off, Swoop would never know.

"Damn, man, what you make of that?" Dundee asked, shaking his head.

Returning Dundee's gaze as they watched the Aston Martin pull out of the parking lot and dart out into traffic, Swoop said, "Your guess is as good as mine, but I'd be willing to put my money on the fact that K.B. wouldn't be too happy if he knew what the hell was going on between nephew and his girl."

They shared a good laugh at K.B's expense, only as he laughed along with Dundee, Swoop's mind was turning a million miles an hour. Though he hated to admit it, his nephew had made a number of major moves in a short period of time and it looked like he had aspirations of climbing way higher in the ranks than Swoop could have ever expected. With that thought in mind, Swoop decided that with Rah-Rah's rapid growth in the city, there was one of two ways that he could come up off him. Being that he had heard through the grapevine that Rah-Rah was moving the work, he could approach him about getting on board, or he could just wait until his nephew stacked his chips and take it all like he always did. Quickly juggling the two options, Swoop made his decision. He would continue to patiently bide his time, and when Rah-Rah blew up he would claim his riches.

"We ain't got a lot of time," Meesa said, unbuttoning her dress and allowing it to flutter to the Motel's floor. She quickly shed her panties and bra as she watched Rah-Rah.

"Look here, Meesa, we can't keep doing it like this," Rah-Rah said, feeling the blood rush into his steadily swelling penis, "We have to be careful."

"Umm hmm," Meesa said, pushing him up against the wall and tongue kissing his mouth slowly. She wanted Rah-Rah badly and that was all to it. Easing her way down his chest, she loosened the drawstring on his sweats, lowered them and pulled his length out through the slit in his boxers. Being the freak that she was, Meesa hurriedly swallowed his head and worked her greedily grasping lips down his length.

Rah-Rah's eyes rolled back in his head as he watched her work through lowered lids, loving every moment of the ecstasy that Meesa's warm mouth provided. Fighting to support his rubbery legs, he was forced to grasp the back of her head and wrap her long hair in between his fingers for support. Gently rotating his hips, he slid himself in and out of her mouth. However, as the pressure became too much and he felt his juices coming, Rah-Rah tried to pull out only to have Meesa force his whole dick down her throat and start to hum.

"Oh shit, Meesa!" was the last thing Meesa heard before she felt Rah-Rah's seed collide with the back of her throat. Her cheeks caved in with the intensity of her suction, draining every drop from Rah-Rah's loins. She then released him from the confines of her mouth as she continued to stroke his length and licked at the cum that covered her lips.

Smiling at Rah-Rah's astonished look, Meesa asked, "What was that you were saying about us needing to stop?"

Rah-Rah pulled his shirt over his head and removed his boxers and sweats, choosing to let his actions be his response. "Stand up and bend your sexy ass over!"

"Meesa loved when Rah-Rah took control, so she quickly stood, turned to face the bed, then bent over and spread her legs. Rah-Rah roughly slid his nine inches inside her tight center and heard Meesa gasp as she grabbed two hands full of the thick comforter and held on. He then began to pump into her at a feverish pace, fucking her brains out.

"Ooooh... Rahsaan... that's my spot!" Meesa cried out loudly. "Slow down, baby!
Please... slow... down!" she begged, burying her face in the comforter.

Spreading her cheeks apart and watching his soaked dick slide in and out, he loved the way Meesa's ass jiggled with each of his deep, pounding strokes. Yet, his excitement grew even more when she began to finger herself in rhythm to his movements.

"Yeah, baby… fuck your pussy. It's all yours!" Meesa cried, rotating her fingers against her clit. "Yes… yesss… oh, yeeeeessss! Sssssss," Meesa's body collapsed on the bed and she began to shake and moan.

Rah-Rah's eruption followed Meesa's causing him to slump against her already prone body. Their breathing and the air-conditioner's grinding sounds were the only noise in the room besides the rustling of the sheets as Meesa and Rah-Rah searched for comfortable positions.

"That was so good, Rahsaan. God! You know how to work me out," Meesa purred, pressing her body tightly against Rah-Rah as he lay on his back and closed his eyes, enjoying the relaxing feel of her hands massaging his chest.

"You weren't too loud yourself," he announced, kissing the top of Meesa's head. Rah-Rah then lifted her chin so that she was able to peer into his eyes, "On a serious note, though, we're going to have to fall back from one another for a while."

"And why is that?" What, you don't want to spend time with me anymore?" Meesa pouted, sitting up on the side of the bed and reaching for her panties.

"Come here!" Rah-Rah barked, pulling her back against his chest. "Me wanting to spend time with you has absolutely nothing to do with it." He now spoke in a soothing tone. "We're beginning to get reckless, and I don't do things this way. You hear me, ma?"

Shaking her head 'yes', Meesa turned her head away so that Rah-Rah wouldn't see the moisture that suddenly clouded her eyes. She was beginning to lose control of herself where Rah-Rah was concerned, and never had Meesa planned to fall so hard and so fast for him. This just wasn't the way that he did things, yet nothing about what had been taking place between the two of them was normal.

"We're going to continue to do what we do. I'm just saying that we're going to have to be more careful when we move. I'm not prepared to bump heads with K.B. yet, ma, so just bear with a nigga. Aight?" Rah-Rah realized that his scheme was moving along a lot quicker than he had originally planned. Even though he hadn't conquered K.B.'s empire yet, the one woman who the so-called five-star general claimed as his wifey really belonged to Rah-Rah, and until she no longer served a purpose, he planned to keep her. Now he just had to make sure that K.B. stayed asleep to his plot.

Chapter Sixteen

"Damn. That nigga Q be trappin' like that, Blood?" Rah-Rah asked, giving the young Blood who stood from his seated position at the table so that Rah-Rah could sit. Nodding at the two other men who helped B-rock count the piles of money that littered the table, Rah-Rah accepted the blunt from B-rock's extended hand and pulled deeply from it.

"Yeah, son don' stepped his game all the way to the moon since you killed his man and gave him the keys to his hood," B-rock joked, smiling.

Thumbing through the stacks of cash, Rah-Rah said, "I guess that means that shit worked out just like I planned then. How much we got so far?"

"Uh, let me see," B-rock said, searching the table until he found what he had been looking far. "Here we go," he announced, picking up a piece of paper and staring down at it. "So far we're already counted up over one hundred, eighty-thousand dollars."

Doing his own count in his head, while listening to the electric money counter that was hard at work, then seeing the pile of untouched bills that sat in the middle of the table, Rah-Rah quickly concluded that they still had one hundred, twenty-thousand left in front of them. This meant that their new man, Q, had moved nearly a quarter of the work that he had held back from the raid on the MS13's supply spot. This was a large feat for one man to accomplish in only three weeks' time. It also meant that Rah-Rah would have to come up with more product and new connect much sooner than he had planned.

"Oh yeah," B-rock stated, snapping his fingers. "He also said that he's been having a problem with a crew of New Yorkers who are trying to set up shop in their hood now that Jamil is dead. It seems that they were the ones who were frontin' dude his work. I told him that we would handle it, tough."

"You told him right, Blood. We're going to handle it alright," Rah-Rah said grinning. "Tell him to find out where them niggas be at, and we'll take care of it from there." Grabbing a stack of cash and fanning it in the air, he added, "As long as he keeps putting it down like this, I'll personally see to any nigga who has a problem with him!"

They all burst into laughter as each of the men shook their heads in agreement. They too needed Q to continue getting money like he was at the moment, because thanks to him, their whole crew, at least the ones who Rah-Rah commanded, were making more money than they had ever imagined. There was no way that they would allow anything to happen to Q or the one man who had changed their lives in a short period of time. Rah-Rah knew this, and he planned to continue breaking bread with the men around him.

"Trooper, you and Weegy come with me," Rah-Rah said, standing and grabbing eight ten-thousand-dollar bundles of cash off the table and handing the now short blunt back to B-rock. "I'm gonna cop us some wheels, Blood. It's about time that we step our whip game up."

"Sounds good to me, man, but what you gon' tell K.B. when the nigga begins to ask where all this extra shit is coming from?" B-rock asked, grinning devilishly.

Never breaking his step as he headed for the door, Rah-Rah arrogantly stated, "Don't you know why by now that I answer to no one. I'm the captain of my own destiny, baby boy." The door that closed behind them shut out B-rock's laughter.

"Great choice," the car salesman smiled broadly, handing the keys to the three Denali trucks to Bulldog. "Would you like to invest in our five year warrantee offer?" the Middle Eastern salesman asked, attempting to increase his commission for the three used trucks.

"Hell nah!" Bulldog stated sharply, reverting back to the cold-hearted ole head that he really was, until he caught the mean-mug that Rah-Rah tossed him and realized that if he didn't play the part that Rah-Rah had cleaned him up and dressed him to play, he wouldn't receive the money that Rah-Rah had for him. "I mean, no sir. I'm fine with things the way they are." He gave the salesman a phony smile.

The salesman gave Bulldog a sour look in response to his uncouth actions and said, "Let me go get your temporary tags and I'll let you be on your way," as he hurried back inside the dealership.

Bulldog turned to face Rah-Rah who stood with his arms folded across his chest and a frown covering his face. Hunching his shoulders and tossing Rah-Rah a smile, Bulldog said, "Youngblood, be easy. Damn, I thought I did pretty good. Look at me, nigga!" he teased, trying to lighten the mood. "I haven't had a haircut and duds anywhere near as nice as this on my ass in years, and then you got the nerve

to give a nigga a hundred and twenty-grand on top of that…
shiiit, If I thought I could outrun you wild youngins, I would
have been got in the wind."

Rah-Rah was unable to remain angry with Bulldog
as the reality of his words and situation brought on a fit of
laughter from the gathered group. "You're crazy as hell,"
Rah-Rah said, slapping Bulldog five, "but you're all right
with me, ole head. Removing the thousand dollars that he
had promised him, Rah-Rah extended his hand towards
Bulldog, "Take it, player. I appreciate you."

"Nah man, I appreciate you!" Bulldog said,
swallowing his pride as he held the crisp bills as if he were
mesmerized. "Rah-Rah, do you have any idea how long it's
been since I've had this much money?"

"Just keep rolling with your boy and I promise you
that your situation will get much greater," Rah-Rah
announced, seeing the gratitude that radiated from Bulldog's
misty eyes. "There's our boy." He added, pointing to the
salesman who headed their way. Grinning as he tossed a
look over his shoulder at the three gleaming, Black trucks,
he decided that after they installed music and an array of
chrome accessories their new vehicles would be worthy of
their growing reputations.

"I'm good right here, young gunner," Bulldog said.

Staring around at the drug traffic that moved through
the block and gun-toting youngsters who kept the addicts in
line, as Rah-Rah pulled the Cadillac CTS to the curb, he
glanced over at Bulldog and asked, "Where you headed, ole
head?" thinking that Bulldog might have wanted to grab
something to quench his thirst in the corner store then head
home.

"I'm about to call it a night," he said, yawning.

"Oh yeah," Rah-Rah stated, giving Bulldog a questioning look. "Well if you don't mind my asking, where do you rest your head at night?" Rah-Rah asked, thinking that he knew the answer but not really sure.

Bulldog's response was given in a defeated tone as he turned from Rah-Rah's gaze. "I live in a large box out behind the store."

'Damn', Rah-Rah thought as he tried to imagine what Bulldog's life was really like. He knew that it was really none of his business one way or another, however his father and Uncle Cross always told him that the only way to survive in the game was to keep a balance by doing just as much good as bad. Rah-Rah decided that there was no better time than the present to heed their lesson.

"Not no more you don't," Rah-Rah said, pulling away from the curb and heading in the opposite direction.

Bulldog looked back at the quickly fading block and nervously muttered, "But, young gun, everything I own is back there. I don't have any family… or any place else to go, man.

Laughing, Rah-Rah said, "Relax, ole head. I got you, man. As far as all the things that you left behind, I'm going to buy you all new stuff. And now that you're on the team, I'll find you somewhere to live. You're my man, so just sit back and watch me work."

No reply was necessary and none was given as Bulldog gave Rah-Rah a pound and leaned back into the plush leather seat. For the first time in many years he had a roll of money in his pockets, and things seemed to be looking up for him. Though it was all happening too fast for him to really grasp, for once the last thing Bulldog felt like was a bum and it truly felt good.

Chapter Seventeen

"The shit we heard about your boy getting dope money out in Norfolk is legit, Blood," one of K.B.'s most trusted soldiers stated with bitterness in his voice. "He's got nigga named Q out there in Tidewater Park trappin' for him."

"Is that so?" K.B. stood and walked to the window. "So lil' Rah-Rah's got his own thing going on, huh? Now ain't that a bitch!"

"You want me to see to that nigga?" His man gripped the butt of his .40 cal wearing a screw face. "You say the word and I'll slay him before the sun goes down, Damu!"

Turning to face his man, K.B. was intentionally stalling when he said, "Let me feel him out and see what's on his mind first, then I'll decide exactly how I want to deal with his lil' ass."

The truth was K.B. liked Rah-Rah and he was aware that many of his longtime associate hated the favor that he showed to the newcomer. However, on the flip side, even though he liked and respected the younger man, Rah-Rah's cold heart and fearlessness scared him. Not to mention the fact that in the very short time that he had been Blood, he had acquired a rather large following of soldiers, for whatever reason, worshipped him. K.B. knew that there was no getting around the fact that regardless of how he felt about Rah-Rah, he was becoming a threat to his reign over the B.N.B Blood set and for that reason alone Rah-Rah had to go.

"Let's ride on the nigga and get this shit out the way, Blood. If I'm going to get to the bottom of this shit, there's no better time than the present," K.B. said, smiling but looking disgusted at the same time.

Meesa took the carpeted steps two at a time as she hurriedly made her way back to the safety of her and K.B.'s bedroom right before she heard the two men leave the office and rushed out of the house. She had heard everything that they had said about Rahsaan and her heart beat out of her chest as she frantically searched for her phone in her haste to call and warm him of the danger that he was in.

"Shit! Where the hell did I put it at?" Meesa was nearly hysterical when she found her phone entwined in their bed linen and began to punch in Rah-Rah's numbers. Counting the rings and praying that he picked up, she closed her eyes unable to control the gush of tears that cascaded over her smooth, dark cheeks. Clicking off and redialing his number once more, Meesa wailed, "Baby, please pick up! Whatever you do… please pick up!"

Rah-Rah and his crew rode through the streets of Newport News with all three Denali truck systems blaring Plies' song 'I got plenty money', drawing the attention of all the women and hustlers who lived and trapped in the many projects that they traveled. They were in full force, rolling at least fifteen deep in the three trucks, showcasing their gleaming new rides and expensive chrome feet.

"Who the hell is this?" Rah-Rah mumbled, feeling the vibrations from his phone against his hip. Pulling it loose and peering at the number, he saw that it was Messa again and returned the contraption back to his belt. He had warmed her to slow her roll, yet regardless of what he said she was determined to have it her way.

Turning the music down and pointing up the block, B-rock said, "I think dude may be one of ours."

Rah-Rah stared out the window, seeing a large group of people assembled around two combatants who were going toe to toe, however, he was surprised to find that one of the brawlers was a female. "Pull over, Blood!" Rah-Rah ordered, jumping out of the truck followed by the rest of his men. He was quickly making his way to the melee when K.B's Benz pulled to the curb and he heard K.B. call out to him.

"Aye, Rah-Rah, let me holler at you," K.B. yelled urgently, slowing Rah-Rah's step.

Rah-Rah was momentarily undecided on which way he wanted to go when he noticed the hate-filled look that K.B's man gave him along with the venom that bled from K.B's eyes. Holding up his index finger in a manner that he realized would be seen as disrespectful, Rah-Rah reached for his vibrating phone, answering it as he yelled to K.B., "Give me a minute." He then said, "Talk to me," while turning his back on the Benz and making his way through the crowd.

"Baby, you're in danger. I overheard K.B. and one of his boys talking about doing something to you behind some nigga named Q that is supposed to be working for you in Norfolk," Meesa's voice was cracking and her sobs made it hard for Rah-Rah to follow what she said.

"They're here right now," Rah-Rah said, causing her to sob harder. "Chill, ma, I'm good," Rah-Rah laughed, feeling the weight of his pistol. "Look, I'm handling something but you can rest assured that K.B ain't about to do shit to me. Relax, and I'll call you back when I get through, aiight beautiful." He ended the call as he paraded into the circle and slapped fire out of the young Blood who was fighting the female.

"Nigga, what the fuck!" the Blood yelled, stumbling backwards before regaining his footing and starting to charge back in. However, as his vision cleared, he stopped in his tracks and un-balled his fists as his hands involuntarily dropped to his sides. "Ruckus," he nervously announced, looking around him at the now legendary elite army who glared at him, "I didn't know it was you, Blood. I'm sorry, man. That's my bad, Damu." He pleaded, staring at his feet.

"Oh hell nah! Move, Ruckus, or whoever the hell you are. I ain't finished with his ass," the female screamed angrily. "I bet you won't fuck with my little brother no more when I finish with your ass, nigga!"

"Look, Blood, I'm sorry about putting my hands on you, but we're gangsters wit' our shit and we don't fight women. You feel me?" Rah-Rah asked, hearing a slew of threats and curses being fired at him and the Blood that he spoke with. "Yo, go ahead and roll out so I can holler at her," Rah-Rah said taking a deep breath and turning to face the she-devil.

"Damu!" he thought when he turned around and laid eyes on her for the first time. She was absolutely stunning, and for a moment Rah-Rah was at a complete loss for words, choosing to stare at the fiery-eyed demon who stood with her hands on her hips, cursing him out.

"And what the hell are you looking at?" the female huffed in a sexy voice, turning her neck in a ghetto manner. Raising her balled fist, she added, "I guess that since you sent your man on his way, you'll have to take his place," as she came towards him.

"What?" Rah-Rah laughed, looking back at his boys as he back peddled out of her reach. "You can't be serious, I'm not about to fight you, beautiful!"

Stopping her pursuit, she angrily barked, "If you weren't trying to fight, then you shouldn't have got in my business, and for your information my name ain't beautiful!"

"Damn, ma, I'm sorry," Rah-Rah smiled, trying to soothe the beautiful beast in front of him. "You mind if I ask exactly what caused you to be out here fighting a dude who outweighs you at least forty pounds?" Rah-Rah asked, wanting to reach out and wipe the blood that seeped from her succulent lip.

Definitely unfolding her arms across her chest and standing back on her slightly bound legs, she said, "I'm tired of these niggas picking on my little brother, and being that all these clowns around here run behind dude, I decided to make an example out of him!" she remarked sarcastically.

Rah-Rah burst out laughing, shaking his head, while thinking that he had never met a female whose heart was anywhere near as big as hers. Not only did he like her, but at that moment he realized that she had been made for him. It was also at that moment that he heard K.B's horn blowing behind him, and Rah-Rah was reminded that he had unfinished business with him.

Rah-Rah tossed a look over his shoulder, seeing the treacherous glares that reflected back at him from the passengers inside the Mercedes then returning his attention back to the beauty before him. "I promise you that you don't have to worry about anyone else out here bothering your brother again. I'll personally see to it. So I don't want to catch you out here fighting anymore, beautiful!" Rah-Rah said walking back through the crowd with his men close on his heels.

Watching the handsome stranger who had to be powerful in some manner that she was unaware of, walk away, Tia couldn't help calling out, "What's your name?" For some reason she felt that their short encounter had ended too abruptly, only she couldn't understand why it even mattered.

A moment before the crowd completely swallowed him up, he turned and gave her a devilish grin, then blurted, "I'll tell you the next time we meet."

Tia's grin was bright and beautiful as she stood on tip-toes, searching for another glimpse of the sexy stranger who suddenly intrigued her. Unable to accomplish her goal, she suddenly found herself hoping that they did meet again. However, as she walked back to her apartment, gently biting on her slowly swelling lip, Tia knew that if it were meant to be then it would be.

Chapter Eighteen

"What's up with them niggas?" B-rock mumbled as he walked next to Rah-Rah on their way to see what K.B. wanted. "Do I need my strap?" he asked, patting his side and the pistol that rested on his waist.

"I'll explain later, but stay on point," Rah-Rah replied, inwardly smiling at the change in B-rock's allegiance now that he had begun to eat with him. Rah-Rah could see the same looks that B-rock wore on the faces of all the men who followed him. It was clear that their loyalty lied with Rah-Rah as well, and he knew that whatever transpired between K.B. and himself in the next few moments, would determine how much longer he allowed K.B. to hold his position at the helm of their Bad News Blood set.

Reaching the Benz, Rah-Rah whispered, "Follow us if they pull off," then winked an eye at B-rock and got in the back of K.B's Mercedes. "What's good wit' ya, Blood?" Rah-Rah asked, ignoring the driver's mean stare and making himself comfortable in the back seat.

K.B. held Rah-Rah with accusing eyes, then said, "Drive, blood," as he turned back around in his seat, ignoring Rah-Rah's question. The threat was evident in K.B's tone when he asked, "Is it true that you're moving my work through some nigga named Q out in Norfolk, son?" His New York accent was intense when he added, " I hope that the shit ain't true, money, because there's no way that I can allow you to deceive me, lil' nigga!" through clenched teeth.

Rah-Rah's jaw flexed and his teeth ground together as he fought to remain calm. His first thought after hearing K.B.'s question and the disrespectful tone was to pull out his cannon and place a slug in K.B. and his driver's head. However, even as he was having that thought, Rah-Rah laughed and replied, "You of all people should know that I would never do anything to put us at odds. I respect your gangster, Damu. However, I have made a move into Norfolk that will benefit everyone in our set, and I plan to take over every project in Tidewater that we're not already getting money in." Seeing the evil looks that passed between the two men, Rah-Rah's hand slowly slid beneath his shirt and grasped his weapon before he added, "I took the work from the nigga that I inherited the project from and I've put a large sum up for you if you want it."

"If I want it, huh?" K.B questioned cutting his eye at his man. "How much money has Tidewater Park allowed you to put aside for me?" K.B. turned so that he could look directly into Rah-Rah's face when he answered.

'Fuck this!' Rah-Rah thought. He wanted to murder K.B so much at that moment that his leg had begun to tremble as he held K.B with an unblinking stare. "I've made enough money to feed myself and my team and put over a hundred grand in the cut for you," Rah-Rah said slowly, trying to contain his fury.

K.B. laughed, blurting, Did you hear this nigga, Blood?" as he continued to hold Rah-Rah in his view. "So you made enough to feed your team, huh? I knew that you're not talking about the same team that I gave you,

- 90 -

nigga!" K.B hissed, adding, "Then you talk about having a measly hundred grand for me when you're riding around here in three fucking Denali's that cost more than that," K.B said, unaware that Rah-Rah had added over forty grand of his own money to make the purchase.

"Look, K.B…." Rah-Rah began ready to explode.

"Look my ass!" K.B snapped, cutting Rah-Rah off. "I don't care if you have to take those damn trucks back in order to come up with it, but you've got until midnight tonight to come up with two-hundred thousand dollars!" Feeling himself, K.B said, "I'm putting Blood here in command of your little crew, and you're going to turn over Tidewater Park projects and your workers to him as well. Now, do I make myself clear?" he asked firmly.

Rah-Rah paused his response in order to get his emotions under control before answering in a grinning voice. "Yeah, Blood, I hear you loud and clear."

"Yeah, lil' nigga… I thought you would!" K.B remarked sarcastically. "Pull over and let this nigga out." When the car slowed and Rah-Rah opened his door, K.B. said, "Be sure to meet me at the club at midnight, lil' Rah-Rah, because 12:01 will be too late and you don't want me to come looking for you!"

Closing the car door, Rah-Rah heard their loud laughter behind him as they pulled off, leaving him in the middle of the street. Smiling in order to mask his fury, when the first truck driven by B-rock pulled up beside him, Rah-Rah reached for the handle and got inside, knowing that he would make their midnight meeting and he would be early. After the way that K.B had spoken to him, there was no way that he would miss it.

"You sure that you don't need us to roll, baby boy, because you know we will? All you have to do is say the word," B-rock urged, swinging his arm around so that Rah-Rah could witness the readiness of the men who stood around them.

Looking at all the faces who stared back at him with battle ready orbs, Rah-Rah felt a sense of pride like none he had ever known. These men were truly elite in every sense of the word, and even though he realized that they had chosen him over K.B. and would gladly fight to insure that their decision was heeded, Rah-Rah had to do this alone. Therefore, grabbing the gym-bag that sat on the table and throwing it over his shoulder, Rah-Rah said, "I appreciate you all wanting to hold me down, but I have to do this one on my own. Don't worry, though, because when I get back we're about to show these lames what B.N.B really stands for. And just in case I haven't made myself clear, we're about to turn it up, my niggas!"

Rah-Rah was ready to see K.B. again and he hoped that he would be able to catch him with the tough-acting Blood who had been with him earlier. If Meesa's information panned out, and Rah-Rah counted on the fact that it would, the two men would not only be together but the key that she had given him to the backdoor of the club would allow him to catch him slippin'.

Parking down the block and taking the alleyway that allowed him to reach the back of the club, Rah-Rah used the key to gain access to enter the strip club and make his way through the dark corridor without being spotted. He was able to hear K.B and another man's voice clearly as he placed an ear to the door and slowly turned the knob, finding them engrossed in a game of pool when he entered the room.

Rah-Rah slung the gym bag on the pool table, instantly garnering K.B and his henchman's attention. The fear was evident when they turned their wide-eyes in his direction. "Nigga, can't you see we playing a game of pool?" K.B snapped, attempting to cover the panic that Rah-Rah's early arrival had caused. They weren't prepared, and the hood that Rah-Rah wore over his fitted hat, highlighting the white contacts that gave him an ominous appearance, filled both men with dread as they looked past Rah-Rah to K.B's desk where their weapons laid.

Holding K.B with a blank look, Rah-Rah reached behind him and locked the office door. He too saw what drew their attention and inwardly smiled at the terror that he knew they were experiencing. "You told me to be here by twelve on the dot or you would have to come looking for me, so I figured that I'd get here at eleven so that you wouldn't have to go through the trouble of finding me." Pointing towards the pool table and gym bag, Rah-Rah said, "Aren't you going to check your money? I did go through a bunch of shit to get this paper, you know?"

K.B looked at the bag apprehensively, then stared back at Rah-Rah who had spread his arms wide as if to say 'what are you waiting on?' Suddenly K.B had lost any faith or confidence in his original idea to harm Rah-Rah in the first place, and as he moved towards the bag, K.B was afraid of what he would find inside.

"Come on," Rah-Rah exclaimed, tainting K.B by glancing down at his watch and saying, "The faster you grab your paper the quicker we can get this whole shit over with, man!"

    K.B's henchman watched Rah-Rah closely as he slowly took steps to distance himself from K.B. Even though Rah-Rah had yet to pull a weapon, his demeanor alone proved that he was strapped, plus the many tales that the Blood soldiers spoke about Ruckus stated that whenever he donned the white contacts, it was a part of his murder disguise. That being the case, the big Blood refused to become a casualty without putting up a fight. When K.B dumped the contents of the bag on the pool table, exposing rolls of nothing but toilet paper, the henchman no longer had to wonder what would come next because as he ran for his weapon he knew.

    "Thwack! Thwack! Thwack!" Rah-Rah's Colt barked, sending their silenced hollow point slugs into the henchman's torso. K.B was in shock as he watched Rah-Rah speed walk to his man and fire two more rounds into his face. "Thwack! Thwack!"

    "Oh God... no!" K.B cried out, dropping the bag. "Rah-Rah... um... listen to me... man!
Please... listen to.....me," he pleaded, staring open-mouthed at the gold-plated .45 with his hands extended outwards, palms up.

    "I thought you said everything that you needed to say earlier today when you and that ho' ass nigga were plotting to kill me muthafucka! Yeah, I know about you, nigga!" Rah-Rah added, seeing the traumatic look that suddenly twisted K.B's features.

    "Come on, Blood, what are you talking about? I... I... would never hurt you, man!"

"Yeah, I'm sure you wouldn't." Sarcasm rang in Rah-Rah's voice as he tossed Meesa's key on the table and saw K.B's shoulders slump with the recognition. "So I guess Meesa lied on you then, huh?"

K.B wiped at the sweat that had formed on his brow and slumped against the side of the pool table. "Man, I've got lots of money…." he began in an attempt at bribing Rah-Rah.

I'm already aware of the dough, nigga! Your bitch already gave me your stash, so save your breath!"

"Why me?" K.B blurted, placing his head in the palms of his hands. Beginning to cry, he said, "Just let me go, man. I promise that I'll go so far away from here that you'll never have to worry about laying eyes on me again. Please, Rah-Rah!"

Rah-Rah was tired of talking and K.B's begging had really begun to disgust him. "Enough, nigga! Damn, can't you at least spend your last few moments on Earth acting like a gangster?" Without awaiting an answer Rah-Rah pulled the trigger three times, "Thwack! Thwack!" and watched K.B's brains spread all over the pool table as his body slumped over on its side. Smiling at his handy-work as he hurried to the door and peeped out into the hallway, before exiting the room Rah-Rah glanced back over his shoulder once more, thinking that he would have to buy another rug and pool table before he moved into his new office.

Chapter Nineteen

Things had been going well for Rah-Rah, and it felt great to be one week away from his nineteenth birthday, yet be in command of one of the largest street armies in Tidewater. Thanks to his elite crew and the take-charge attitude that B-rock quickly showed no sooner as K.B.'s murder was uncovered, he easily slid into the position of King Blood. What little opposition they had encountered behind the regime change, was been easily wiped out as well. And after the bodies were found in whatever disarray Rah-Rah's men had left them, any other Bloods who may have planned to put up resistance thought better of it. Now, weeks later, Rah-Rah tooled his brand new Audi A8 through the city streets thinking about the family that he had left behind in the Dominican Republic, and for the first time in weeks his heart ached to be reunited with them. However, so much had changed that going back, at least right now, was totally out of the question. Only as he reached for his phone and keyed in a sequence of numbers, he figured that the next best thing to actually seeing them was to hear their voice.

"Hello!" the attitude-filled voice that rang through the receiver brought on instant smile to Rah-Rah's face. It belonged to a gorgeous female that owned his heart.

"Hey, lil' sis," Rah-Rah said, removing the phone from his ear at the sound of her loud shriek.

Boy, why haven't you called me? We've been worried sick about you!" Rahsaanique argued, yelling, "Ma, Tania… Rah-Rah's on the phone!"

Rah-Rah laughed at his little sister's excited response to his call, thinking that even though he loved his big sister Tavia to death he and Rahsaanique's bond had always been much tighter. "Ronnie," he called out, using the nickname that he had given her when they were little in an attempt to get her attention.

"I'm here, boy, and you still haven't answered my questions," Rahsaanique complained, adding, "You know Mom, Dad and Uncle Cross have been plotting on coming down there to see about you, boy," she confided, lowering her voice.

"Is that so?" Rah-Rah questioned, glad that he had caught Rahsaanique at home so that she could give him a heads up.

"That's all you can think to say?" Rahsaanique blurted. "Well, Rah-Rah, Dad and Uncle Cross think that you are up there doing something that you're not supposed to be doing and I'm seriously starting to sway my thoughts toward that direction as well."

"Nah, I'm straight, lil' sis. I ain't doing nothing wrong," Rah-Rah lied.

"Umm hmm, tell that to someone who don't know you, Rahsaan!"

"No really!" Rah-Rah laughed. He realized that no one on Earth knew him better than Rahsaanique. "I'm good, Ronnie."

"You sure, Rahsaan, because you knew we worry about you and we love you?"

Rah-Rah could hear the emotion in her voice and he too was forced to swallow the lump that had begun to form in his throat in order to get his own emotions under control. "Believe me, baby girl, I'm great and you all have no need to worry. I love you, Ronnie, and let the rest of the family know that I'm fine and I love them also," Rah-Rah stated, hearing Tavia and Bonni's voices.

"I have to go, Ronnie."

"Hold on, Rah-Rah, Mom and Tavia want to..." were the last words that Rah-Rah heard before he push the button to end their call and turned his phone off. Though he missed Bonni and Tavia just as much as he did Rahsaanique, at that moment he felt terrible about the fact that he had a wonderful family back in the Domincan Republic who loved him and cared about nothing more than his safety, yet he continued to deceive them by living a double life. The only problem was what he now presided over. In fact, he planned to turn the heat up in the streets and there was nothing that anyone could do about it.

"Yo, have you had any luck with finding out anything about the lil' cutie that was fighting Blood out in Dickerson Court that day we were rolling through?" Rah-Rah asked B-rock as he waited for Bulldog to miss a shot on the new pool table that he had installed in his new office.

"Damn!" B-rock snapped, causing Bulldog's concentration to waver, making him miss his shot. "I got that for you last week and forgot all about it, man!"

Bulldog gave B-rock an evil eye, then grabbed his drink off the table's ledge and moved aside, giving Rah-Rah room to shoot his shot.

"My bad, Bulldog." B-rock winked his eye at Rah-Rah as Bulldog sucked his teeth and walked to the wet bar.

Banking the nine ball off the rail and sending it into the opposite corner pocket, Rah-Rah snatched the hundred dollar bill that bulldog had bet him off the table and smiled broadly. "Thanks for the free money, ole head, and I'll gladly take a few more of these off your hands anytime you like."

"If you want to thank a muthafucka, thank your man there for throwing that bullshit in the game!" Bulldog retorted, draining his drink and heading towards the door. "When you're ready to try your hand again, minus the interruption, I'll be out in the club mingling with the ladies."

Rah-Rah placed his stick on the table and grinned as he watched Bulldog walk out of the room, thinking that he hardly resembled the old bum that he had encountered the day he had introduced himself at the corner store. In the place of the old drunk, a sharp-dressed, game spitter had been born and Rah-Rah was glad that he had played a part in the newly created Bulldog. The crazy part was Bulldog had proved himself to be invaluable in so many ways, and the game that he brought to their drug franchise made the house, car and salary that Rah-Rah provided well worth it.

"Her name is Tia, my dude, and she lives in Dickerson Court," B-rock said, interpreting Rah-Rah's thoughts.

"Does she deal with any of these knuckleheads out there?" Rah-Rah asked, hoping that she wasn't spoken for, but planning to see her again regardless of her relationship status.

"Nah son, my niggas say shawty be on her 'stay away from me' shit, so dudes give her plenty of space." Laughing, B-rock added, "She was slinging her hands when you met her, so you already know that ma don't play 'bout hers, Damu!"

Joining in the laughter, Rah-Rah shook his head in agreement, recalling the dark-chocolate beauty that he hadn't been able to get out of his thoughts ever since their brief encounter weeks before. Even now, her long black hair and dark bottomless eyes have a hypnotizing affect on his thoughts, and the lusciousness of her body, clad in jeans and a sweatshirt caused his blood to flow into his private parts.

"What else did they find out, B?" Rah-Rah asked, needing to know more.

"Uh" B-rock began, trying to remember everything, "She takes care of her brother because her parents are dead, and she works at the mall."

"That's good money, baby boy!" Rah-Rah exclaimed giving B-rock a pound. He couldn't wait to see her again; it had already been long enough since he had laid eyes on the woman that he wanted all for himself.

"On that other thing you asked me to look into, Rah, Q wasn't able to find out where them New York niggas lay their heads, but it seems that their whole crew be up in Liquid Blue strip club every Friday night. He said that one of his home girls works in the joint and them niggas be in the club stuntin'."

"Now that's really what I wanted to hear!" Rah-Rah announced, thinking that they only had two days left to prepare a party for the New Yorkers. A plan immediately came to mind, and Rah-Rah's excitement was evident when he drained his drink and slammed the glass down on the table. "Check it out, B, get in contact with Q and tell him that we need his home girl to handle something for us that's worth an easy five G's to her." Smiling, Rah-Rah couldn't help but think that the news that he had received in the last few minutes made his night. In fact, little did B-rock know, he had actually presented Rah-Rah with the most perfect Birthday present ever, even if no one but him knew that he turned nineteen that day.

Chapter Twenty

Rah-Rah couldn't understand what was wrong with him, but as he headed through the mall in search of the clothing store where Tia worked, he found himself experiencing nervous jitters. This was unlike him being that he had always been the aggressor when it came to females, yet this was no appearance in the glares, finding himself to be flawless, Rah-Rah took a deep breath, hand-combed his thick, silky waves and walked into the store. Taking time to acquaint himself with his surroundings, he noticed an array of sexy sales clerks but Tia was nowhere to be found. After having such high expectations for their reunion of sorts, Rah-Rah's mood began to rapidly sink.

"Excuse me, sir, but is there something that I may be able to assist you with?" the female asked, walking up behind him.

Quickly turning towards the voice that carried a trace of a smile and a sense of familiarity, Rah-Rah was shocked but happy to find that it was Tia who stood behind him with her arms folded over her breasts. Unable to form his words as he openly stared at what he felt was the epitome of perfection, his only response was a smile.

"So we meet again after all, huh?" Tia asked shifting her weight from one high heeled foot to the other as she openly gazed at the handsome man who stood before her. His smile alone had her heart twisted into knots.

Eyeing her as he watched her eyes take him in, Rah-Rah cleared his senses as best as he could and replied,

"Didn't I tell you that we would? And just so you know, when I say things, I mean then!"

"Is that so?" Tia smirked.

"Yes, that's so." Rah-Rah shot back, imitating the pursed lipped look that she held him with.

Tia smiled showcasing her beautiful dimples, then asked, "Mr. I say what I mean... do you have a name?" even though she found out who he was within an hour of their last meeting.

"My name is Rah-Rah, but from this point on when you address me, I would appreciate it if you would call me Rahsaan." Rah-Rah took a step forward, slightly closing the gap between them.

"And why would I call you Rahsaan if your name is Rah-Rah?" Tia asked, trying to act as though she wasn't affected by his invasion of her space even though he had her heart doing summersaults.

Rah-Rah knew that he was taking a big leap when he opened his mouth to give his answer but figured 'what the hell?' and said it anyway. "Because you're going to be my body, and I can't have you using a nickname, Tia."

Blushing, Tia was shocked by Rah-Rah's response. However, as she replayed his words and recalled him using her name when she had never given it to him, she knew that he too had been checking for her. Therefore, with that knowledge in mind, Tia decided to play a little hard to get.

"So Rah-Rah," she began, purposely using his nickname, "Why do you want to be my man, and what makes you think that I don't already have one?" Tia asked, holding him with a questioning stare.

Rah-Rah inwardly smiled at Tia's little game and threw her completely off balance when he closed the distance between them, backing her into a clothing rack. "Well first of all, the next time you refer to me, it better be by Rahsaan, and if by chance you did already have a man, call him right now and let him know that you're mine!" Rah-Rah pushed his phone into her hand.

Though Tia was somewhat startled by Rah-Rah's aggressiveness, the strength that emerged from his words and actions turned her on immensely. Thus, as she looked from the phone back to Rah-Rah's stubborn gaze, Tia said, "Look, Rahsaan, I don't have a man, but that doesn't mean that I'm about to just fall head over heels for the first one who comes along."

"I was hoping that you wouldn't," Rah-Rah said, returning his phone back to its place on his side. "Being that I'm the best man to come along, I figure that you made a damn good choice," he added, placing a gentle kiss on her lips then turning to leave. However, before doing so, he announced, "I'm coming to pick you up around eight o'clock tomorrow night for dinner, so wear something nice like what you're wearing now and I look forward to seeing you then."

Watching him walk away with a huge grin on her face and a rapidly beating heart, Tia said, "I'll go out to dinner with you, but I'm still not your girl, Rahsaan."

"Sure you are, Ms. Tia… you just don't know it yet," were the words that reached her ears as he exited the store.

"What's the business, baby?' Rah-Rah asked B-rock as he and Trooper exited a dark colored Malibu and gave pounds to B-rock and Q.

"They're in there like he said," B-rock stated, nodding his head towards Q who quietly stood bedside him.

Glancing from Q who seemed nervous, back to B-rock, Rah-Rah pulled the large hood on his Crown Holder sweatshirt over his head and donned his white contacts. "How many men are with him, and did his homegirl take care of that like I asked?"

Rah-Rah shook his head in acknowledgement of B-rock's statement; only he was more interested in Q and needed to know where he stood. The last thing he needed around him was a scared man, because his father and Uncle Cross had always taught him that scared men talked. "You seem a little nervous over there," Rah-Rah said, eyeing Q.

"Nah man, I'm straight," Q lied, looking away from Rah-Rah's piercing, white eyes.

"I'm glad to hear that, my nigga," Rah-Rah said, suddenly foreseeing a change of plans in the night's events. "Let's get this show on the road then," he added, tossing his arm around Q's shoulder and leading him towards the club's entrance.

B-rock followed them, glancing over his own shoulder at the line of Bloods who brought up the rear wearing the same hooded sweatshirts and white contact lenses as Rah-Rah. Though he wasn't quite sure how Rah-Rah planned to deal with the New York crew, as they entered the club to the thunderous sounds of booty-shaking music, and made their way to the bathroom where weapons had already been stashed, B-rock knew that death would undoubtedly be the end result.

"Is that them, right there?" Rah-Rah asked Q upon laying eyes on a group of men who were tossing back drinks as they threw bills into the air and watched them flutter down onto the scantily dressed females that paraded past their table.

"Yeah, that's them. The one wearing the blue and grey Yankees hat is their leader and he's the nigga that used to hit Jamil wit' the work."

At the completion of Q's words, Rah-Rah, Q and a few of the men who had come with them headed across the floor and walked straight up to the New Yorkers' table. The New Yorkers immediately stopped what they were doing before the group of men intruded on their festive evening, and stood ready to take it wherever the hooded men may have wanted to go.

'What the fuck you niggas want, and who the hell invited you to this party?" the man who Q pointed out as the leader spat, grilling Q then turning evil eyes on Rah-Rah.

Rah-Rah took a seat and poured himself a drink from the bottle of Patron Silver that sat in front of him and swallowed it, inwardly smiling at the foolish courage of the New Yorker as he stood with his fists balled up at his sides. Little did he know, he would have no need for his fists when he was in the midst of a gun fight about to erupt.

"Son, which are you, fucking retarded, or just plain stupid?" The New Yorker barked, snatching the Patron bottle from in front of Rah-Rah.

Upon seeing the arrival of the hooded men and realizing the tension that ensued between them and the New

Yorkers, the strippers quickly retrieved their discarded clothing articles and money that was left strewn on the floor, then hurriedly scampered away from the two groups of men.

Shaking his head at the outlandish show of emotion before him, Rah-Rah said, "Relax, New York, and take a seat so we can talk like two bosses do." His voice was calm and it apparently had some effect on the New Yorker, because he reluctantly pulled out his chair and dropped his six foot plus frame down into it.

"What do we have to talk about, and who the hell are you in the first place?" the New Yorker questioned, heated.

"They call me Ruckus, and if you think that you're going to continue getting money in my trap, we have plenty to discuss," Rah-Rah got straight to the point.

"I'm getting money in your trap? What the hell are you talking about, duke?" New Yorker snapped.

Watching him closely, Rah-Rah was beginning to tire of the fake tough man act that the New Yorker was putting down, but he still kept his calm demeanor. "Look, New Yorker, I'm not good at doing a whole lot of talking, so all I'm asking is that you relocate your product away from Tidewater Park, and let my man here," Rah-Rah cut his eyes at Q," get his paper in peace."

New York's eyes traveled from Rah-Rah to Q and back again, then began to laugh as if Rah-Rah had said something that was extremely humorous. "So let me make sure that I heard you correctly... You expect me to stop bubbling my shit out the Park so this bird-ass nigga can bang your work in its place? Yo, how the fuck you sound right now, son, 'cause it's apparent that you've got me twisted!" New York angrily remarked, banging his fist against the heavy charm that dangled from the diamond chain that hung on his chest.

Rah-Rah patiently waited for the New Yorker's academy award winning performance to end before he downed the remainder of his drink and stood with his hands flat on the table to support him as he leaned far enough forward so that he and the New Yorker were close enough for the man to hear his whispered response, "Hear me and hear me good, New York. Even though I don't know you personally, just for the sake of doing so I'm going to give you the benefit of doubt that you're smart enough to know when you're dealing with a nigga who's playing for keeps, and believe me when I tell you that I'm that nigga, New York. Now I murdered your man Jamil and his team to gain my entrance into the Park, and I don't have a problem with repeating the process in order to keep it all to myself, Rah-Rah said, standing with a smile in place.

"What!" New York yelled, jumping up out of his chair and knocking it over in the process as he watched Rah-Rah walk away. "You niggas act like we ain't 'bout ours, son!" Fuck that! I'll bang my shit wherever I want, and if you don't like it see me, kid!" New York stunted for the club patrons who heard his outburst.

"I see you now, nigga!" Rah-Rah yelled over his shoulder, sweeping his hand over his head to alert the four men who were stationed around the perimeter of the club with M1 machine pistols that it was a go, as he and the bulk of their entourage exited the club.

Swoop's patron Dundee was stationed at the bar, mingling with a stripper when he noticed the encounter with the New Yorker and his man's nephew. Finding their encounter interesting, he had just begun to dial Swoop's number when Rah-Rah walked out of the club and swept his arm in the air. However, before Swoop answered, he saw four men wearing hoods run up on the table where the New Yorker's sat and opened fire with automatic weapons. Though the weapons fire only lasted a matter of seconds, when it was over, all five men laid twisted and full of holes as their blood flowed into an endless puddle.

"What the fuck is going on? Dundee heard Swoop's voice yelling through the receiver as he stood and watched the crying strippers and scared patrons running as they hurried to escape the club and the horror that had just taken place inside.

"Swoop, it's me, Dundee," Dundee said exhaling. "Man, we need to talk."

"About what, man? What was that noise? You all right?" Swoop questioned, sounding worried.
"Yeah, I'm good, man... but your nephew is a problem, player!"

Chapter Twenty-One

"You leaving so quickly, baby?" Meesa questioned, stretching her overworked limbs and pulling the covers back above her naked breasts.

"Yep," Rah-Rah answered shortly as he continued to dress, noting the time on his watch. Seeing that his sexual escapade with Meesa had gone over the time he'd expected, Rah-Rah was now in a hurry to reach Tia and the dinner date that they were scheduled for. Brushing his waves that were still wet from his quick shower, he checked his appearance and was happy with what he saw.

"Rahsaan, you look good enough to eat, with your fine ass," Meesa poured, unknowingly increasing his already inflated ego. However, no sooner as the words were out of her mouth, another thought came to mind that caused her to sit up in bed and let the covers slip to her waist. "Where are you going that's important enough that you're damn near running from my bed to get there?"

Rah-Rah continued to inspect his image in the large mirror, but he was still able to observe the jealous look that Meesa wore as her eyes bore into his back. He figured that if he ignored her, she would get the message and give up on her interrogation. However, he was wrong and as he watched her climb out of bed and grab a sheer robe, Rah-Rah grabbed his shades off the dresser and headed out of the bathroom.

"Rahsaan, don't you dare walk away without answering me!" Meesa argued as she followed him down the stairs and blocked the door.

"Come on, Meesa, I don't have time for this right now!" Rah-Rah was in a hurry and she was starting to annoy him. "Move!" he said, grabbing her arm and gently trying to move her aside.

"Stop, Rahsaan, you're hurting me!" she whined.

Releasing his hold on her arm even though he knew that he hadn't hurt her, Rah-Rah stepped back and asked, "Do you really want to know where I'm headed, Meesa, because you and I both know that sometimes you have to be careful of what you ask for?"

"Yes, Rahsaan, I do want to know," Meesa said, shaking her head furiously. However, the truth was she wanted to retract the question as soon as Rah-Rah said that she may have wanted to be careful what she asked for.

Folding his arms across his chest as he scrutinized her stubborn stance, Rah-Rah hated to put it out there this way but if nothing else, he owed it to Meesa to keep it real with her. Therefore, being that he was already late, he casually stated, "Look, Meesa, I've got plans tonight and I'm running a little late, all right?"

'Plans!' Though she heard him clearly and she had been around long enough to know exactly what plans meant, for some reason she was unable to think clearly and felt like she was suffocating at the thought of her Rahsaan, the same Rahsaan that she had gambled her future and the life of her ex on, going to meet another female. No longer able to hold her composure, Meesa whispered, "I don't think I heard you correctly. Please explain what you mean by plans."

"I've got a date with a special female that I want to get to know much better," Rah-Rah clarified, knowing that there was no need to sugar-coat the situation any longer when Meesa would undoubtedly find out sooner or later anyway.

Meesa's face carried a sour look and her eyes filled with evil intentions as the magnitude of Rah-Rah's words began to sink in. Her chest began to heave as sobs racked her body. Sliding down the door and sitting on the floor with her robe open and her pride gone, Meesa's voice was chocked when wailed, "Why Rahsaan? What haven't I done to make you happy?"

"It's not you, Meesa. You're great, and I do love you," Rah-Rah said, wanting to embrace her but knowing that she needed her space. "The thing is, I feel something even more powerful for this female and until I'm able to see what the magnetism between us really is, I think it's best if you and I take a little break from one another."

"A break, huh?" Meesa's laugh was crazed as she said, "What the hell makes you think that you can just fuck the hell out of me then get up and tell me some shit about we need to take a break? Nigga, miss me with that sucker shit!" She hissed angrily, then gave him a hate filled look and said, "Don't forget that I know how you murdered K.B., and it was me who put you in charge of that club and passed off K.B's product, nigga! You might want to make sure that this little bitch that's got you all open is worth everything that you stand to lose if you walk out this door!"

Rah-Rah's first thought after hearing Meesa's threatening words was to pull his pistol and deal with her, but two things kept him from acting on it; he had never killed a female and he did love her. Only as her words continued to reverberate through his mind, Rah-Rah knew that something had to be done about her because he refused to take her warning lightly. Opening the door and pushing her out of the way, Rah-Rah said, "I hate that it had to come to this, Meesa, but I'm going to act like you never made the threats that came out of your mouth a moment ago. In fact, when you're no longer angry and you come to your senses, give me a call and we can continue to be friends."

As he walked out the door and closed it behind him, the words that followed him down the driveway made him cringe. "Fuck you, Rahsaan! I meant every word I said, and if you don't believe me now, you'll believe me when your ass is doing a fuckin' life sentence!" However, as he got in his car and pulled off, he did believe her and now he had to decide how he was going to deal with it.

"This nigga's living real fat now! Swoop blurted, turning to Dundee with a smile etched into his features. "Nephew or not, we 'bout to cake off with his lil' ass!" he added, giving Dundee a pound.

Dundee's eyes were glued to the rear of Rah-Rah's Audi A-8 as they trailed him through the city streets in an attempt to see what type of surprise he may have had in store for them today. After following him and one of his Blood associates to a suburban community in Hampton the day before and receiving the shock of a lifetime when Bulldog, the neighborhood bum, met them at the door looking like a million dollars, wearing linen and gators that had to cost a grip, Dundee realized that anything was possible where Rah-Rah was concerned.

"I agree, my nigga, but after what I witnessed from him and them wild youngens that he commands, we got to bring our A-game, Swoop."

"Huh!" Swoop exclaimed. "Come on, nigga, don't let me find out that my nephew got you on some shook shit. When you start that, Dundee?" Swoop taunted, shaking his head.

"Shook? Pssst, come on, man. You already know how I get down, but on the real, it ain't about being scared, Swoop, and you know it. Dude just don't seem like one of these average knuckleheads who be running around in circles out here. He's got his shit in order, and I'm just saying that we need to be careful… that's all." Dundee turned his attention back to Rah-Rah as the Audi veered into the projects.

"Whatever!" Swoop snapped, downplaying Dundee's statement and Rah-Rah's importance as he followed his nephew into the projects from a safe distance. Only in all truth he had already come to the same conclusion as his partner after replaying all the moves that Rah-Rah had strategically orchestrated in the city since his arrival. Since he had killed Chico and Manuel, throwing the MS13 army into chaos, then robbed one of their biggest stash houses, he had somehow been able to kill K.B. and capture the Blood throne in the process. What Rah-Rah had done in such a short period of time was big to say the least, but even though Swoop was in awe, no way would that deter him from capitalizing on his nephew's growth in the game. It wasn't really personal and Swoop somewhat hated that it had to happen to his family, but he was in no way planning to half step when the time finally arrived to obtain his riches.

Rah-Rah tried to clean the drama that he and Meesa had just gone through from his mind as he pulled in front of Tia's apartment building and exited the car. He wanted to give her one-hundred percent of himself on their first evening together, without any distraction. Thus, as he reached her door and knocked, he exhaled and awaited the first look at the woman who had been on his mind ever since their last meeting, days earlier.

"Terry, get the door for me, please!" Rah-Rah heard Tia yell, causing him to smile. His smile slowly faded when the door opened and a six foot, five inch man who outweighed him by at least 30 pounds said, "What's up, man?" in a deep voice with a mouth-filled with potato chips.

Openly staring at the young giant who all but blocked the door, Rah-Rah asked, "Is Tia home?"

"Tia, dude's down here!" he yelled through the apartment as he turned and walked away.

Watching as the man walked away, Rah-Rah didn't know whether to enter the apartment or stay where he was. He was also trying to figure out who the young giant was when his eyes were drawn to the stairs. The vision of pure bliss walked down the steps minutes later. As his eyes tripped from her Giuseppe stiletto heels over her perfectly formed ankles and calves, taking in the impeccably rounded curves that her thin wrap dress encased, he wanted nothing more than to caress her when she smiled at him and tossed her hair in a manner that caused the long, silky braid that she wore it in to lay over her right breast.

"Whoa!" Rah-Rah muttered, grabbing his chest as he held her with wide eyes. "You get more and more beautiful every time I see you," he said, meaning every word.

"Thank you, Rahsaan, and you look extremely handsome in your button down and Prada shoes," she said, finding his grown-up attire sexy, adding, "Damn, Rahsaan, you're killing me with that Giorgio Armani Code cologne. I love the smell of it."

"How about we get started on making you love the man who's wearing it." Rah-Rah gave Tia his boyish smile, laying his charm on thick.

Lowering her eyes as she cleaned the stairs and gave him a short hug, she laughed, then replied "Well have to work on that one."

Enjoying the closeness that they shared, Rah-Rah was about to enfold her in his arms again when the giant reappeared.

"When you coming back, T?" He stuffed his mouth with Ruffles as he awaited an answer.

I'm not sure, but it won't be too late," Tia replied soothingly. She then turned to Rah-Rah and asked, "I see you met my little brother, Jerry?"

"Little brother?" Rah-Rah exclaimed, smiling. "That's the little brother that you were talking about when we met?" Rah-Rah asked, and his surprise evident as he stared from Tia to her brother and back.

Tia laughed, then began to make introductions. "Rahsaan, I'd like you to meet my brother. Jerry, this is my friend Rahsaan.

"What's good, Jerry?" Rah-Rah gave him a pound, cleverly adding, "Your sister mistakenly called me her friend, but for the record I'm her man."

They all laughed when Tia playfully punched Rah-Rah in the arm and said, "Stop lying to that boy and come on here, Rahsaan." Giving her brother the evil-eye, Tia said, "Be on your best behavior while I'm gone, Jerry, and I mean it," as she closed the door behind them.

Tia felt like she was about to burst as she and Rah-Rah walked along the Virginia Beach boardwalk. He had been the perfect gentleman ever since their date began. From the moment that he opened the car door for her and helped her into the passenger seat of his exquisite automobile, all of the many stories that she had heard about Ruckus no longer seemed to fit. The man who she soon found to be extremely smart, charismatic and funny shared no relation to the cold-blooded killer and leader of the Bad News Bloods. However, being street-bred herself and having her own secrets, Tia of all people knew how easy it was to lead a double life. Plus, since she had done a thorough investigation on Rah-Rah herself, regardless of how hard he tried to separate his two identities, she knew exactly who he really was and Tia had not only chosen him to be her man, she had chosen him to be her first.

"How about I give you a penny for your thought? Rah-Rah asked, slowing his stride.

"A penny?" Tia gave a look that said 'are you serious!' "Man, we're in a recession and you and I both know that a penny ain't buying nothing!" Tia teased.

Rah-Rah smiled at her wit as he felt his phone's vibration for what seemed like the hundredth time since he and Tia started their date. Even though he hadn't answered it, after checking the number the first few times and finding that it was Meesa, unbeknownst to Rah-Rah Tia had already come to the realization that a female was blowing his jack up.

"Come with me", Tia announced excitedly, removing her heels and leading Rah-Rah onto the sandy beach. Walking along, hand in hand, with no sound besides the waves crashing up against the rocks off in the distance, Tia said, "Do you really want to be my man, or are you just trying to get some ass?"

"I really want to be o your man." Rah-Rah's response was quick as he abruptly stopped and held her in a gaze filled with sincerity. "Now don't get it twisted, a little ass to go with it wouldn't be a bad thing either," he teased, causing Tia's beautiful features to blossom.

"Shut up, Rahsaan. I'm trying to be serious right now."

"Aight, my bad." Before he could say more, his phone began to vibrate again. Both of their eyes dropped to his waist.

"Well if you really want me to be your girl, the first thing you need to do before we can even think about embarking on any type of relationship is answer your phone and let her know what the deal is, unless you would rather I do it?" Tia held her hand out.

Pausing to consider how he wanted to handle their dilemma, Rah-Rah said, "I want to be with you, Tia, and that's real... the only problem is I told her about you," he pointed to the phone, "and she made some really dangerous threats that I can't take lightly." Rah-Rah exhaled and lowered his head with the weight of his explanation.

"Rahsaan, do you trust me?" Tia asked, raising his chin so that their eyes met.

"Yeah, I do." Although he wasn't sure why he trusted her, there was something about Tia that allowed him to let his guards down.

"Then give me the phone," she stated flatly, extending her hand towards him.

Without a second thought, Rah-Rah removed the still vibrating phone from his belt and handed it over.

Tia turned it off, then winked her eye at Rah-Rah and tossed the phone in the ocean. Enfolding her arm in his, she said, "I'll buy you another phone tomorrow, but tonight I want you to tell me everything about this chick who thinks that she can threaten my man and get away with it."

Chapter Twenty- two

"That's cute as hell, girl." Meesa complimented one of the regular customers on her hair as she strutted through the beauty parlor looking as glamorous as ever. "Tanya, I'm ready for my wal- in now. Send her back," she called to the front of the shop, directing her friend and receptionist. Returning to her chair, Meesa had just turned up a bottle of Evian water when she noticed a new, but beautiful female coming towards her with a big pair of Gucci frames covering her eyes.

"Hello," the newcomer said, smiling brightly. "Make yourself comfortable, and please tell me what you want me to do with this pretty stuff of yours?" she questioned, marveling at the silky texture and length of hair that the newcomer possessed.

Taking her seat and removing her glasses, the female said, "I don't know myself, I'm just here to make my boyfriend happy." Frowning, she said, "You know how that goes, I'm sure. Anyway, I guess he'll be straight with a conditioned wash and flat iron. At least, I hope that will make him happy."

"Umm, if you excuse my saying so… fuck that nigga, boo. Men ain't shit fo'real, so you would be better off doing you. Believe that!" Meesa blurted, preparing that female for the sink.

"Girl, I feel where you're coming from on the real. I'm to the point where I'm getting tired of these niggas altogether. Shit, if I wasn't afraid of trying my hand, I would probably see what it was like to get with another bitch," the female divulged.

Leaning the female's head back and allowing a warm spray to run over it as she worked the shampoo into her scalp, the newcomer's words replayed in Messa's head, causing her to scrutinize the dark beauty more closely as she looked directly into Meesa's probing eyes. Meesa was forced to blink and drop her eyes as the female's dark bottomless orbs held her hostage, hypnotizing her with their intensity. As Meesa continued to lather her head, trying to avoid eye contact, she unconsciously found herself drawn to the female's breasts that were virtually straining the material of her small Gucci tee. The nipples were large and swollen, and the woman's dark tone indicated to Meesa just how chocolate and delicious her areola and nipples would be. The thought alone caused her own nipples to harden and her mouth to water uncomfortably. Although it had been a long time since she had tasted female flesh, the unspoken initiation as well as the thought of all the things that she could do to the bootylicious beauty made Meesa yearn for the chance to feel the female's succulent lips wrapped around her clitoris.

"What is it that you're afraid of?" Meesa asked in a low tone, glancing around to make sure that no one heard her.

"I don't know... I've just never had the heart to approach another female," she mumbled shyly. "Plus, I wouldn't even know where to begin, so it would have to be with someone who would be gentle and take the time to teach me," the newcomer said expectantly.

"There's nothing to be afraid of. Just look at you, you're beautiful," Meesa flirted." I'm sure that you could have any woman that you want. In fact, what type of female would interest you, or do you even know?"

The newcomer paused to think about the question, then looked up into Meesa's eyes and gently bit her bottom lip. "I hope that I'm not being too forward, but if I had to choose someone, you would fit the bill perfectly. I'm sure that you're not interested, though.

Meesa's hands began to tremble and her juices flowed down the inside of her thighs as she began to think about the many tricks that she would inact on the young dimepiece. Moving her eyes around the shop to be sure that no one was paying them any attention, Meesa dropped her towel on the female's chest and pushed her hand beneath the short tee and began to finger her nipples. As the female closed her eyes and breathed harder, pressing her large breast more firmly against the hand that massaged it, Meesa whispered, "Not only is this your first lesson of the day, but I hope that this answers your question."

Meesa paced the floor of the Hotel room, drinking from a crystal flute with Chardonnay as she lit the dozens of candles that she had placed throughout the room. Standing back to admire the luminance of shimmering lights and multitude of fragrances that wafted through the air, Meesa exhaled and smiled at the mini utopia that she had created for the evening of sexual tutelage that she planned for her young friend from the beauty parlor. As she rotated her shimmering hips and gently jiggling her behind to the Trey

Song's C.D. that flowed through the surround sound speakers while smoothing the transparent material of her lingerie over her breast and flat belly, for the first time since Rah-Rah's departure and disappearance from her bed and life, Meesa actually felt enraptured. Though she still planned to deal with him in the worst way for his disloyalty, at the moment, he was the furthest thought from her mind. The chocolate Goddess who she expected to arrive any minute was the only thing that Meesa could think about.

Hearing a light tap on the door, Meesa's heart began to race as she did a last minute check of herself, finding her attire to be as sexy and tempting as planned. Taking a deep breath and releasing it, she made her way to the door and opened it. Meesa smiled brightly as she stood aside to allow her companion of the evening to enter, locking her eyes on the bulbous ass that shook like gelatin in the zebra striped tights.

"Wow, you have really outdone yourself," the female complimented, setting her overnight bag on the floor near the bed and turning to face Meesa who quickly closed the door and the distance between them. Removing her big shades and large Gucci hood, the female watched Meesa closely.

"I'm glad you like everything," Messa said, doing a slow turn for her companion's benefit. "What do you think about this?"

"Nice… real nice!" the female stated. She couldn't lie; Meesa's body was tight as hell, and even though she wasn't the jealous type, she had to admit that the older broad had it going on.

Leaning forward, Meesa gently kissed her, feeling the reluctance to return the kiss. However, thinking that she was nervous and slow to oblige her attempt at seduction, Meesa grabbed the female's ass and pulled her close, then slid her tongue into the girl's mouth.

"Hmmm," the female moaned, liking the feel of kissing another woman. Regardless of how good the new and different feeling was, the female pulled back and broke their embrace. She felt butterflies in her stomach as she nervously blurted," I need to shower and prepare myself for you before we get started." She quickly grabbed her gym bag and headed for the bathroom.

"Hey, there's no rush, boo. If you like we could have dinner and a few glasses of wine, and then we could shower together?" Meesa suggested, leaning back on the bed with her legs open and her bare pussy in view.

Quickly turning her eyes away from Meesa, the female walked inside the bathroom and said, "This will only take a minute. I promise." She then gave Meesa a forced smile and shut the door behind her. Locking the door and turning the shower on, the female began to move quickly as she unzipped the gym bag and removed a pair of thin leather gloves and a 9 millimeter with a suppressor attachment. As she put the gloves on, she angrily stared at her reflection in the mirror. Removing the safety and slowly jacking a round into the chamber, she took a deep breath in order to calm her nerves and release some of the sexual tension that she had acquired from kissing and pressing her body against another female. Gripping the gun tightly as she disengaged the lock and turning the knob, she was mad at herself because she had enjoyed their kiss and her anger intensified tenfold when she entered the room to find Meesa naked with her eyes shut tight, pleasuring herself with one of the many toys that lined the bedside table. Momentarily halting her step upon witnessing the intensity of Meesa's pleasure, she waited for Meesa's orgasm to subside and her eyes to flutter open in acknowledgement of her presence before raising the gun.

"Wha… what the hell is going on?" Messa stuttered, crawling backwards until she was plastered against the glass headboard. She clutched the thin sheets to her chest and began to cry. "Why are you doing this to me? I don't even know you."

Even though the female felt a level of sorrow for the cowering woman before her, there was really nothing left to discuss. Therefore, closing her heart and mind to Messa's pleas, she compressed the trigger of the 9 millimeter until the clip was empty and Messa's wide eyes remained still. She then moved around the room wiping down anything that she may have touched since her arrival and retrieving her bag and shades. After doing a double-take of her search, she gave Meesa one last glance and said, "I appreciate you taking the time out to teach me a few things." Blowing her a farewell kiss, she laughed and closed the door behind her as she left the room and hurried out of the Hotel.

Reaching the Hotel's exit without a hitch, she felt like a seasoned killer as she walked through the parking lot like a true Diva and popped the passenger door of the car that awaited her and slid into the plush leather seat. The female leaned back and exhaled.

The car quickly pulled out of the parking lot and moved into traffic. "You aight? Did everything go as planned," the driver asked, flicking his eyes back and forth between the road and the passenger.

Boldly leaning over and giving him a tongue kiss, Tia gave Rah-Rah a big, beautiful smile and bragged, "you see me, don't you? Well that means I'm straight. As far as Meesa is concerned, didn't I tell you I would handle it?"

Rah-Rah laughed as he gazed at his woman. He had never met, nor dreamed, that any female who embodied all of her characteristics would come into his life. Now that she had arrived, he planned to give himself 100% and prove to her just how much he appreciated what she had done in order to prove herself to him. After that night, their relationship was solidified and there would be no turning back. However, before the sun came up, there was one more thing that needed to be done before Tia could truly belong to him, and so he placed his hand on her pussy, and she fully understood what was next.

Chapter Twenty-three

"Man, we're wasting our time chasing this nigga all over Tidewater when we already know where the work is," Dundee argued. "While we're sitting out here in the Hotel parking lot looking stupid, that nigga's up there fucking the shit out that lil' fine bitch he got with him."

Like Dundee, Swoop was also tired of playing Detective when they had pretty much figured out that the work was at Bulldog's house. After doing surveillance on the house for a couple days and witnessing a number of high level Bloods coming and going from the residence at all times of night, it was clear that he was either holding Rah-Rah's work or money.

"So what you want to do, playboy?" Swoop asked, yet he already knew the answer to his own question and he was ready to get paid.

Smiling, Dundee said, "Dawg, you already know what I want to do! Let's go holler at that nigga Bulldog!"

Returning his man's smile with a wicked one of his own, Swoop started the car and backed out of their parking space. They had waited long enough, and the time had come to put in work. As they pulled out of the Hotel parking lot and merged into traffic, Swoop took one last look through his rearview mirror at the Marriot's entrance. Even though he was on his way to see Bulldog and hopefully cake off with Rah-Rah's riches, the hater that resided in him still planned to deal with his nephew as well. With that in mind, he knew that he and Rah-Rah had unfinished business.

Tia's body was on fire as she watched Rah-Rah place a trial of wet kisses from her collarbone down to her breasts. His mouth and tongue felt so good as they double teamed her torso that Tia could hardly keep her eyes open as her head tossed from side to side and her breaths came out in short gasps while he sucked on her right breast and squeezed and pinched the other. Tia's nipples were hard and swollen and her pussy was throbbing and moist as she caressed the back of Rah-Rah's head, forcing his head tighter against her breast.

Rah-Rah allowed Tia's moans to determine his direction, and by her erratic breathing alone he knew that she was ready for further stimulation. He slipped his free hand into her lace thong and gently began to rub her pulsating clit. Increasing his pressure as her moans intensified, Rah-Rah stepped up his suction on Tia's breasts and squeezed her clit before sliding two fingers into her center. Tia was tight and wet, causing Rah-Rah to dig deeper inside her.

"Sssssh, damn baby!" Tia moaned, kissing and sucking on Rah-Rah's lips as she forced her pussy down on his probing fingers. Without warning, she felt Rah-Rah rip her panties off, and she watched through sex-gazed eyes as he removed his boxers and allowed his dick, which was big and thick, to bob freely. Tia's eyes widened at the size as fear suddenly began to set in. Gazing from his dick to his handsome face, she whispered in a small voice, "Rah-Rah, it's not going to fit."

Seeing the pain in her gaze, Rah-Rah said, "I won't hurt you, Tia. I promise," in the most soothing voice that he could muster. Pulling her to the end of the bed, Rah-Rah held her in an unblinking stare as he kneeled between her outstretched legs and began to kiss and lick her chocolate inner thighs, making her squirm. Blowing on every inch of her moist skin as he traveled to the valley that housed her pearl, he placed the tip of his tongue against Tia's clit and rapidly began to flick it. Her loud moans, groans, facial expression, euphoria, and intake of breath intensified his wish to make her experience worthy and unforgettable.

"Oooooh, my God! Rahsaaaaan!" Tia cried out, staring down at the head that was wedged between her trembling legs. She had never experienced anything like what Rah-Rah was doing to her at that moment, and although he was unaware of it, Tia was a virgin. Thus, as he picked up his pace, licking her inner walls then sucking and licking her lips and clit, the explosion that rocked her body was unexpectedly beautiful.

Rah-Rah paused his actions and waited for Tia's orgasm to subside, while standing and climbing on the bed between her outstretched legs. Placing himself at the moistened lips of her opening, as he gazed into her lowered lids, Rah-Rah eased the head inside and slowly began to inch further inside of the glove tightness that enveloped him.

Tia bit into Rah-Rah's shoulder to stifle the scream that slid from her lips as she felt his dick stretch the confines of her pussy. It hurt like hell but felt so good at the same time, making her cry out in a mixture of pain and pleasure as Rah-Rah pumped all nine inches into her tightness in a slow, grinding motion. He was tearing her pussy up, and was loving every minute of it.

"Rahsaaaan, fuck me hard, baby!" Tia whimpered through moans and groans.

Rah-Rah abruptly pulled out. His dick was covered in Tia's juices as he stood and said, "Turn over and get on your hands and knees." She quickly complied with his wishes, wanting to feel him back inside her so bad that she would have done anything he asked.

Assuming the position, Tia placed her face in the pillow and arched her back as she felt Rah-Rah massaging her ass. He then re-entered her drenched depths and began to pump himself into her slowly as he squeezed her ass firmly, catching a rhythm.

"Aaaaaahhh. I love the way you feel, Rahsaan," Tia cried out as Rah-Rah fucked her with no mercy, slamming her hips back into him. Their moans and breathing increased as their pace accelerated, and Rah-Rah added to Tia's sensation by stroking her nipples and kissing her back. "Ooooh baby, I'm cumming!" Tia yelled, feeling her climax at the same moment that she felt Rah-Rah's seed collide with the walls of her pussy.

As they collapsed onto the bed, breathing loudly, they were both sated from their bout of lovemaking but pleased with the outcome for totally different reasons. Enfolding Tia in his muscular arms, Rah-Rah truly felt that she was his woman after what had just transpired. However, as Tia molded her body to her man and slowly stroked the piece of flesh between them that had brought her so much pleasure, she was proud to think that after what had just taken place between them, she was finally a real woman. Only then they both realized they belonged to one another, and anyone who tried to come between them would end up paying a dire price.

"Little mama, you're in for one hell of a night!" Bulldog bragged, hefting his crotch for the benefit of the young hood chick that exited his Lincoln. "I'm tearing that shit up," he said watching her thickness as she strutted next to him and draped her arms through his.

"Bulldog, you're so crazy," she laughed and leaned against his shoulder. She liked Bulldog and the money that he gave up whenever he rolled through, but she found it hilarious that he actually thought that he was tearing anything up with that little ass dick of his.

"Come on in and make yourselves comfortable," Swoop said, motioning the pair to have a seat on the couch as he openly stared at the thickly proportioned light-skinned chick who nervously glanced from him to Bulldog.

"Bulldog's mind was moving a million miles a minute as he surveyed his surroundings, seeing the ripped furniture and general destruction of his home. The reality of their situation had just set in when he felt a heavy object crash into the back of his head, sending him to his knees as the sounds of his companion's screams followed him into the darkness that he slipped into.

"Omigod…omigod," the girl cried, shivering in the cold porcelain Jacuzzi where they had tied her naked body up and placed her beside Bulldog's unconscious body.

"Bitch, not even God can help you now, so you may as well stop calling him!" Dundee barked, throwing the handful of popcorn he had been eating at her. "And shut that damn crying up before I let this bitch go up in that shit," he added, pointing his gun in the tub.

Her sobs turned to light whimpers as she trembled violently. The female was petrified, and the only thought that continued to eat at her was, 'why the hell didn't I stay with my daughter instead of forcing her off on my grandmother again so that I could go trickin' with this nigga?' She cut her eyes at Bulldog and tried not to look at the man who rubbed himself as he ogled her naked flesh. She hoped with all of her being that when Bulldog awoke he would get them out of their dilemma so that she could go home to her child.

"Damn, this nigga still ain't up?" Swoop barked, entering the room with a bag of money. "Thanks to your quick-tempered ass we're stuck in this bitch waiting for his ass to wake up instead of somewhere splitting up this paper and the bricks that I know they stashed up in this joint somewhere!"

"Hey, the nigga acted like he wasn't trying to sit his ass down... so I just helped him," Dundee stated, hunching his shoulders and shifting his eyes from the naked girl to the bag of money.
"How much you got there, dawg?"

"Not nearly enough," Swoop announced, cutting his response at the sound of Bulldog's moans. Peering over the edge of the tub, he said, "Well it looks like our boy has finally decided to wake his ass up."

Bulldog's head felt like it would explode any moment, and a blinding light forced him to blink numerous times as he tried to adjust his vision to his surroundings. The voices that he heard above him, as well as the warm flesh that lied beside him, brought on immediate remembrance of his predicament, causing him to struggle against whatever material that his captors had used to bind his legs and arms.

"There's no need for that, ole head. You ain't going nowhere, nigga!" Swoop sat on the edge of the tub and looked down at Bulldog and the teary-eyed female as Dundee's laughter filled the room.

"Now I just need you to answer a couple easy questions for me, then we'll leave and you two can get back to whatever it was that you were about to do." Biting on his bottom lip as he scrutinized the fine piece of meat that lay beside Bulldog's bum ass, Swoop said, "Damn, you're fine! But anyway, if we don't get the answers that we want, although I hate to do it, I'm going to blow your pretty little head off, ma."

The floodgate instantly opened upon hearing the man's plans for her, and there was no stopping the female's loud sobs as the realization of her fate suddenly revealed itself. As Bulldog listened to his company's sobs, he steered his heart and mind of any fear that may have entered had he not already known what was coming. He had been around long enough to know that whenever jack boys came at their victims without masks they had already planned to leave no witnesses to the crime. As he peered into the pleading eyes that stared back at him, Bulldog was truly sorry for what he was about to do.

"Okay, now that we've got that out of the way," Swoop began, swinging the pistol into the tub, "Where's that nigga Rah-Rah's stash at, playboy?" Staring at Bulldog, Swoop saw nothing but contempt in his face as Bulldog held him with a closed mouth look and an inferno in his eyes.

"Well, if that's how you want to carry it, your bitch has until the count of ten. One," Swoop began pointing the gun at her head.

"Two," the female heard the gunman say as she jerked her head towards Bulldog and yelled, "Tell them what they want to know! Don't let them kill me."

"Three… Four… Five… Six."

She was frantic as she fought with everything she had to free herself, to no avail. "I have a little girl who needs me!" she screamed in a quivering voice as tears of frustration poured from her eyes.

"Seven… Eight… Nine."

"Please, tell 'em," she begged Bulldog. However, the tears that she saw in his cold eyes confused her as they shared a tense silence.

"Time's up, beautiful!" Swoop announced, pulling the trigger. Blood and brain matter exploded all over the Jacuzzi, and covered the walls and Bulldog's face and chest. "Damn, I forgot to say ten, didn't I?" Swoop joked, turning the gun on Bulldog. "Okay, ole head, there ain't going to be no more countdowns. I'm going to ask you one more time, and if you continue to play this fake ass gangster game that you're playing, I'm going to twist your fuckin' cap back. Now where's the muthafuckin' stash at, nigga?"

Bulldog knew that he was about to die, but the one thing that gave him solace in his last few moments on Earth was the knowledge that his murderers would experience the same fate that he was about to suffer. He was also proud of the fact that he hadn't cracked under pressure and given Rah-Rah's stash up. After all that Rah-Rah done for him, he felt that he owed him that much. Even in the face of death, he found it funny that the two men had no idea that they had not only missed out on a multimillion dollar stash but their whole fiasco had been caught on a number of surveillance cameras that the house been fitted with and he always activated whenever he left.

Breaking into a fit of laughter as the two men gave one another disbelieving looks, Bulldog said, "I'll see you two bitch ass niggas in hell, real soon!"

Their pistols erupted in unison as they watched Bulldog's body jerk with the force of each slug that entered. Although they would have killed him regardless of whether he gave them the stash or not, he had chosen not to and his disrespectful comment had only assisted in his imminent demise.

Chapter Twenty-Four

"Say what?" Rah-Rah's outburst woke Tia from her comatose state. "When did you get there, Blood?" he asked, climbing out of bed and reaching for his clothing that was strewn all over the room. Dressing as he listened closely to the caller, he said, "Clean the house out and put everything in the other spot, then torch that shit. We'll tip a few bottles for the OG later, but right now we need to clean up shop. Meet me at the club when you're done."

Hanging up the phone and turning to Tia who had a questioning look on her face, Rah-Rah was startled by what B-Rock had just informed him. He truly liked Bulldog, and he hated that the ole head caught a bad one. However, as he turned to Tia and said, "Get dressed, I've got to take you home," he recalled his Uncle Cross once stating that in order to survive in the streets you had to adopt a money over everything mentality.

"Baby, what's wrong?" Tia asked, her voice filled with worry as she got out of bed and complied with his wishes. "You all right?" she added, noticing the fleeting look of sadness that he had on his face when he turned to her.

"Yeah, I'm good, baby. I just found out that one of my dudes got murdered tonight," Rah-Rah said dryly.

"I'm so sorry to hear that, Rahsaan." Tia gave him a big hug, then said, "I'm not going home, boy... I'm going with you."

Pulling back and breaking their embrace, Rah-Rah said, "I'm taking you home, Tia. I'm not sure what's going on yet, and I'm not going to have my woman out in the streets where she may be in danger. Besides, you need to be at home with Jerry."

Folding her arms across her naked breasts, Tia's stance was defiant when she insisted, "I'm not going anywhere but with you and that's all to it. If Jerry needs me, he'll call, and I'm sure that I'll be in no more danger while I'm with you in the streets than I normally am, so don't even come at me with that weak shit. Besides, my gun ain't broke."

Shaking his head and walking into the bathroom, Rah-Rah wasn't trying to deal with Tia's stubbornness at the moment. Although he wasn't about to tell her, he found it kind of sexy that she was prepared to ride with her man. Only if that was how she wanted to carry it, Tia needed to pick up her pace. As he headed into the bathroom, Rah-Rah announced, "If you plan on being the Bonni to my Clyde, you might want to put some clothes on that lil' pretty ass of yours before I come out of this bathroom or I'm leaving you here."

"Yeah, picture that," Tia replied sharply, smiling at Rah-Rah's back as he closed the door behind him. However, as she hurriedly got dressed knowing that she had gotten her way, Tia decided that just in case he had truly meant what he said she wasn't about to get caught unprepared for his exit.

"Where's B-rock?" Rah-Rah questioned a group of Bloods who stood in front of the club as he exited his car with Tia close behind.

"He inside waiting on you, Damu," one of the men answered, holding the door open for Rah-Rah and Tia.

"Good looking out, man." Rah-Rah tossed him his car keys and said, "Put my shit out back," as he led Tia into the club and through the mass of bodies that were crowded inside.

'Wow' Tia thought as she allowed Rah-Rah to lead her through the parting crowd. She had never been in a strip club, and she found something extremely sensual about seeing women in various stages of undress sliding down poles and giving lap dances. Tia also felt a thing of jealousy at the realization that Rah-Rah spent so much time around such beautiful women, even if she did feel that none of them could hold a candle to her.

Entering the hallway that led to his office and nodding at two hulking Bloods that stood guard, Rah-Rah barged into the office and was met by a group of his elite men who were engrossed in whatever they were watching on the flat screen television. However, upon seeing Tia, the screen immediately went blank and everyone stared.

Rah-Rah understood that his bringing Tia to their meeting was unusual and he had more than likely made his men uncomfortable, but since she was going to be a presence in his life, he figured that they may as well get used to her being around. Therefore, he broke the silence and got straight to business. "Baby, these dudes are my people, and I want you all to meet my girl Tia," Rah-Rah announced, looking around the room. "She's going to be here, and she's a soldier in every sense of the word as you all need to get used to her. Now, is all of our shit in order and what do we know about the niggas who murdered Bulldog?" Rah-Rah asked B-rock.

"They found the fake stash, but the real stash was in order when we arrived," B-Rock said, tossing the remote control to Rah-Rah. "As for the niggas that did that shit, it's all on the surveillance tape, bruh."

"Oh yeah!" Rah-Rah blurted, thinking that they had just signed their own death warrant when they foolishly ran up in his house and killed his ole head for a little over a hundred grand. Hitting the play button as he took a seat and pulled Tia down into his lap, the face that came into view stopped Rah-Rah's heart. As he watched his uncle murder Bulldog and his companion, he knew that it wasn't a random stick-up when Swoop specifically asked where his stash was. At that moment it also became crystal clear to him how Swoop's treachery had to be repaid, and as he stood to leave, the only thought he had in mind was, 'two can play this game.'

Swoop leaned back in his chair and disgustedly blew out a breath of air. "Man, look at this bullshit!" he snapped, staring at the money on the table.

"What bullshit?" Dundee exclaimed excitedly. "Nigga, I don't know about you but I'm good with my cut. Shit, I would have gladly deaded their asses for much less."

Swoop was forced to smile at the truth in Dundee's statement, knowing that he too would have and had killed for much less in his lifetime. The only thing that bothered him about doing so tonight was the fact that he had wanted to hurt his nephew's pockets, and he realized that the money they received from the night's caper was nothing more than peanuts to Rah-Rah.

Placing the stacks in his jacket pocket and standing, Dundee said, "As usual, I've enjoyed putting in work with you, my nigga, but after seeing all that ass on dude's girl earlier, I think I might need to go holler at one of my pretty little young things."

Giving Dundee a pound and retrieving his half of the money from the table as well, Swoop watched Dundee leave, thinking that he would more than likely blow his share of the heist on a couple of young bitches like he always did. He grabbed his keys and headed towards the door. Swoop's plans were totally different but the same as every time that he ever came up on a decent sum of money. He was going to drop past his mother's house and leave her a few grand, so that she could add it to the hefty nest egg that she already had put away. Smiling to himself as he headed out the door, Swoop kind of saw himself as the modern day Robin Hood because he robbed from the rich and gave to the poor. It never occurred to him that maybe he should have picked a safer victim this time around, because little did Swoop know he and Dundee had just become shark bait.

"Baby, what are you doing, sitting here in the dark?" Rah-Rah's grandmother asked, walking in the living room and clicking on the light.

"I'm just sitting here, thinking, grandma," Rah-Rah lied, feeling the weight of the gun and silence that rested beneath his hooded sweatshirt.

"That's funny, I didn't see your car when I looked out the window," she said as if the thought had just come to her, before adding, "Why didn't you wake me? And you need to call your father because he has been calling here every day looking for you, and I can't even tell him where you are when I don't know myself. Where are you staying, honey, because you don't even come and see your poor grandmother?" She vented, having a one-sided conversation.

Rah-Rah forced himself to smile at his grandmother, even though he was far from happy at that moment. However, before he could respond, he heard the front door close and his Uncle's voice. He involuntarily reached beneath his sweatshirt and gripped the handle of his Colt .45.

"Ma, what are you doing up?" Swoop asked, walking into the living room with his head down, counting out a number of banded bundles of money. "I brought you something, "he said, lifting his eyes and coming face to face with Rah-Rah's wild-eyed stare. As he held Rah-Rah's unblinking stare with one of his own, Swoop hated to admit it, but his nephew had the drop on him and by the way his hand visibly shook beneath his hooded sweatshirtshirt, it was also clear that Rah-Rah had a weapon and he knew about the robbery. Swoop just couldn't imagine how he had found out, or what he planned to do about it with his grandmother in the room.

"God is good," his grandmother announced, smiling from ear to ear as her eyes darted from her son to her grandson. Reaching for the money and giving Swoop a big hug, she was oblivious to the animosity that was being directed between the two when she said, "How lucky can I be to wake up and find my grandson here, then you pop up with all this money for me?" Bay, where did you get all this money anyway?"

"Yeah, Unc, where did you get all that money?" Rah-Rah asked though clenched teeth. He wanted to kill his Uncle so bad that his head hurt, and the only thing that kept him from doing so right then was the fact that his grandmother stood between them and he respected her too much to kill her son in her presence.

"I won it in a dice game, ma," Swoop lied, ignoring Rah-Rah's question all together. He was somewhat comforted by the fact that Rah-Rah hadn't pulled the gun that rested in his hand yet, but was planning to remain in the doorway and keep his mother between them until he was sure of his nephew's intentions.

"I bet you did some serious shooting to get that paper, unk, but from what they tell me you almost made off with a U-haul full of money." Rah-Rah spoke in a manner that only he and Swoop could decipher. "Maybe you could have come up in a major way if you would have slowed your roll."

"You think so?" Swoop asked, refusing to let Rah-Rah get out on him. Flashing a number of tightly wrapped bundles and grinning, he bragged, "If I may say so myself, I think I did just fine for my first night out. Plus, I was always taught that you can't ever get it all. However, you can bet your ass that I'll do much better next time."

"Is that so?" Rah-Rah said sliding to the edge of the couch. His teeth were clamped so tightly together that his jaw shook.

"You better believe it, lil' Rah-Rah," Swoop boldly stated, adding, "If I'm lucky, maybe I'll be able to catch you at the next game."

Glaring at his uncle's smiling face, Rah-Rah's heart banged against his chest as he stood and hugged his grandmother tightly. He had to get out of there as quickly as he possibly could before the explosives that lied dormant in him detonated. Thus, he broke their embrace and said, "I'll be back to see you as soon as I can, grandma." As he walked past Swoop with hatred blazing in his eyes and heart, Rah-Rah whispered, "Your stupid ass should have worn a mask if you planned to kill my man on camera, but just so you know, I'll be back to see you much sooner than I will grandma, nigga!"

Swoop could only stare at Rah-Rah's departing back with his mouth open and a stupid look on his face. However, Rah-Rah had put him on point with the warning, so he no longer had to wonder whether they knew. His only worry at this point was staying alive. With that thought in mind, Swoop decided that he needed to put a little security on his life and he knew exactly who he was going to see.

Chapter Twenty-Five

Stink could no longer shake the feeling of dread that resided in his mind and the pit of his stomach as he reached for his phone and pondered his last conversation with Jose over a month ago. Although Jose had promised him that Rah-Rah was fine and he had nothing to worry about, even with the magnitude of trust that Stink had in Jose, something just wasn't adding up. Not-to-mention, Jose had agreed to call him back with any additional information that he was able to learn about Rah-Rah's new associates, and after a month of waiting, he still hadn't heard one word from him. This wasn't the Jose that Rah-Rah once knew, and as of late he was finding it hard to determine exactly who he was dealing with. What bothered Stink the most was the fact that he was beginning to share Cross' sentiment that their good friend and mentor was on some bullshit. Nevertheless, as he closed his eyes and shook his head in an attempt to clear his head of the negative thoughts that clouded it, Stink decided to give Jose the benefit of the doubt and call him. Maybe he had allowed his stress and Cross' constant opposition to Jose to sway his thoughts as well.

Dialing the numbers that he now knew by heart, Stink involuntarily counted the rings as he awaited an answer.

"Hello," a soft, sultry-sounding voice answered.

"Yes. Is Jose in?" Stink asked. He was surprised to hear a female answering Jose's phone, because it had never happened before.

"I'm not sure, sir," the female said, a slight pause in her tone. "I'll have to check, but who may I ask is calling?" she added, walking towards Jose's office door and knocking lightly.

Momentarily pausing at the sound of the voice on the phone, Stink couldn't quite place it, but he knew that he had heard the female's voice before. "Tell him that Stink is on the phone.

Hearing the name and voice that had played her thoughts and dreams for many years caused the female's heartbeat to increase to a feverish pace as she opened the door and walked inside Jose's office on rubbery legs. Though she tried to hide the nervousness that gripped her, as Jose and his associate turned and stopped talking when she said, "Okay, Mr. Stink, I'll check for you. Please hold," her voice suddenly sounded as if it belonged to someone else. Staring at Jose, she wore a blank face as she awaited his response. When he shook his head 'no' and waved her away, she walked out of the room and closed the door behind her. Exhaling a breath of air, she stilled her nerves as much as possible and said, "I'm sorry, Sir, but he's not in at the moment."

"Okay," Stink said, his mind running a million miles a minute. "Have him get in contact with me as soon as he returns, aight?"

"I'll give him the message, sir," she replied in the most business manner that she could muster, hating for the call to end.

Stink held the phone, listening to the labored breathing on the other side. "Excuse my forwardness, Ms., but do we know one another, because your voice sounds so familiar and I feel as if we've met?"

"Umm, no sir," she replied, slouching down in her chair and biting her bottom lip.

"Aight then, give Jose my message. Thanks," Stink announced before ending the call.

"That was his father on the phone," Jose announced, observing the men who sat in front of him. "He has been a loyal friend of mine for over twenty years, and now this." His words tapered off. "How do you know this?" Jose's question was directed at Miguel.

"I was contacted by a man named Swoop who claims to be his uncle, Patron. He says that he witnessed Chico's murder," Miguel replied. His words caused Jose to lean back in his chair with a questioning look on his face.

"Why is he giving his own nephew to us this way, and what do you know about this man?" Jose asked.

"It seems that he and his nephew are at odds, Patron, and from what we've learned so far, he's a man who uses his gun for a living," Miguel said, adding, "He wants to meet with us and discuss terms of assisting in his nephew's elimination.

"And what do you think?" Jose turned his attention to Santiago. "Did Rah-Rah have anything to do with the death of my nephew, Chico?"

Santiago shook his head 'yes', saying, "He's been involved in a number of deaths in the city, Patron, and it's rumored that he carries a gold-plated Colt .45 like the gun that Chico used to have."

"Umm hmm," Jose hummed, cradling his chin. Standing and walking around his desk, Jose's face radiated calm but his eyes and tone of voice defined the rage within him. "I want you to set up the meeting with Rah-Rah's uncle, Miguel. Santiago, I want every soldier we have in that city to be prepared for an-all-out war within the week… and not even the two decade relationship that Stink and I have shared can stop me from demanding that one of you bring me his son's head and place it right here!" Jose barked, slamming his palm down on the desk, causing the two men to jump as their heads shook up and down in unison.

Though Jose and his associates thought that their words were being spoken in silence, outside of anyone's earshot besides their own, little did they know someone else had heard. And as she quickly moved away from the door where her ear had just been pressed, the female was caught between a rock and a hard place. She had just stumbled across information that was detrimental to the only man that she had ever really loved, yet she realized that in order to warn him, she had to cross the man who had given her the utmost loyalty and helped her put the pieces of her once crushed heart back in place. Teary- eyed as she stumbled through their enormous house and ran out the front door, she didn't know what to do. However, as she sped down the long, winding driveway with thoughts of her past colliding with those of her present, she realized what she had to do, as well as what her actions would cost her. As the wind whipped through her long, sandy curls, with her mind made up, she lifted the phone and scrolled back to the last caller where she found exactly what she needed.

Pushing the digits and holding the phone against her ear and shoulder, the woman's heart beat out of her chest as she anticipated revealing herself to the man that had never been far from her thoughts.

"Hello," Stink spoke into the receiver.

"Hello, Stink?" the females voice trembled.

Stink twisted the top off the beer he held and sipped it, "Yeah, this is Stink, who is this?"

The caller was experiencing second thoughts, and she was about to hang up and forget about her hair-brained scheme when Stink pulled her from her thoughts, "Hello, are you there?"

"Yes, Stink... I'm here." She paused, the mumbled, "It's me... Melody."

Chapter Twenty-Six

"Your own uncle did that shit? Damn, Blood, that nigga cold as hell," B-Rock stated, shaking his head angrily.

"That's fucked up, fo'real!" Tia hissed, gently removing her palms over Rah-Rah's waves as he leaned his back against her in the large armchair. "What you going to do about it, boo?" she asked.

Opening his eyes, Rah-Rah's response was quick and straight to the point. "I'm gonna push his dome back next time I see him… that's what I'm gonna do!"

Watching his man stand and stalk across the room, B-Rock understood Rah-Rah's anger and knew that he too would have felt the same had it been his uncle who ran up in their spot and murdered Bulldog, but regardless of how hard a man carried it, only a special kind of individual could kill his own family member. B-Rock realized that he didn't posses a heart as cold as that, therefore, without questioning Rah-Rah's gangster, he decided that he would offer him an alternative.

"Aye, Blood, how about you let me handle this one for you?" B-Rock asked, watching Rah-Rah's body language as he turned to face him with fire in his eyes.

"Naw, Dawg, I got this!" Rah-Rah blared. "I appreciate it, though."

"Baby, I know you're mad, and I can't blame you… but B-Rock does have a point.

Dude is your uncle, Rahsaan, and if he has to get what's coming to him, you wouldn't be the one to give it to him. Think about it, he is your uncle," Tia said, trying her best to be persuasive.

Frowning at Tia's words, Rah-Rah barked, "Fuck that nigga, Tia! I understand that he's my mother's brother, which makes his clown ass my uncle, but I don't know his shiesty ass !" Pacing around the room as he spoke, he said, "If he gave a damn about me, he wouldn't have done that lame shit to Bulldog, so now I'm about to show him what happens when I don't give a damn about a muthafucka. I'm murdering his ass and that's all to it!" he argued, storming out of the room.

B-Rock watched Rah-Rah angrily exit the room and disappear up the steps, thinking that Swoop was in big trouble. He had also received the answer to his question as to how cold Rah-Rah's heart was, and for the first time since meeting him, B-Rock no longer thought that his man was crazy, he now realized that Rah-Rah was a mad man. Turning back towards Tia, B-Rock was about to ask her to help him talk some sense into Rah-Rah when her huge smile stopped him in his tracks.

"What's so funny?" he asked, hoping that she could help him shed some light on what she found humorous about their impending situation.

Tia stopped picking at her immaculately manicured nails and looked up at him. "I was just wondering if maybe my boo would let me tag along when he runs down on his uncle?" Smiling, she added, "If he's already got his mind made up, then I may as well go with him to make sure that it's done correctly. You feel me, right?" Tia looked at B-Rock expectantly.

B-Rock was in disbelief as he stared at the dark

beauty before him. Unable to respond to her words, he could only shake his head as he turned and walked out of the apartment with Tia's laughter ringing in his ears. Suddenly laughing himself, B-Rock reached his car and got inside, and couldn't stop thinking that Tia and Rah-Rah were made for one another. They were both nuts, and wherever Swoop was at that moment, B-Rock hoped that he knew that he was a walking dead man.

Against his better judgment Dundee had allowed Swoop to talk him into meeting with two of the head members of the MS13 organization, and as they entered the prearranged location, finding it filled with Latino soldiers, he instantly began to have second thoughts.

"Man, I'm not feeling this shit," Dundee spoke in a voice that only Swoop could hear as they followed the man who had intercepted them as soon as they exited their vehicle. Many eyes traveled along with them as they entered the restaurant and made their way into the kitchen and down a flight of stairs.

"Relax, my dude. I got it all under control," Swoop replied calmly. "I told you that I had you, so watch me work.

Dundee loved his man like a brother and couldn't think of anyone else that he would rather have beside him when things got rough, but he understood who they were up against now that the secret was out that they robbed a Bad News Blood stash house and murdered one of their members. Now to make matters worse, they were walking into a hornets nest, surrounded by Latinos who hated their guts. As far as Dundee was concerned, he was already seeing the results of Swoop's work in living color, and thanks to him, they were forced to run from one group of killers right into the arms of another.

Reaching a large steel door, the Spanish man who led them stopped and knocked two times then gave another three knocks, pausing for a few seconds between each knock. When the door opened, the men were ushered into the room and patted down by four huge, tattooed men and relieved of their weapons.

"Hey, what the hell you doing?" Swoop argued, reaching for the weapon that the large, baldheaded man had just taken off his waist. "Pass me that back, amigo!"

Before the huge MS13 soldier could react, the man who had escorted them through the restaurant stepped between them and spoke. "No guns are allowed inside the meeting, and your weapons will be returned to you when you're ready to leave, Senor." Waving the grimfaced soldiers off, he turned to Swoop and Dundee and said, "Follow me."

Neither man liked the idea of parting with their weapons, but they grudgingly followed the man in front of them through the corridor, shooting mane glares at the four soldiers as they passed. However, as another door opened and the man who led them abruptly stopped and waved them inside, they came face to face with the men that they had come to see.

Miguel and Santiago sat in comfortable high-backed chairs, wearing Armani suits and Gucci loafers, looking the part of high level members in one of the countries most renowned criminal organizations. Openly scrutinizing the men who stood before them with smug looks, although they felt that the two Blacks were beneath them and they would have never entertained the thought of meeting with them had Jose not gave the order, it was Miguel who greeted the men first.

"Take your seats and let us get started," he said, pointing towards the row of chairs that stood across the table from where he and Santiago sat, wearing expressionless looks.

Although Swoop and Dundee sat in the chairs that they had been directed, Swoop felt disrespected by the two Spanish men. From the moment that they entered the room, it was painfully obvious that the men viewed them with a level of contempt. However, when they neither stood nor paid them the complimentary acknowledgements that a mere handshake would have accomplished, Swoop instantly realized that their meeting would more than likely be rocky.

Miguel clasped his hands in front of his handsome face and gave his attention and words to the bigger and more intimidating of the two men who sat across from him. "Okay, you asked to meet with us, now that we're all here, what would you like to discuss?" His demeanor was nonchalant as he peered down at his time piece.

"Well, umm," Swoop cleaned his throat suddenly unsure of himself, "I'm aware that your people have been combing the streets in search of Chico's killers, and like I told you in our initial conversation, I know the man who is responsible."

Dundee jerked his head in Swoop's direction. What he had just heard was new to him, and he assumed that they were there to collect on a reward, which now made it easier for him to understand why Swoop had been so adamant about him coming along for the meeting. Inwardly smiling at Swoop's scheme, the next words that he heard from the Spanish man caused his inward smile to turn to an-all-out look of bitterness.

"You said that your nephew, Rah-Rah, was the one responsible for the murders," Miguel remarked. "Tell me more," he said, sitting back in his chair.

Swoop ignored the stink look that Dundee held him with as he began to tell the men what he recalled from the night of Chico's murder in the hopes of saving his own skin. He knew that his chances of living increased ten-fold if he helped the men before him in their pursuit of his nephew.

"He killed both men with throwing knives, catching them off guard as they left the restaurant. After murdering the men, he retrieved his knives from the bodies and took a gold-plated gun out of Chico's hand," Swoop said, avoiding Dundee's accusing eyes.

"Where were you throughout the ordeal, and how do we know that you are not involved as well?" Santiago questioned. His dark eyes bore into Swoop as if he could see into his soul, yet his tone was flat and casual.

"What are you implying, man?" Swoop blurted defensively. "I didn't have shit to do with Chico's murder, man… I just happened to run into it when I followed my nephew and some if his partners, that's all!"

Witnessing Swoop's nervousness and becoming agitated himself, as Dundee watched the stoic faces of the Spanish men knowing that a series of commands from either of them could end their lives at any moment, he found himself holding his breath as he awaited a response from one of them.

After sharing a tense silence, Santiago tossed Swoop

a patronizing glare and said, "We have been ordered to work along with you to annihilate this problem that your nephew has become," pausing his statement upon seeing the utter relief that radiated from Swoop, Santiago continued, "But let's make one thing clear before we carry on, I don't like you, and I think that any man who would sell his own blood out for any reason should be put to death. However, what I think doesn't matter."

Swoop's mouth hung slack; no man had ever spoken to him in such a manner and lived to talk about it. "Hey who the hell do you think you're…."

"He's speaking to you!" Miguel cut Swoop off, finishing his sentence in the process. He then completely disregarded Swoop's complaint, "Anyway, now that we've gotten that out of the way, what do we owe you for this information, because I'm assuming that you didn't just hand your nephew over to us as a gift, am I correct?"

Dundee remained quiet throughout the exchange, listening to everything the men said. Like the two Spanish men, he couldn't believe that Swoop had actually crossed his own nephew. It was one thing to hit his pockets, but Dundee didn't agree with snitching in any form, especially when it was to a group of people who planned to murder your family as soon as the chance arose.

Grilling the men, Swoop said, "Nah, it wasn't a gift! The first thing I want is any money or product that we find when we catch him. I want no harm to come to any of my other family members, and I want twenty-four hour security for the two of us until my nephew is killed."

"It's done," Miguel announced, glancing at Santiago. "Is there anything else?" he asked his colleague.

"See yourself out!" Santiago stated, his voice defining the disdain that he felt for the pair. "Well be in touch."

Standing and walking to the door, as Swoop exited the room, he made a vow to himself that if he lived long enough to carry it out, he was going to murder the two arrogant Spanish men for disrespecting him. They would regret that they had ever laid eyes on him, and as he tossed a glance over his shoulder at the men before the door swung closed in his face, he closed his eyes so he would never forget their faces.

Chapter Twenty-Seven

"I hate to say it, but I told you so, high!" Cross announced, watching Stink throw an array of clothing articles in a Louis Vitton bag.

"I don't need to hear that kind of shit right now, aight?" Stink remarked, angrily cutting his eyes up at Cross, then returning to the task of packing.

"Aight, nigga, my bad," Cross stated. He understood that his man wasn't in the mood for any foolishness. "What did Bonni have to say about Melody's call?" he asked, his voice ringing in the room.

"Sssshh!" Stink said, jerking his head toward the door then turning back to Cross. "Keep your voice down, man. I haven't told her, because I don't need her worrying about Rah-Rah anymore than she already does."

"Whoa!" Cross exclaimed. "So you're planning to just go back, get Rah-Rah and return to the Dominican Republic as if nothing has ever happened back in America. Come on, High, be fo'real. Do you really think that Jose is going to let everyone live happily ever after? Rah-Rah killed his nephew and friend, Jose not going to allow his actions to go unpunished."

As much as Stink wanted to believe that Cross' words were wrong, he couldn't deny the truth. Jose would not only take revenge on Rah-Rah, but he would gladly give the order to have their whole family massacred, and not even the twenty plus years that they had been friends would sway him from his objective.

"Okay, Cross, I'm all ears… so how about you tell me how I should handle this, because right now I honestly don't know where to begin?" Stink said, taking a seat on the California King sized bed and massaging his temple as he blurted, "I can't believe that Rah-Rah has put us in this kind of danger."

Taking a seat beside him, Cross said, "Look High, what's done is done and there's absolutely nothing that we can do about that. The first thing that you must do is let Bonni know what's happening, then you have to send her and the girls somewhere safe until we can take care of this shit…."

"Slow down, Cross… you lost me," Stink interrupted Cross. "Where did you get we from when I'm the only one who's going back to America?"

Grinning, Cross said, "Come on now, High, you already know that I'm not about to let you go back alone. We're a team, bruh, and that's the way that it's always been. Plus, you know that we do our best work when we're together.

Stink know that Cross spoke the truth and he would have loved to have him at his side, but unselfishly he realized that it wasn't possible. Cross was wanted in the United States on numerous charges including kidnapping, murder and escaping from a prison where he was already serving a lengthy sentence.

"You can't go on this one, Cross!" Stink blurted seriously. "I need you to hang back and call the plays for me. Not to mention, there's no one else that I can trust to watch over my girls, bruh." Stink played the only real card that he knew would have some sway over Cross, because he knew how much Cross loved Bonni and the girls.

Cross fully understood what Stink was doing and as he stood there and smiled at his best friend, he said, "That's the way you want to play it, huh? You really want to go up against Jose on your own, Stink?" He held Stink with keen eyes, searching for the doubt that he knew lived within his soul.

Speaking slowly in the hopes that he could make Cross believe him when he wasn't even certain himself, Stink said, "I got everything covered, man. All I ask is that you make certain that my ladies remain safe in my absence. Can you promise me that, Cross… huh bruh, can you?"

"I promise you that I will see to it that Bonni and the girls are safe until this thing with Jose is over, High," Cross pledged. However, as he returned the brotherly hug that Stink stood and enfolded him in, Cross uncrossed his toes as he ran a series of schemes through his mind of ways that he could guarantee the safety of Bonni, Tavia and Rahsaanique and still return to the United States and assist Stink and Rah-Rah. Smiling at the thought of returning to battle once again, though he wasn't quite sure how he would pull it off. Cross was a firm believer that whenever there was a will there was a way, and he was going to find it.

"My plane leaves in an hour, sweetheart, and you have got to get yourself together," Stink said, sad himself as he rubbed Bonni's head, feeling her unrestrained tears coating his neck.

"I'm so afraid, Rahasaan," Bonni sobbed. "What if something happens to you, baby? There's no way that I could carry on without you."

Stink allowed her to get it all out of her system as he

softly kissed and rubbed her head. Like Bonni, he too had entertained the thought that he may not return and this may have been the last moment that they had to share with one another. A lump formed in his chest when the realization hit him that he, Bonni, Tavia, Rahsaanique and Rah-Rah may never be the happy family that they had once been, ever again. However, putting forth a level of strength that he didn't really feel, he said, "Baby, there's no need to be afraid. Nothing is going to happen to me. I'll always return to you, Bonni. That, you will never have to worry about."

Lifting her head and staring at Stink with misty, red-rimmed eyes, Bonni said, "Promise me that you will not only return to me, but you'll bring Rah-Rah home as well, baby. I need to hear those words from you, Stink!" Bonni pleaded, her tears blurring her voice.

Stink was unable to hold his wife's gaze as he blinked away the tears that threatened to erupt from his own eyes. "I promise you that we will return home, Bonni. Now get yourself together, baby, so we can go break the news to the girls." As Stink helped his wife dry her tears, he hoped that her last memory of him wouldn't be that he had lied to her in their last moments together.

Chapter Twenty-Eight

"What?" Rah-Rah yelled. He couldn't believe or understand what he had just heard.

"So far, with the exception of our spots in Dickerson Court, Newsome Park, Harbor Homes and Tidewater Park all of our other traps were overtaken by large groups of armed Hispanics. They were being led by a big baldheaded older dude from what we've been told so far, and it seems that they were looking for you, Blood," Trooper informed Rah-Rah.

Rah-Rah noticed the uneasy look that Trooper sported as he walked from one end of the room to the other, thinking his report over in search of any logic that he may have been able to retain from it. Stopping his pacing and turning o face his soldiers, Rah-Rah asked, "Do you recall if they said who exactly was asking about me?"

"Umm," Trooper frowned as he tried to remember. "Oh yeah, it was the Black dude who asked the questions."

"Were any of our people killed?" Rah-Rah questioned, though his mind was busy processing the news that Trooper had brought and formulating a number of counter measures.

"We lost three people, but with the exception of a few injuries, it seems that they virtually walked into four of our neighborhoods and snatched them right from beneath us without having to fire a single shot. If you ask me, the first thing we need to do is assassinate every single Blood that was working those traps, then kill any Spanish bangers that we encounter when we go take our shit back!" Trooper spoke with a ferociousness that defined his rage.

"Nah, Blood, take it easy," Rah-Rah said more calmly than he actually felt. He had already calculated the vast sums of money that they had lost when Stewart Gardens, Ridley Circle, Marshal Courts and Seven Oaks were commandeered from their grasp. However, his greatest lesson in life, the one that had been drilled into him more than any other, was patience. "There's a time and a place for everything, Blood, and when the time is right, we will strike them. Until that time arrives, I need you to relay the word to B-Rock that I want double shifts posted in the remainder of our traps and triple our perimeter guards. Also, from this moment on, I want four of our elite soldiers to watch over Tia when she's not in my presence. Do I make myself clear?"

"Yes, Damu... but what about you?" Trooper asked, wearing a troubled look. "Who would you like to protect you, because it's clear that they're after you?

Seeing the apprehension in Trooper's features and replaying his words, Rah-Rah was unable to hold the laughter that spilled from him. He actually found the thought of needing someone to protect him humorous, and felt that if Trooper and the others had any idea of how dangerous he had really been trained to be, they would have found themselves and their positions as elite soldiers unnecessary.

"I'm straight, gangster," Rah-Rah stated, ending his laughter and adding, "But for the moment I think it may be best if I get low. I'm gonna keep it moving for a while and you may not be seeing me as much as usual. In my absence,

B-Rock will relay any orders that I deem necessary, is that clear?"

"I got you, Ruckus," Trooper replied. Giving his general their customary Blood handshake and turning to leave, he blurted, "Be careful, even if you don't need us to protect you." He smiled and removed his phone to call their soldiers and relay Rah-Rah's instructions.

The grin instantly disappeared from Rah-Rah's face when Trooper walked out and a frown took its place as he reached for his phone and dialed Tia's number. After what he had just learned, Rah-Rah had no doubt knew that his uncle had aligned himself with the MS13 organization, and although he wasn't aware of how he had pulled it off, he was highly mindful of the fact that Swoop's power had grown tremendously. RahRah quickly called Tia and when he heard her voice, he barked, "Pack some things for you and your brother. I'm on my way!"

"That's his girl, right there!" Swoop spoke to the group of Spanish men who sat in the Virginia Power van. All the men wore hard hats and Virginia power uniforms that had been stolen along with the van. They had spent the morning sitting and waiting for Rah-Rah or any sight of his girlfriend, in the hopes of catching him slipping.

"Rahsaan, what are you talking about?" Tia laughed. "Why do I need to pack, and why are you yelling?" Listening closely as she dumped the trash, Tia looked around her when Rah-Rah said that she may have been in danger but thought nothing of it when her surroundings reflected nothing out of the norm.

Grinning at her man's paranoia, Tia said, "We'll talk about it when you get here, but I don't plan on leaving the place that I've lived in my whole life because of a threat that we're not even sure of." Tia removed the phone from her ear and glared at it in disbelief, trying to listen to Rah-Rah's loud demands. She then cut his ranting short and calmly said, "Baby, if it will make you feel any better, I'm going to go grab one of your weapons right now and we can continue this conversation when you get here. I love you too. Bye"

Smiling at the thought of how crazy her man was, Tia allowed her eyes to sweep through the neighborhood one last time before she picked up her trashcan and headed back into the house. Even though she didn't feel that there was any reason to be worried, deciding that she would rather be safe than sorry, Tia locked the door and headed up the stairs to retrieve one of Rah-Rah's weapons as promised.

"Let's go get her," Swoop said as soon as he saw her end the call to walk back into the apartment. He needed to flush his nephew out in the open, and he was sure that if they snatched his girl Rah-Rah would show his face.

The five-man team exited the van with their toolboxes and made their way across the street. Though it was relatively early, the Project bustled with traffic, and with so much going on, no one paid attention to the men as they headed up the walkway and slipped their hands inside the toolboxes. It wasn't until the big Black man slammed his foot into the door sending it crashing in, that people began to notice the five gun-toting men. Only no one intervened in the home invasion, mistaking the men for police and the home invasion for a drug bust.

Barging into the apartment Swoop waved the Spanish men in different directions, he then began to move stealth-like through the floor level in search of Rah-Rah's woman. He kept his gun held out in front of him just in case an unexpected surprise awaited around one of the corners. However, the loud boom that erupted behind him, followed by a painful scream, caused him and the two men that followed close on his heels to turn and run back in the direction that they had just come from.

Pressing the trigger again, Tia braced herself for the powerful kick of the silver Mossberg pump as she watched the surprised look on the Spanish man's face right before the deadly slug tore half of it off, sending him tumbling back down the stairs beside his dead comrade. Tia's adrenaline was racing as she heard feet running across her tiled floor. Just as she plastered herself against the wall, a volley of automatic weapons' fire erupted, tearing chunks of wood out of the ceiling and peppering the wall only inches above her head. Tia said a silent prayer and tried to fight down the fear that had her heart beating out of her chest, but the footfalls that she heard on the stairs alerted her to the eminent danger lurking. With that thought in mind, she gripped the pump tightly and tried to close in on the number of stairs that separated her from her assailant. When she felt that he was close enough, Tia pushed herself off the wall and fired down the stairs as she ran across the hall and slammed the bathroom door. Although she wasn't sure, due to the gunfire that erupted, sending angry bee sounds past her ears as she dashed into the bathroom, Tia thought that she heard a body tumble down the stairs. Only how many men stood on the other side of the door, she wondered. Tia made her mind up that even if she didn't make it out of her present dilemma alive, whoever tried to come through the door would share the trip to hell with her.

Speeding into Tia's projects and observing a crowd of people staring at her apartment then seeing the door wide open, hanging by a hinge, Rah-Rah drove up on the grass and jumped out of the car before it had come to a complete stop. With a gun in both hands, he ran to the door and stole a glance inside andsaw three bodies sprawled at the bottom of the stairs and a booted foot that had just cleared the top step. With no other thought in his mind besides saving his girl, Rah-Rah stepped into the apartment with his weapons held high. Tiptoeing over and around the multitude of spent shells that littered the floor at his feet, he was aware that a major fire-fight had taken place before he arrived. Quickening his step as he crouched at the bottom of the stairs and began to ascend them, Rah-Rah held a Spanish shooter in his sights but was hesitant to open fire on him due to hearing the low voice of another man that was concealed from view. However, when the man popped a fresh clip in the Mac-11 that he leveled at the bathroom door and pressed the trigger, Rah-Rah stood from his crouched position and let his own guns go. Catching the shooter by surprise, the shells from Rah-Rah's .45's sent him crashing into the bathroom door only to be slammed back against the opposite wall when another shell exploded through the door, blowing a large hole through the wood and the man's back. Running up the stairs, Rah-Rah heard the sound of shuffling feet followed by breaking glass. By the time he reached the bedroom and peered out the window, Rah-Rah saw his uncle turn the corner of another building moving at breakneck speed. He planned to catch up with him at a later date, but as he moved back through the hallway witnessing the bloody floor and bullet-riddled walls, Rah-Rah prayed that his baby was alive and unharmed.

"Tia, are you all right in there?" Rah-Rah called out, refusing to stick his head in the door uninvited. Though he was racked with worry, he tried to keep his voice steady when he said, "Baby, it's me, Rahsaan. Is it okay for me to come in?"

Tia's body shook violently as she held the riot pump ready, awaiting the men who had come to harm her. Even though she heard the familiar sound of Rah-Rah's voice, after what she had just went through, Tia couldn't trust herself to make the right decision as to whether it was really him or she had subconsciously summoned him there.

Hearing footsteps approaching, Rah-Rah stole a glance down the stairs and saw a heavily armed group of his men entering the apartment. Mouthing the words, "I'm good" as he waved them back, he gently announced, "Baby, it's over now. I'm here with you, Tia, and you no longer have anything to worry about." Though she gave no response, the sound of her low sobs reached his ears. "Baby girl, I'm coming in to get you, so please don't shoot me." Taking a deep breath, Rah-Rah walked through the door.

When Tia saw Rah-Rah walked through the door, her tears ran unrestrained down her face as the riot pump slipped from her hand and clattered into the bathtub. No words were needed to explain what had just happened, and as Rah-Rah lifted her from the tub and cradled her in his arms, he allowed her to release the sobs that would cleanse her soul. Exiting the apartment and placing her in the car, Rah-Rah turned to the group of men that had been dispatched to guard Tia and said, "I want you to retrieve a bag of weapons that are in the bedroom closet and get rid of the riot pump in the bathtub."

"What do you want us to do about the bodies, Blood?" One of the men asked.

Thinking about it, Rah-Rah said, "Leave'em. Too many people saw what happened here, so there's no way that we can act like nothing ever took place." Tossing a look over his shoulder at Tia, Rah-Rah said, "Find her brother and bring him to me."

"It's done." The men scurried off to accomplish their task as Rah-Rah and Tia exited the projects.

Chapter Twenty-Nine

Exiting New York City's LaGuardia Airport with his Louis Vuitton baggage, Stink fished his Aviator shades out of his Gucci khaki shorts' pocket and placed them on his face. The bright sun's glare was much more bearable, thanks to the tint that now covered his eyes, and as Stink searched the sea of vehicles that populated the front of the Airport in the hopes of finding his ride, his attention was suddenly drawn to a car that sped into the parking area. Before he was actually able to see the driver clearly, Stink smiled at the knowledge that no one but Melody would arrive in a convertible Aston Martin DB9. However, as the car came to a screeching halt and the two of them laid eyes on one another for the first time in thirteen years, Stink's smile broadened at the fact that the woman before him was even more beautiful than she had ever been since the last time he saw her her.

'Oh my God!' Melody thought when she saw Stink standing only mere feet away from where she sat. Her heartbeat seemed to elevate with each second that their eyes locked with one another, and even after all of the time that had elapsed, though she couldn't understand why she felt this way, Melody was nervous and anxious at the same time. However, as she breathed in a gust of air and tried to calm her racing nerves, Melody placed her vehicle in park and a dimpled smile on her face as she opened the door and exited the car.

"Wow!" Stink exclaimed, his eyes wide with

admiration at the sight that Melody presented as she strolled around the car. She had always been stunning, but the older, thicker Melody that strutted towards him was not only gorgeous, her beauty now bordered on exotic proportions.

Blushing as she closed the distance between them, Melody swept her view over Stink's body and shivered at the memory of its touch, texture and the many tricks that it was able to perform on her own body. Nevertheless, she knew that these thoughts belonged to another place and time and it was understood that they could never recapture that which was lost. He was there because of his son and nothing else. Thus, as Melody reached for one of his carry-on bags, she placed her own feelings on the backburner and spoke as nonchalantly as she possibly could.

"Hello, Rahsaan." Melody wiped all traces of emotion from her face and voice. "I hope that your trip was to your liking. Let me grab that for you." She cried, staring into the crowd.

Stink was at loss for words as he held Melody captive with his eyes. Although he heard her words, after he had been with her for so long, he knew Melody well enough to understand that she too was experiencing emotions that had lay dormant far too long. There had never been any real closure between them, so their unexpected reunion of sorts was much greater than him coming to check up on Rah-Rah and they both knew it.

"Rahsaan, is everything okay?" Melody asked in an unsure tone, trying to avoid his piercing glance.

Dropping his bags and holding his arms apart, Stink saw the uncertainly in her stance as she shifted her weight from one leg to the other. However, when he said,

"Regardless of what you must have thought, in the last thirteen years I've never stopped thinking about you." Melody's façade evaporated as she walked into Stink's embrace.

"I never stopped thinking of you either," Melody announced reluctantly disengaging herself from the muscular arms that she had dreamed of holding her for so long. Clearing her throat as she nervously looked around them she added, "There's so much that we need to discuss, and I think that it's best that we go somewhere private to do it. You'll understand my paranoia better when I'm able to explain it all better, all right?"

"I agree," Stink replied, feeling somewhat paranoid himself as he retrieved his bags and followed Melody to the car. He had to remember that Jose had eyes everywhere and if Melody was close enough to him to hear a private conversation then there was a chance that someone was watching their every move at that very moment. With that thought in mind, as they pulled out in traffic Stink found himself wondering just how close Melody and Jose were as he looked more closely at the woman who he may have known as well as he thought he did. She decided to pull the top on the convertible for more privacy, before taking off.

Moments later, Melody pulled up at the Renaissance Hotel and gave the keys to a valet. Stink was unable to suppress his feelings for Melody and the inevitable seemed to be lurking from the moment their eyes met.

"Follow me," Melody said with lowered, sex-glazed eyes. She then mumbled, "In case you're wondering, I reserved the room the day we spoke so that we could have somewhere safe to talk."

Stink refrained from responding. His mind was filled with thoughts as they boarded the elevator and headed to their room. So many memories clouded his mind as his eyes devoured Melody's succulent frame, the same frame that he once owned. When they exited the elevator and reached their room, before the door had shut completely they were all over one another. An animalistic desire overcame them as their lips and tongue melded together, fighting for dominance.

"Umm, damn!" Melody moaned, pulling away and unbuttoning her silk shirt. She let it flutter to the floor behind her, and stood before Stink in her satin bra and heels while she waited for him to remove his clothes. Seeing him naked caused her mouth to water.

Stink's dick instantly filled with blood at the sight of Melody's panty-less body. Her juicy light-complexioned body was so deliciously put together that he lost all control when he lay down on the bed with her on top of him. Their kiss intensified as Stink gently released the snaps on her bra and allowed her breasts to bob free. His lips and tongue slowly sucked and liked at the elongated pink nipples that sat at their center.

"Yeeeeesss! That feeeeels so goood!" Melody drew the words out in a long moan. Reaching behind her to grasp Stink's rock hard length as she positioned her thighs on either side of his body, she felt her juices sliding down her inner thighs as she raised upwards and looked longingly down into his dark eyes.

Holding Melody's glance with his own wanting look, Stink witnessed the same vulnerability in Melody that he always remembered being there right before he entered her. However, as he said, "Regardless of where our paths take us when we leave this room, you will always belong to me," Stink lowered Melody's hips onto his dick, feeling her soaked center engulf him.

"Oooooohhh, Rahsaan! Ooh, God!" Melody cried out, tossing her head back and holding his ankles as she ground her pussy on his hardness. Her long hair framed her face as she violently bounced up and down on Stink's dick, biting her lip in an attempt to concentrate. The pleasure she felt was beyond anything that she had felt in years.

"Shit, Melody! Work that shit like I taught you, ma!" Stink felt every crevice of Melody's wet center as she shifted her ass on his shaft, and he loved every moment of it. Not only had the years been kind to her in the looks and body department, but her sex game had gotten much better as well. Feeling himself getting close to ejaculating, Stink rolled Melody over on her back and placed her legs on his shoulders. He then began to pounce her pussy with the force of a jackhammer.

"Oh! Ooh! Oooooh!" Melody whimpered, wide-eyed. Stink was killing her pussy and she loved every minute of it. " Keep it right there, dammit! Right there! Rahsaan,...." She screamed, "I'm dummying!"

Stink's eruption was only moments from arriving thanks to the muscles that Melody milked him with as she gripped him. Closing his eyes tight, Stink fought with the decision of whether to pull out of Melody or cum inside of her. Quickly deciding that he had awaited this moment for years and he wasn't about to pass it up, Stink's body suddenly began to spasm as he shot spurt after spurt of warm liquid into the depths of Melody's pussy, watching her grip the sheets.

"That's right, Rahsaan! Cum with me, baby… cum with meee!" Melody screamed as her body shook with the intensity of her orgasm. "Ohmygod!" she groaned collapsing on Stink, their breaths coming in short gasps as they laid in a tangled mess of sweaty flesh and moist sheets.

"Damn, Mel, that was good, ma!" Stink blurted, laughing and wiping her damp hair out of her face.

"No, that was great," Melody corrected Stink, laughing as well. "Thanks, boo… I needed that," she added seriously. Sliding out of bed and heading in the bathroom, she returned with a soapy rag and towel and started to cleanse Stink's body. When she finished, she cleaned herself up and began to get dressed.

Stink took her silence as his cue to dress as well. Thus, he retrieved his clothes and quickly followed suit, watching the look of sadness that suddenly appeared upon her face as Melody took a seat and waited for him. Taking a seat on the opposite side of the table, he allowed their silence to permeate the room.

"Rahsaan, when you left me, my life was in shambles and I thought that I would go completely out of my mind," Melody began, looking at him with sad eyes. Wringing her hands as she exhaled, she said, "If it hadn't been for Jose, I'm not sure whether I would have made it."

Stink could tell how hard it was for her to explain whatever it was that she was trying to say, so he remained quiet and allowed Melody to vent in whatever manner that she needed to.

Reaching in her purse and bringing out a wallet, Melody skinned through a number of photos before removing one and sliding it across the table. "She's six years old, and her name is Soana. She's my daughter and the reason why I awaken each and everyday.

Staring at the picture of the beautiful little girl who smiled back at him with long curly hair and missing teeth, before Melody could even say the words, he already knew who her father was. Though he had no right to feel the way he did, Stink's heart ached with the realization.

Melody knew that her secret was out when she saw the hurt in Stink's face, but what was done could never be undone and there was nothing left to say besides, "Jose is her father and my husband."

Allowing the picture to slip from his hand and flutter to the table, the magnitude of her words resonated through Stink's mind as he tried to make sense of why Melody had called him to inform him of Jose's plan to murder Rah-Rah knowing that he would kill Jose.

"Melody, what kind of games are you playing?" Stink spat, standing. "Is this a trap?" he asked, stepping around the table with his fist balled up.

Melody was aghast. "I'm not playing any games, Rahsaan. And hell no it's not a trap!" Glaring at him as she spoke, she said, "Jose will kill me if he ever finds out that I've been with you again and not even our daughter could make him forgive me. I loved you more than I loved myself back in the day, and if you doubt my feelings for you right now, never forget that I've put my life in danger so that you can save the life of your son. Now I'm not sure how you feel about that, but from where I stand it's not a game!"

Dropping his head, Stink was at a loss for words. She spoke the truth, and the only thing that he hoped for besides Rah-Rah's safety was that Jose never learned of Melody's deceit because if he did Stink knew that not even he couldn't save her.

Chapter Thirty

Cross' face held the promise of death to anyone who tried to deter him from completing his task of delivering Bonni and the girls to safety as he stalked through the airport with his hand gripping his favorite weapon beneath his shirt and his loved ones close on his heels.

"Pan Am flight seventy-three is now boarding at gate twelve," the Spanish females voice blared over the P.A. system alerting Bonni, Tavia and Rahsaanique that they were really about to abandon their lives in the Dominican Republic and traipse halfway around the world to a place that they had never been. However, as they followed Cross, each engrossed in their own thoughts, they were all aware that their unplanned excursion was for their benefit. Not to mention, they each loved Cross and trusted him with their lives. They trusted his decision to go to Dubai until the danger blew over.

Reaching the departure gate and turning to face the trio who stood behind him, Cross fought with the turmoil that resided inside of him as he noted the expectant looks that they gave him. At that moment, he truly found himself wondering whether he was making the right decision by sending them all the way to Dubai. Only, the flipside of his skepticism clearly stated that not even their enemies would think to search for them in the United Arab Emirates.

"We'll be just fine," Rahsaanique announced as if she had read Cross' mind. "There's no need to worry, Uncle Cross," she added, smiling brightly as she stepped into his tight embrace and gave him a big kiss on the cheek.

Cross was sad as he watched his now grown niece walk through the scanning machine, waving back at him as she strolled up the aisle.

"Hey, I'm starting to get jealous here," Tavia teased as she stood with her arms folded. "Can I get some love too?" She smiled brightly as Cross turned and gave her a hug as well.

"I love you and your sister alike," Cross said, pulling back and gazing at Tavia who resembled her mother so much that they could have been twins. "And just in case you're not aware, Ms. Lady, I'm going to miss you both so much."

Bonni quietly stood back and watched the interaction that took place between Cross and her daughters. Even though they were twenty-three and eighteen respectively, it never ceased to amaze her how they still had the ability to turn Cross' cold heart into putty with a simple smile and soft words. The funny thing was, they never would have guessed that their loving Uncle was once a cold killer, and if it was up to Bonni, they would never have to find out. Thus, as she watched Tavia give Cross another hug and follow her sister, Bonni walked up to him and grabbed his hand.

"Bonni, I hope that I'm doing the right thing," Cross said, looking down at his feet then off into the crowd. "I promised Stink that I would take care of you all, I feel that the best way to guarantee your safety is to send you away. Also, by placing you all out of harm's way, I can go where I'm really needed."

Inwardly smiling at what Cross was trying to say, though Bonni already had an idea of what he planned to do, she felt like a weight had been removed from her shoulder, and she was suddenly able to breathe a little better. Reaching out to grasp his chin, she turned his face to look at her and said, "Cross, you are a good man, and not only have you been a loyal friend to Rahsaan and myself, you have been an even better uncle to our children and they love you just as much as we do."

"But, I promised Stink that I…." Cross began before Bonni cut in.

"You are fulfilling your promise right now, and I agree that we will be better off in Dubai than here in the Dominican Republic any day. So with my blessing, go where you're needed, Cross, because whether Rahsaan realizes it or not, he can't go up against Jose without you." As Bonni gave him a hug and walked away, she saw the fire return to Cross' eyes after she freed him to go assist Stink and Rah-Rah. However, as she headed to the plane with tears in her eyes, Bonni's gut feeling told her that regardless of how badly she wanted all of them to return unscathed, it wasn't going to happen.

Cross packed his Range Rover on the uneven dirt road and checked his weapon before he exited the truck. He observed the rough looking men sitting off to the side of a ramshackle dwelling, playing cards as he made his way towards the small plane and pilot who was busy working on the grease-filled engine. Watching the men through his peripheral view as he passed them, Cross was also aware of the AK-47 that leaned against an old tire and the M-16 assault rifle that laid across the lap of one of the men. Being that they were drug runners and it was rumored that they would transport anything anywhere for the right price, after checking their credentials with his people in the Dominican Republic, Cross was sure that he had come to the right place.

"What you need?" the man who was working on the plane growled, staring in the direction of the three card players as he wiped his greasy hands on his dirty pants.

Cross ignored the man, choosing to impact the place instead. As he checked out the plane, Cross made sure that he kept the men in sight. However, upon seeing the growing displeasure on the pilot's face, Cross said, "What can you do with this thing?"

"What the hell are you talking about?" the man questioned in broken English, getting angrier by the moment.

Cross saw the three men stand and grabbed their weapons upon hearing their associate's loud outburst, but he continued to talk as if he didn't have a worry in the World. "You asked me what I needed, and I need to know if you can really fly this thing?" Cross said impatiently.

"Huh?" the Spanish man exclaimed, looking from Cross to his plane and back again. "I fly the best in the Dominican Republic!" he boasted, shaking his head up and down.

"So you're telling me that there's nothing that you can't do with this piece of metal?" Cross asked, raising his brow in a questioning manner.

"I'm the best, I say!"

Cross quietly contemplated his next move, then he tossed the pilot his Range Rover keys and said, "You see that truck over there?"

Looking over at the Range Rover, the man shook his

head 'yes'.

Do you like it?"

The man's head-nod gave the same response.

"Well, if you take me where I need to go, you can have it and the fifty thousand dollars that is in the glove compartment." Cross saw the interest in the man's face as soon as his words left his mouth.

Bouncing the keys in his hand as he stared at the truck, the man glared at Cross suspiciously. "Where is it that you need to go?"

"Miami, Florida," Cross replied, gauging the looks that passed between the four men.

"How much coca will we have to transport?" the man asked. He suddenly seemed upon to the idea.

"Huh?" Cross asked, then it dawned on him that the man had misunderstood what he meant. "No, there won't be any coca. It will only be me and a duffle bag filled with toys." Cross smiled.

"Okay." The man smiled also. "When do you want to go to Miami?"

"Now," Cross said.

Looking at his men, then staring at the pretty truck while thinking about the fifty grand that sat in the glove compartment, the man said, "We go to Miami now, but we can only fly as far as Puerto Rico then my associates there will take you to the United States I very fast cigarette boat."

"Sounds good to me," Cross said. As long as he made it back to the United States, that was all that mattered to him. He knew that Stink and his nephew needed him and with them going up against Jose, every moment that he procrastinated could be their last.

Chapter Thirty-One

Melody continued to replay the sexual encounter that she and Stink had undertaken hours earlier through her mind. Now that it was over, she couldn't quite determine how she felt about it. On the one hand, her body exalted in the pleasure that Stink had brought her, yet Melody realized that her heart wasn't strong enough to mend another break and it was clear that Stink had moved on with his life. However, it was thoughts of Jose and their daughter Soana that caused Melody the greatest guilt, because she understood that she had not only cheated on the one man who treated her like a Queen, but she had placed them in jeopardy when she exposed Jose's plans to Stink. Though she knew that she could never take back what had already been done, Melody's heart ached with the knowledge that no matter what happened one of the men that she loved would be hurt if not killed because of what she had put in motion. These thoughts and more had her mind in turmoil as she drove around the city for hours trying to sort it all out. Only Melody had put off going home long enough, and as the wee hours approached, she knew that she had to go face the music. Melody pulled the Aston Martin to the side of the road and lowered her vanity mirror. Viewing the red-rimmed eyes that reflected back at her, she reached in her bag and grabbed her make-up. Only a mile separated her from her home, and she planned to be on point when she arrived. Thus, as Melody began to work on her face, she prayed that everything else that she had done would work itself out as well.

Jose's mind was confused as he tried to imagine a number of scenarios that could possibly explain why Melody had been away from home so long. Though he let her come and go at her own free will and had never been the type to monitor her movements, Melody had never done anything remotely like this. Throughout their marrying, unless they had gone out together, Melody never even left the house at night. As Jose stared at the clock that illuminated the dark room, noticing that it was nearly 2 a.m., his nerves were on edge as he keyed her number into his phone for the umpteenth time. Hanging up after he was directed to voice mail, Jose was about to call his own people and have them comb the streets when the video surveillance screen showed Melody's car driving up through the gate. Watching her closely as she drove into their sprawling estate, Jose saw nothing in her solemn look. Other than the timeless beauty that made his heart race every time she entered any room, her face gave no clues as to where she had been. Jose's features gave off an aura of cool and calm. Only in all truth, a violent rage lied beneath the surface.

Melody entered the cavernous   mansion and looked around her nervously. As she strolled through the immense foyer area and made her way up the spiral staircase, hearing her heels connect with the marble floor, it sounded much louder to her than usual. Melody realized that she was probably experiencing a level of paranoia when she stopped and removed her shoes, but as she climbed the stairs, the only thing that traveled through her mind was being as quiet as possible. She planned to look in on her daughter, take a quick shower and slide in bed without awakening Jose. Melody wasn't up to answering any questions and she hadn't devised a lie that would stand up under Jose's scrutiny. She just wanted to be left alone. When she reached their room and entered its darkness, Melody's heart dropped when she heard Jose's voice.

"I waited up for you," Jose stated flatly, watching Melody jump in alarm as she turned in the direction of his voice. Unlike Melody, Jose had the advantage of seeing her every move as she tried to adjust her eyes to the darkness.

"You… you shouldn't have, sweetheart." Melody's voice wavered.

"Where were you, bonita?" Jose affectionately questioned, wanting to give Melody the benefit of doubt before he jumped to conclusions. However, he noted the silence that engulfed the room after her question.

Melody's breath was caught in her chest when Jose asked where she had been, but when he referred to her by bonita, which meant beautiful in Spanish, any lie that she would have answered with seemed unbelievable before she had even told it. Thus, she decided to give him a half truth instead.

"I went to dinner in the city and then I caught a late movie. After that, I just drove around to try and clear my head," Melody unconvincingly replied.

"Is that so?" Jose said more to himself than Melody, adding, "I was worried about you bonita. You are Mi-vida, and I can't imagine what I would do without you and Soana." Though Jose truly felt that Melody was his life, his words possessed a dual meaning. "Do you understand me,

Melody?"

"Of course I do, Jose," Melody replied in a hushed tone.

"Is there someone else that you aren't telling me about, bonita? If there is, this is your one and only chance to tell me," Jose said, genuinely meaning every word of what he said.

Melody was shocked by his question as well as his offer to come clean. Although she knew him well enough to believe that his honor wouldn't allow him to go back on his proposal, every bone in her body told her that not even Jose's honor would keep him from punishing her for being with Stink. There was no way that she could confess her infidelity.

"Jose, there's no one else! Why would you ask that when you know how I feel about you?" Melody asked incredulously. "I can't believe you," she added as she turned to leave the room.

"Where are you going, bonita?" Jose's tone was not only cold and hard, but it was commanding.

Stopping in her tracks, Melody's nerves were on edge as she turned back to face her husband. "I'm going to check on Soana, and then I'm going to take a shower."

Jose could sense Melody's fear, and he was aware that no matter how defensive she tried to act she had lied to him. At that moment, he hated himself for the feeling of weakness that overtook him, only he had no control of the jealousy that consumed him. Nevertheless, even in his anger, he found himself wanting her.

"Soana is fine and your shower can wait. Come here, bonita," Jose said, unsnapping his silk pajama bottoms and releasing his length.

Melody was momentarily frozen as the reality of what her husband wanted from her sunk in. At that moment, she felt dirty as she recalled what had just transpired between her and Stink. However, as she walked to Jose in a daze and dropped to her knees, when she grabbed his dick and placed it in her mouth, the only face that she saw in her mind when she closed her eyes was Stink's.

Jose closed his eyes and leaned back in the chair. As he guided Melody's head in his lap, he experienced a mixture of pleasure and pain, both as a result of what his wife was doing to him. The pleasure was due to the wet suctioning, but the pain was due to the fact that as soon as he found out who she was creeping with, he was going to kill her.

Chapter Thirty-Two

Turning over and finding the warm body that she had become accustomed to being besides her missing, Tia's eyes instantly opened in alarm. Searching the dark confines of the large room, she found Rah-Rah sitting upright in a chair watching her. Even though she already knew what was bothering him, Tia rolled out of bed and grabbed a silk robe to cover her nakedness as she walked across the room and sat in his lap.

"Why are you sitting up in the dark, Rahsaan?" Tia asked, rubbing his head.

Thinking of how lucky he was to have Tia in his life, as well as the fact that he had almost lost her due to his own negligence, Rah-Rah wrapped his arms tightly around Tia's waist and reveled in the feel and smell of her body. At that moment, he wanted to do nothing more than hold her.

Kissing him softly, Tia felt Rah-Rah's heartbeat through the thin silk rob that separated them and for the first time in her twenty years on Earth, she truly understood how it felt to be loved by a man. "Come back to bed, baby... it doesn't feel the same without you," she said, glancing down into the dark eyes that held her captive.

"Nah, ma, I just need to sit here and clear my head... you know? Go back to sleep though. I'm not going anywhere." Rah-Rah had no plans on leaving Tia's side after the move that Swoop had pulled the day before.

Tia laughed, then gave Rah-Rah a look that said 'are you serious?'

"What's so funny?" Rah-Rah asked.

"You. You're what's funny, baby." Tia sat upright and smiled at Rah-Rah .

Though Rah-Rah found nothing funny about himself or their present dilemma, he forced a grin and said, "Being that you find me so humorous, how about you share the joke with me."

"It's just funny how you act as if I'm so fragile that you must put your plans on hold just so you will be able to protect me day and night. Well, that's not the man that I met and fell in love with, Rahsaan. I fell in love with the fearless leader that was known for taking the battle to his enemies, instead of waiting for them to come back and attempt to kill us again." Tia exhibited more strength than she actually felt in order to bring Rah-Rah out of the slump that he had been in ever since the attempt on her life. "Well I'm not fragile, and you already know that my guns go off just like theirs. Therefore, when the sun comes up, I want to see my Boo back in rare form, and I want your uncle to repeat the day that he crossed us."

Tia never ceased to amaze him, and as Rah-Rah stared at her seeing the strength and devotion that resonated from her beautiful face, he loved and wanted her with a vengeance. Thus, as he rose from the chair with her in his arms, he knew that he had to strike Swoop and his Spanish cohorts with deadly force when the sun came up like his woman said. However, as he laid Tia on the bed and peeled the robe from her body, he planned to punish something else until the sun came up.

"Man, I don't want any parts of this shit," Dundee said, teasing a glass of Bourbon back and frowning at the burning sensation.

"What the hell you mean you don't want any parts of this shit?" Swoop asked incredulous. "Are you serious, nigga? Don't you realize that you can't be out here on your own, man?"

Dundee gave Swoop a look of annoyance and poured himself another drink as he glared at the Spanish men who waited for Swoop at the other end of the bar. Shaking his head and gulping the liquor down, Dundee grouched, "I'm not with the way you ran to those muthafuckas and gave your own blood up, Dawg. I've rolled with you on a lot of shit that wasn't kosher, but that was the foulest shit that you're ever done, by far, and I'm not about to sanction it. And as far as me being by myself, I'd rather roll alone than with those snakes!" Dundee pointed his drink at the Spanish men, and then turned his attention back to the stripper that flaunted her stretch-marked ass on the stage.

Swoop's jaw trembled with the force of his clenched teeth as he replayed Dundee's words. Even though he was already aware of how grimey is decision had been to cross his nephew in such a manner, Swoop didn't appreciate Dundee or anyone else trying to check him about any move that he chose to make. "So I take it that you're saying that after all that we've been through, you're not with me anymore either, huh?" Swoop spat, eyeing Dundee evilly.

Dundee returned the mean look that was reflected at him as he placed his glass on the bar and his hand inside his jacket, turning the barstool to face Swoop. He had been

Swoop's partner for many years and was well aware of the malice that lied beneath his words, yet he went just as hard, if not harder, than Swoop and he wasn't about to bow to the challenge that had been directed in Swoop's question.

"Take it however you like, nigga! Just miss me with the bullshit you're on!" Dundee snarled.

He no longer felt any allegiance to Swoop, and he was ready for whatever.

The tension was so thick between the two men that it could be sliced with a knife as they ice-grilled one another. However, Swoop's chuckle somewhat lightened the situation as he shook his head from side to side and said, "Look at us, nigga! What the fuck are we doing beefing over another muthafucka that we don't even really know? We've got too much history between us for that shit, partner."

Dundee said nothing. He remained distant, taking no part in Swoop's reminiscing on their past, because he had already made his mind up that Swoop couldn't be trusted and there would be no future partnership between them.

Swoop noticed Dundee's reluctance to communicate with him, as well as the fact that his hand still lingered inside his jacket where his weapon undoubtedly resided. As he continued to ramble on, smiling and keenly peering into the crowd that stood around the bar and stage, he grabbed a clean glass and reached for the bottle of Bourbon Dundee's eyes never wavered from. There was nothing unnatural about Swoop pouring himself a drink. However, when he swung the bottle and caught Dundee square in the forehead, sending him crashing to the dirty floor with a loud thud, Dundee was unable to react as Swoop removed the gun from his hand and slashed the jagged edge of the broken bottle across his face. He then commenced to beat Dundee in his face and head with the butt of his own pistol.

"I'm taking it exactly how you knew I would, you bitch ass nigga!" Swoop grunted swinging blow after blow. He was in a zone as he glared at Dundee's bloody face. "Take this ass whipping for talking slick out your mouth!" Swoop hawked a glob of spit in Dundee's face then stood and straightened his clothes. Turning to leave, he barked, "The only reason why you're still alive is because we've been through so much, but the next time we meet, you better duck!"

The crowd parted, giving Swoop room to leave the club with the three Spanish bangers on his heels. As soon as they disappeared through the exit, two young men who had been preoccupied with getting lap dances when the commotion erupted, pushed their way to the front of the bystanders and gawked at Dundee's injuries. Instantly recognizing the two men from the stash house robbing, although they didn't know what had transpired between the men to cause their riff, the younger men immediately took advantage of their good fortune.

"Grab his arm and help me lift him," B-Rock told Trooper as he reached for the opposite arm and began to hoist the bloody, unconscious man to his feet. They carried him through the club and out the door without any interference. Tossing him in the back of the truck and climbing inside behind him, B-Rock tossed the keys to Trooper and retrieved his .40 caliber from beneath the seat just in case their vic woke up.

"Where you want to take this nigga?" Trooper asked,

pulling out of the club's parking lot.

"Go to the spot out Newsome Park, Blood," B-Rock said, thinking that Rah-Rah's uncle had really fucked dude up. However, as he removed his phone and punched in Rah-Rah's number, he knew that the beating that Swoop had given dude was nothing compared to what Ruckus would do to him when he reached Newsome Park.

Rah-Rah and Tia had just stepped out off the shower and were finally preparing to get some well needed rest when his phone began to ring incessantly, making it impossible for him to ignore.

"You want me to grab that for you, baby?" Tia asked, rubbing the towel over her long, wet tresses.

"I'll get it, T." Rah-Rah walked out of the bathroom and picked his phone up off the dresser.
He knew that B-Rock wouldn't be calling him at 4 A.M. unless it was of the utmost urgency, so he answered the call. "Talk to me, Blood."

"We got the nigga who was with your uncle the night that Bulldog got hit." B-Rock got straight to the point.

"Word? How did you pull that off, and did you dead him?" Rah-Rah questioned eagerly.

"It's a long story, Damu, but Ill explain it all when you get to the spot out Newsome Park. We're on our way right now."

"Can't this shit wait until later?" Rah-Rah yawned.

B-Rock knew that his next words would change Rah-Rah's mind, "I'm not sure because I saved him for you, but if you would rather I do the deed…."

"I'm on my way!" Rah-Rah exclaimed, ending their call.

Chapter Thrity-Three

Stink couldn't stop thinking about the news that Melody had revealed to him, concerning her relationship with Jose and the daughter that they shared. Even though he had left her behind, choosing to be with Bonni instead, he would have never guessed that Melody would find solace in Jose. After thinking about the situation, it suddenly made sense to him why whenever he had inquired about Melody through the years, Jose would either downplay his interest in her or ignore the request altogether. Thanks to Melody's disclosures, Stink now understood that he had gone from Jose's friend and son that he never had, to a threat without even knowing it. The worst part was, thanks to Rah-Rah's negligence, the most dangerous man that Stink had ever known had become his adversary, and he had absolutely no idea how he was going to beat him.

After arriving in Virginia, Stink's gut feeling was correct, it wouldn't be easy to locate his son, especially if what Melody told him about Rah-Rah's war with his uncle Swoop and the MS13 organization was true. Rah-Rah had been trained well in the ways of war, so Stink was sure that he would be keeping a low profile. Nevertheless, as he pressed his foot more firmly on the accelerator, the only thought that traveled through his mind as the rented Lincoln LS dipped in and out of traffic, was reaching Rah-Rah. Nothing else mattered.

Cross' heart began to beat out of his chest at the first sight of lights off in the distance. Straining his eyes in an attempt to see better as he leaned forward in his seat, every time the speedboat bounced over a wave and South Beach shoreline appeared closer, Cross' heart rate increased. Even though he loved the Dominican Republic and had accepted it as his home, he had always longed for the day when he could return to his place of birth. The moment that he had dreamed of had come to pass, and as the cigarette boat veered away from the city lights and headed around the tip of Miami, Cross was drawn out of his train of thought.

"We're going to have to dock in a private inlet on the other side of the city," the driver yelled over the loud engine. "Sit back and hold tight, though, because we may encounter the Coast Guard." Smiling he added, "Then I'll be able to show you what this baby can really do!"

Returning the man's smile, Cross was game for whatever obstacles they may have come across as long as they reached their destination. After traveling from the Dominican Republic to Puerto Rico in a drug smuggler's plane, then making the second phase of his trip in a supped up speedboat, if necessary, he would swim the remainder of the way. He was within sight of the United States and nothing short of death would keep Cross from setting foot on American soil. The thought alone caused his smile to broaden. However, as he recalled his reason for returning in the first place, Cross' smile disappeared. Though he had known Jose longer than Stink, no man living or deceased had ever shown him more love and devotion than Stink. Thus, his allegiance belonged to his brother Stink and no other. As the speedboat cut a swath through the surf, bringing the craft closer to their desired destination, Cross couldn't wait to reach Newport News. A war was in progress, and he needed to be fighting side by side with Stink and Rah-Rah.

Chapter Thirty-Four

Dundee's right eye was swollen shut and he could barley see out of his left when he finally regained consciousness. Slowly accustoming himself to his surroundings, he flinched with the pain of his wounds as he tried to sit up straighter in the bathtub filled with water. The seriousness of his dilemma didn't really dawn on him completely, until he felt the chains that had been attached to his arms grind into his skin, forcing him to slump back into the tub. Gasping loudly, Dundee tried to stifle the sharp cry that rang out as his head smashed into the porcelain rim of the tub nearly sending him back into oblivion. Only refusing to go out without a flight, he took deep breaths and regained his lucid state in an attempt to get a bearing on exactly where he was and what was happening.

Listening closely, Dundee was able to discern a number of voices over the rap music that played in the other room. Though none sounded familiar to his ear, by their slang and Ebonic usage of words, he was easily able to determine that they were young and urban. His discovery immediately triggered an alarm in his mind, ruining any prior hopes that he may have harbored that Swoop had brought him there after the attack to scare him. Had it been Swoop, Dundee felt that his chance of survival would have been greater than the people who he hoped weren't responsible for his predicament. However, as he heard the front door slam and the music abruptly go off, Dundee's heart skipped a beat at the loud voice that blared from the other room.

"Where is the nigga that had the guts to rob my stash house?" Rah-Rah growled loudly as he and Tia entered the tiny apartment. He was amped as he looked around the room at a number of his men with angry eyes.

"Relax Rah, he's safe and sound in the bathroom," B-Rock announced, coming out of the kitchen with a sandwich and bag of chips. "Oh, hey Tia," he added before closing the distance between them and giving Rah-Rah a pound.

Rah-Rah immediately removed his gold plated Colt and cocked it. Tia's gun instantly appeared in her hand as well. They began to walk towards the bathroom.

"Whoa, you two! Let me at least put you up on game before you do that," B-Rock said, stopping them in their tracks. Shaking his head as he peered at the awestruck faces around him, the often occurring thought that Rah-Rah and Tia were made for one another returned.

"Make it quick!" Rah-Rah said, staring from the bathroom door back to B-Rock. "We're in a hurry, so let's get this over with!"

B-Rock could tell that Rah-Rah was impatient, so he pulled him to the side and said, "He may be able to help us locate your uncle."

"That's his man, Blood, so what makes you think he would do that?" Rah-Rah asked, annoyed.

"We snatched the nigga up out of Magic City after your uncle smashed a bottle over his head and pistol whipped him with his own gun. I'm not sure how you see it, but it damn sure doesn't sound like they're still good friends to me." B-Rock's face was twisted in a silly questioning smirk.

Rah-Rah smiled. "Well you might have a point, B. We may need to question him before we kill him after all," Rah-Rah said, placing his gun back on his waist. Cutting his eyes in Tia's direction, she did the same. Taking a moment to think, he asked, "Where exactly do you have him at in there, Blood."

"He's chained up in the bathtub." B-Rock answered

Rah-Rah traipsed through the room until he found what he was looking for. Quickly closing the distance between himself and the flat screen television, he unplugged it and yanked the cord out of the back, disregarding the looks of the men who were watching it. Checking the ends of the wires that dangled outside of the plastic covering, Rah-Rah inwardly smiled. He turned around and walked back in the direction that he had come.

"Come on, T," he motioned for Tia to follow him as he reached the bathroom door and turned the knob.

"How the hell did I get myself in this shit?" Dundee mumbled as he fought to contain his steadily warming courage. He had never been helpless in his life, and after all the dirt that he had done to others, Dundee finally knew what it felt like to be defenseless. It was not only a scary feeling, but in his case it was karma. He heard footsteps outside the door and then saw the doorknob turn in slow motion. He prepared himself for whatever was going to happen next.

Rah-Rah and Tia entered the bathroom and shut the door behind them. There were no words spoken between them as they stared at the badly beaten man inside the bathtub. They saw nothing dangerous about the man who looked small in stature and scared as he shivered in the cold water.

"So you're my uncle's partner, huh?" Rah-Rah stated, locating a socket near the tub and plugging the cord into it. Splitting the wire down the middle, he touched them together causing a crackling sound to resonate and sparks to shoot from their tips.

Dundee jumped at the sound of the electric current, but said nothing as he saw Rah-Rah come closer. His heart was racing at the knowledge of what he realized Rah-Rah planned to do with the wires. He began to say a silent prayer.

"Damn, the cat musta got a hold of your tongue, my man, because I know that you can talk," Rah-Rah said, letting half of the cord dangle over the rim of the tub. He saw Dundee's body tense up, then he pulled the cord back and said, "Baby, this nigga had mad shit to talk about the night they murdered Bulldog and took my money. You saw the tape just like I did, T."

"You sure that's him, baby?" Tia asked, coming closer to get a better look. "The dude I remember was tough as hell." Grilling Dundee, Tia said, "Give me that cord, boo!" I'm sure that I'll be able to loosen his tongue."

Handing it to her, Rah-Rah stood back and folded his arms across his chest. He wanted to see how Tia worked. However, as he observed the no nonsense look upon her face as she removed her 'Bebe' hooded sweatshirt and glared down at the wide-eyed man, he was glad that she was on his side when Tia allowed the wires to slide into the water.

Dundee's scream echoed off the bathrooms walls as he violently flopped around the tub.

Watching the spectacle that Dundee made of himself with a smile on her face, hearing Rah-Rah clear his throat much louder than necessary, Tia pulled the cord out of the water.

"Okay, now let's try this all over again," Rah-Rah announced taking his place back at the side of the tub. Dundee's groans filled the room as his body trembled like a leaf. "Are you going to talk or do I have to put my girl on you?"

"I'll…talk!" Dundee blurted weakly, violently shaking his head up and down. "I'll tell you whatever you want to know."

Sharing a conspiratorial look with Tia who wore a smug look as she leaned against the sink, Rah-Rah said, "You can start by telling me why my uncle did that to you." Rah-Rah pointed to Dundee's butchered face.

"He… he was… mad because I… because I cut him… off." Dundee fought to get his words out.

"Why would you do that? I thought that was your man," Rah-Rah questioned.

Dundee swallowed, and spoke slowly. "He told the top dope in the MS13 organization that you were the one who killed Chino. He claims that he saw it with his own eyes." Dundee began to cough loudly prompting Rah-Rah to hold his next question.

Tossing a questioning look over his shoulder at Tia, he was surprised at the news that Dundee had just divulged to him. Things were suddenly much clearer to him now. Swoop had joined up with the MS13, and they were increasing their efforts to capture him at all costs. The only thing that he didn't understand was why Dundee would have a problem with joining forces with a team whose strength rivaled that of the Bad News Bloods when that the Bloods were after them, Dundee's reasoning truly intrigued him.

"How does my action cause you to cut him off?" Rah-Rah suspiciously.

Thinking about his response for a moment, Dundee said, "First of all, we were the ones that crossed you, and whatever beef that comes behind it is supposed to be between us and you. Second, I'm not a snitch and I have no allegiance to snitches. The last thing that I will ever accept is the friendship of a man who has no problem with setting his own blood up to get murdered. There are rules to this game, and I refuse to play it any other way besides the right way."

Rah-Rah was stumped after hearing Dundee's response because like Dundee, he too had been taught that there were certain rules that had to be adhered to in the streets. However, those same rules stated that he had to receive retribution from Dundee for his part in robbing their stash house and killing Bulldog.

"Where is my uncle hiding out?" Rah-Rah asked flatly, clearing his mind of any emotions that he had allowed himself. "You tell me where to find him and I promise that I won't kill you for taking my money and murdering my man."

Tia's eyes shot up in alarm as she rose up from the sink and hissed, "How can you just let this nigga walk away after what he did? Rahsaan, I don't believe you…."

"I'm calling the shots, Tia!" Rah-Rah snapped, giving her an evil look. He then turned his attention back to Dundee. "Now, what's it going to be?"

Dundee felt that Rah-Rah's proposal was a no brainier. As his heart began to race with the anticipation of surviving his present dilemma, he excitedly stated, "He's camped out in Seven Oaks with a lil' broad named Pam. There's at least three Spanish dudes with him at all times, and they're heavily armed." Dundee used the last of his strength to sit up in preparation for his restraints to be removed.

"Is there anything else that you may have forgotten to mention?" Rah-Rah asked cooly.

"No, that's everything," Dundee quickly answered.

"Okay, Rah-Rah announced turning to face Tia. "When I said that I wouldn't kill him, I never said anything about you."

"Huh?" Tia asked, not quite sure what he had meant.

Smiling, Rah-Rah saw the look of dread that contorted Dundee's features when he said, "He's yours, baby. Handle your business."

"You promised, man! Come on, you don't have to do this!" Dundee pleaded as he struggled in vain to free himself. "Please, don't," he begged.

Strolling past Rah-Rah with a sure step, her gun in one hand and the electric cord in the other, Dundee's pleas fell on deaf ears as Tia stared at him with a mixture of disgust and pity. She recalled every moment of the tape that she had watched where Dundee had not only shown himself to be heartless, but exhibited no remorse when he murdered the female whose only crime was that she was in the wrong place at the wrong time. Now that the tables were turned, Tia couldn't believe that he had the nerve to beg for his life all the dirt that she knew he had done to others.

"I still have my half of the money that we took and I'll give it back, man! Just tell me what I need to do!" Dundee begged, his eyes traveling from Rah-Rah to Tia.

Rah-Rah hunched his shoulders and pointed at Tia as if to say 'it's out of my hands'.

"Nigga, you're killing me with all that bawling you're doing! Damn, have some self-respect, man!" Hearing Rah-Rah giggle behind her, Tia said, "Pick your death, nigga! You want it with this or this?" she asked raising the electrical cord and then the gun.

Dundee couldn't believe that this was happening to him. It wasn't supposed to end like this, and as he looked at his choices for death neither one appealed to him. However, as he peered into the cold eyes of his beautiful assassin, he saw that there was nothing that he could possibly say that could break her resolve to kill him. Therefore, he refused to be remembered as a bitch after all the work that he put in over the years to be to be known as a gorilla.

"You pick it, bitch!" Dundee yelled, barely missing Tia with a glob of spit.

"Now that's what I'm taking about!" Tia's smile stretched the contours of her large mouth as she tossed the electrical cord in the tub, then leveled the nine-millimeter into the tub and opened fire. When Dundee's body lay still, Tia returned her weapon to its resting place on her hip and turned to a smiling Rah-Rah. "What?" she asked, sarcastically.

Shaking his head, Rah-Rah asked, "Don't you think

that was a little much?"

"Nope. He said choose and I couldn't, so being the bitch that he said I was, I just gave him a little of both," Tia said, looking down at the dead eyes that stared back at her.

Rah-Rah draped an arm around her shoulder as they exited the bathroom and headed for the door. Oblivious to the eyes that followed them out of the apartment, he said, "B-Rock, get a couple of the homies to clean that mess up and lose that nigga's body." He then turned his attention back to Tia and said, "I think you're starting to enjoy this shit a little too much. Let me find out that I created a monster."

Tia's only response was her dimpled smile and the tight hug she gave Rah-Rah as they walked to the car. There was nothing to be said when he had said it all. Tia loved the new power that she now possessed; there was nothing that compared to taking a life. Thanks to Rah-Rah, she finally found her calling, so just maybe, he had created a monster.

Chapter Thirty-Five

"What you want us to do, Blood, they're everywhere?" B-Rock said in frustration. "Every one of them that we kill, two more pops up!"

Rah-Rah surveyed the room filled with glum faces, then turned to Tia and shook his head. As far as he was concerned, the answer to B-Rock's question was easy. "If two more targets pop up each time you slay one, then kill their ass too!" he snapped, throwing his hands up in disgust.

Tia's laughter resounded through the room as she sucked on a lollipop as if she didn't have a care in the World.

"Come on, Rah... it's just not that easy." B-Rock gave an exasperated sigh and waved his hand in a wide arc, adding, "Look around you, Damu. Every one of these niggas are going through pure hell in those streets. Our army is no match for the number of Spanish bangers that they're sending at us. I swear to you, I've never seen anything like this."

Although Rah-Rah attempted to play down the threat that B-Rock had so vividly defined, he realized wholeheartedly what they were up against. However, what ate at him the most was the knowledge that his killing of Chino was responsible for the immense force being released against them. Now that his uncle had thrown him to the wolves, he had to find a way to conquer Swoop and the beast that combed the city in search of him. The only problem was, as he stared around him at all the men who expected him to give them direction, Rah-Rah had no idea what to tell them.

Hearing a loud commotion outside the door, Rah-Rah lost his frame of thought. Everyone in the room turned their attention to the door, and a number of weapons were drawn as the voices in the hallway increased in volume. Then to everyone's dismay, the door flew open against the wishes of the Bloods who attempted to block its path.

"Let him through!" Rah-Rah said sharply. The utter surprise that he experienced was written all over his face as he held the man with an unblinking stare.

The room was silent as everyone's eyes traveled from Rah-Rah to the man who stood in the doorway. Tia stopped sucking on her lollipop and gazed at her man with a questioning look, only her question was immediately answered when the man says the words that no one in the room expects to hear, leaving them all in shock.

"Hello, son!"

"How did you find me, pop?" Rah-Rah asked as soon as the room was cleared and the initial shock of his father's arrival eased.

"I have my ways, son. In case you don't recall, I once ran this city," Stink said, embracing his son then parting so that he could view the change that had taken place in Rah-Rah in the short period of time that they had been apart.

"Unghhh umm!" Tia cleared her throat loudly as she stood near the door, trying to determine whether she should have left the room with the others.

Both men turned their attention on her. Rah-Rah smiled, then said, "Excuse my manners, baby. Come and meet my father, Tia." He then glanced at his father whose brow was raised in appreciation and announced, "Pop, meet my baby."

"Wow!" Stink whistled, gently grasping Tia's hand. "You're absolutely gorgeous, and it's good to meet you!" he said meaning every word.

"It's nice to meet you as well," Tia announced, blushing. She then gave Rah-Rah a peck on the lips and said, "I'm going to leave you two alone."

"Aight, baby; but let the others know that no one leaves until I speak with them," Rah-Rah said.

Tia shook her head in understanding and left the room.

As soon as the door closed, Stink exhaled then grinned at his son while looking disgusted at the same time, "Rah-Rah, how did you get yourself into so much shit in such a short period of time? My intentions were to send you back home for a while to keep you out of trouble, now look!" Stink said, throwing his hands up in despair.

"Pop, it's not as bad as you think," Rah-Rah lied. He couldn't help but to wonder how his father even knew what kind of troubles he faced.

"So you don't think it's bad, huh?" Stink asked slyly.

"Nah, I got it under wraps," Rah-Rah answered, looking away from Stink's probing eyes. Though he was Ruckus the fearless Blood leader to the men who followed him, when it came to his father, he was just little Rah-Rah and the last thing that he wanted to do was let Stink down.

"Well, Rah-Rah, I beg to differ," Stink announced. He then said, "Whether you know it or not, you have managed to step on some very powerful toes and the last thing that you have is things under wraps. Thanks to your antics, Bonni and your sisters are in hiding and I've been forced to come back to the U.S.

Rah-Rah's shoulders slumped as he listened to his father talk. The last thing that he expected was that his actions in America would place his loved ones back in the Dominican Republic in danger. After hearing this, it suddenly became painfully obvious that the beef that he was involved in was much more serious than he thought.

Seeing the distance that his words had brought Rah-Rah, Stink said, "What's done is done, and regardless, I'll always have your back. Now, what I need you to do is start from the beginning and tell me every detail of how you arrived to this point. Okay?" Stink asked calmly.

Shaking his head 'yes' and dropping down in the chair beside his father, Rah-Rah said, "It all began the day that I met B-Rock....

Chapter Thirty-Six

Cross walked through the door of the old pool hall and allowed his eyes to grow accustomed to the dimly lit place. Although he was surprised that the place still existed, the décor that he already recalled as being ancient, was ever more offensive and decayed then he remembered. However, as he walked further into the establishment smelling an array of tobacco, alcohol, musk and urine, Cross searched through the faces of old whores, junkies and hustlers until he came across the person he was looking far. As he closed the distance between them, never taking his eyes from his mark, Cross couldn't believe that Cole Slaw was still in a pool hall hustling people.

Sinking the eight ball and snatching a few bills from the table, Cole Slaw lit the Newport that was wedged in the corner of his mouth and slurred, "Who's next?"

Cross walked through the crowd that loitered around the table and grabbed the pool stick that the last player had discarded. "I'll try my hand, my man. What's the wager?" he asked, removing a wad of cash from his pocket and placing it on the wooden rim.

Staring across the expanse that separated them with lowered lids, Cole Slaw blew a gust of cigarette smoke out and casually said, "Twenty dollars a game, nigga, and it's your rack."

Cross grunted at the word 'nigga' that Cole Slaw used. Being that they never liked one another in the past, his reference to Cross as 'nigga' carried a level of disrespect that ate him. However, being that he was there for more important reasons, Cross grabbed the rack and set the balls in their respective places. Holding his growing anger in check as he stepped away from the table and let Cole Slaw break the rack, he patiently waited his turn.

Making eight straight slots in a row, Cole Slaw removed his twenty dollars from the table and said, "Rack'em, or step aside and let another sucker get his shot at me." He smiled as he watched Cross tremble, knowing that his words were finding their mark.

"I got your nigga and your sucker!" Cross' tone was cold and hard, yet he flashed Cole Slaw a phony smile as he racked the balls.

Busting the rack and slowly moving around the table to gauge his best shots, Cole Slaw said, "The last I heard, they were searching high and low for you. The word was you supposedly escaped from prison up in New York or something." Cole Slaw chalked up his stick and took his shot in one fluid motion. He then tossed a glance over his shoulder at Cross and asked, "Did you ever get that straightened out?"

Cross wanted to knock the arrogant smile off Cole Slaw's face, but as hard as it was for him to refrain from doing so, he said, "Shoot the damn ball, and don't worry about my legal issues."

"Hey, you know me, I shoot pool and spread the news," Cole Slaw exclaimed, sinking a bank shot.

Looking at his watch, Cross was instantly reminded the he was wasting vital time listening to Cole Slaw's bullshit. "Look, man," Cross stated impatiently, garnering Cole Slaw's attention. "You and I both know that I can't beat you at this shit, so let's cut the games and get to the reason why I'm really here."

"I agree," Cole Slaw said, extracting another twenty dollars bill from Cross' bankroll. "That's for the game that you were about to lose, nigga!" he said when Cross shot him a mean look.

Cross' blood was boiling at nearly dangerous levels as he subconsciously added up the amount of disrespectful acts that Cole Slaw had committed since his arrival. Nevertheless, he exhaled and said, "I need some information, and I'm sure that you can help me."

"You're probably right, but if I can help you what's in it for me?" Cole Slaw grinned.

Staring at the wad of bills on the table then back at Cole Slaw, Cross said, "There's nearly five grand in that roll, and it's yours if you're able to help me." The greed in Cole Slaw's eyes was unmistakable as he eyed the cash.

"Aight, what you need?" He questioned, giving Cross his first glimpse of the missing and rotten teeth that were scattered throughout his mouth.

"How do I find a young dude named Rah-Rah?" Cross asked, immediately noticing the change in Cole Slaw's demeanor. "You know him?"

"Who doesn't know him, and why are you looking for him?" Cole Slaw asked suspiciously, his eyes roaming through the crowd of onlookers.

"That's not a part of the deal!" Cross spat. "Now do you want this paper or what?"

"Come here," Cole Slaw said, leading Cross away from anyone who may have been intent on hearing their conversation. "Look Cross," he began, a serious look etched into his features. "The lil' nigga that you're asking about is bad news with a capital B, you hear me? And even if I could tell you where to find him, which I can't, it would take a whole lot more money than that," Cole Slaw announced, pointing towards the pool table and money that sat on top of it. "Contrary to what you may think, I don't have a death wish and lil' Ruckus ain't got no problem with deadin' cats!"

Inwardly smiling at the fear that Cole Slaw showed at the mention of Rah-Rah, Cross said, "Tell me a little about him and who he rocks with and the money is still yours."

"Yeah, I can do that." Cole Slaw leaned his pool stick against the wall and said, "The word is he murdered the top Blood nigga K.B. and took his stash and his place in the organization, then he started a war with the MS13 in order to snatch their turf."

Cross took pride in the knowledge that Rah-Rah had used all of the tools that he had taught him to his advantage. From the sounds of what Cole Slaw was telling him as well as the reverence that he used when he spoke of Rah-Rah, it was clear to Cross that Rah-Rah had the city under siege. However, pride aside, Cross also experienced a level of displeasure at the knowledge that he would be responsible for any harm that came to his nephew if Jose was allowed to carry out his scheme to have him killed.

"Being that you can't tell me where to find him, point me in the direction of one of his men and I'll work from there."

"Damn, nigga! Let me live!" Cole Slaw remarked, missing the evil look that transformed Cross' features at the third and final reference to him being a nigga.

Cross remained silent, choosing to ball his fists and allow Cole Slaw to finish talking.

Seeing that Cross wasn't budging, as Cole Slaw tossed one last glance at the bankroll that he not only wanted but needed, he said, "Rah-Rah's road dog goes by the name of B-Rock. Find a body that's marked in chalk, surrounded by yellow tape and one of them young niggas won't be far behind."

Before the words had completely exited Cole Slaw's mouth, Cross' ham-sized fists slammed into it catching him by surprise and dropping him to his knees. Cross then grabbed the back of his head and slammed his knee into his face. When Cross released him, Cole Slaw crashed face first into the dirty linoleum floor. Stepping over the unconscious body that lay at his feet, Cross strolled to the pool table and snatched his money up, mumbling to himself as he walked through the pool hall.

"I never liked his bitch ass anyway," Cross hissed, pushing through the crowd of on-lookers in his haste to leave. As he exited the dim-lit pool hall and headed to his rented Malibu, finding B-Rock was the next thing on his agenda.

Chapter Thirty-Seven

Swoop watched the custom Mercedes Benz Conversion van's approach with a level of dread. Meeting with Miguel was the last thing that he wanted to do. He would rather be combing the streets in search of his nephew, yet as the van came to a stop beside his car, he exhaled and exited his vehicle.

"Drive," Miguel ordered as soon as Swoop entered the back of the van and closed the door. Though he never looked up from the computer screen as he felt Swoop's presence and the van's movement, Miguel's carried a trace of venom when he said, "What good are you to us?"

"Excuse me?" Swoop answered, caught off guard by Miguel's question.

"What good are you to us?" Miguel repeated, closing the lap top computer screen. "It's been weeks since you came to us with the proposal to flush your nephew out, and since then the only thing that you've done is get a number of our people killed."

Swoop shifted uncomfortably in his seat upon hearing Miguel's words. Peering at the two large Spanish men who quietly sat in the back of the van with them, then noting the presence of the driver and passenger, Swoop knew that he had to remain composed. However, he hadn't forgotten their meeting and his vow that he would deal with Miguel when the time permitted.

"What do you have to say for yourself?" Miguel spat, snapping Swoop out of his contemplative state.

"Uh," Swoop's response eluded him as he felt hostile eyes burning into him from every direction. "You're correct, we have experienced losses but so have they," he announced, his confidence returning. Allowing his words to sink in, he added, "So far my nephew has eluded capture, but we will catch him. The only way to bring him out into the open is to continue putting presence on the Bloods organization."

"Pssssst!" Miguel blurted, his loud laughter mocking Swoop. "Those were bold words coming from someone who hasn't made a bit of difference in anything that we've done against the Bloods. Maybe that's not really true," Miguel spoke his thoughts out loud. There was no longer any trace of humor in his voice when he hissed, "Actually, you are the only one who has gained from our conflict with the Bloods, and I don't like it."

"What are you talking about?" Swoop asked, knowing that Miguel spoke of the money and dope that had been confiscated and turned over to Swoop, every time that they took over one of the Bloods trap spots.

"Don't play dumb when you know exactly what I mean!" Miguel's words came out in a growl as he angrily glared at Swoop. "However, I can care less about the measly scrapes that you've obtained. What I do care about is the fact that your vault grows larger at the expense of our organization, yet you have failed to deliver the Blood leader and man who's responsible for Chino's murder!"

"I will make good on my promise, and you can believe..." Swoop began.

"I care not to hear anymore of your promises!" Miguel exclaimed, cutting him short. "You have seven days from today to deliver your nephew's head to us, or we will take your head, your mother's and every one of your family members' heads that we can locate in exchange!"

"Wait a minute! The deal was that none of my family members would be harmed," Swoop yelled aggressively leaning forward in his seat. Feeling strong hands grasp his shoulder and slam him back. "That's our new deal and the terms aren't up for discussion, so I suggest that you get a move on." Nodding his head at one of his associates who instantly opened the door Miguel said, "Get out!"

Doing what he was told, Swoop exited the van and stood transfixed on Miguel until the door was closed in his face. Watching as it pulled off the shoulder of the highway tossing dirt and gravel on him as it merged into traffic, for the first time since going to them and informing on Rah-Rah, Swoop truly regretted his decision to do so. Turning around, Swoop began to walk back in the direction that would take him back to his car, dropping his hand in disgust for the first time in his life, Swoop had absolutely no idea what he was going to do.

"That's her with the two little girls," Tia directed her words to Stink who was sitting behind her.

Spying the pretty young girl and her daughters through the tinted window, Stink noted that the little girls were the spitting image of their mother. Yet, his heart ached for them due to their circumstances, but his heartache turned to pure anger when they came close enough to the car for him to observe the girls black and purple eye and the bruises that covered her yellow face.

"Damn, you see that, baby!" Tia cringed as she stared at Rah-Rah, then looked back out the window.

Rah-Rah shook his head and continued to follow the trio with his eyes as he wondered whether his uncle was responsible for the beating that the woman suffered. Coming to the immediate conclusion that he was the culprit, he turned to his father just as he began to speak.

"There's got to be another way," Stink said what Rah-Rah and Tia were already thinking. "I wouldn't normally back out on something this big at the last minute, especially with things being as serious as they are, but my gut feeling tells me that kidnapping her and her daughters isn't the way to go about this."

Rah-Rah and Tia shook their heads in agreement, but it was Tia who responded with an idea of her own. "Hear me out and tell me what you two think about this," she began, receiving no interference from either man. "She just picked the girls up from pre-school, so I'm willing to bet that she does this everyday at the same time."

"Okay, she picks the girls up everyday," Rah-Rah said, frowning. "What does that have to do with us getting at my uncle.

Seeing Tia's agitated look, Stink blurted in. "Let her finish, son. I'd like to hear what she has to say."

"Anyway," Tia said, rolling her eyes at Rah-Rah then smiling at Stink. "My girl told me that Pam loves her daughters to death, and other than her knack for choosing bad men, she's real sweet. So if your uncle is beating her and I believe he is, I think that she would be glad to get him and his associates out of her house and away from her daughters." Seeing the questioning looks that Rah-Rah and his father wore, she added, "Give it a few days and when we come back, let me talk to her. I'm sure that a little girl-talk and a few well placed dollars will get us everything that we want."

Sharing a moment of silence between them, Stink thought Tia's proposal over and decided that there was a chance that it might work. "I'm open for that. What you think, Rah-Rah?"

Cutting his eyes at Tia, he could tell that she held her breath as she awaited his answer, and he was aware that she held him and his decisions in high esteem. So, when he said, "Grab as much money as you think you'll need and handle your business," he wasn't surprised by the big kiss that she placed on his lips and the beautiful smile that she wore when she leaned back in the seat.

As they pulled away from the curb and merged out into traffic, everyone in the car felt good about the day's choice. Now only time would tell how Pam reacted to Tia's proposal.

Jose could hear Melody humming her favorite 'Trey Song's tune in the shower as he entered the room undetected and peered in the bathroom. Though the glass shower was fogged up, he was able to get a glimpse of Melody who was engrossed in her bath. Backing out of the bathroom, he closed the door and stared around the room until his eyes came across what he was searching for. Heading in the direction of Melody's Chanel bag, Jose quickly rummaged around in the bag until he grasped her phone. Removing it and the special recording device that was no larger than a needle, he slid the battery compartment off the back of the phone and placed the gadget inside. Hearing the shower and his wife's humming come to an abrupt stop, he closed the compartment and placed the phone and bag back in their proper place. Before he took a couple of steps away from the dresser, the door opened and Melody appeared.

"Hello, beautiful," Jose said, catching his wife by surprise.

Quickly raising her head, Melody fumbled with the towel that she held at her side in an attempt to cover her nakedness. "I… I didn't know…you were home." Melody stammered.

"I needed to come back for something," Jose said flatly. His smile never wavered, yet his disgust grew greater each moment that he watched the woman he loved, knowing that she had deceived him. He quickly turned away before Melody could witness his slowly deteriorating strength, because the last thing Jose wanted her to see was the emotional turmoil that he was fighting with. "I'll be out late this evening, so don't wait up for me," were the last words he said before he left the room.

Watching Jose leave, then peeking through the curtains and waiting until she saw his Bentley roll through the gates of their estate, Melody dropped down on their bed and breathed deeply. She had been holding her breath ever since she walked into the room and found him there, and ever since the night that she slept with Stink, this was how it had been. The thing that worried her the most was she was neither smarter than Jose nor talented enough to fool him. There was no way that he wasn't aware of her betrayal. Melody's fear was warranted and she suddenly realized that it wasn't based on the premise of paranoia like she had previously led herself to believe. The thought of her husband knowing of her deceit caused Melody's heart to race; fear of the unknown sent her racing around the room in search of clothing to wear in her haste to leave.

Melody dressed as quickly as she could. She then rushed to her closet and rummaged through its vast contents until she found the article of clothing that she was looking for. Snatching it from the rack and extracting a small key and piece of paper from its hidden pocket, Melody placed the safety deposit box key inside her bra and ran over to her Chanel bag and retrieved her phone. Keying in the numbers that Stink had given her, Melody's mind swirled in a million different directions as she attempted to devise a plan that would keep her alive and allow her and her daughter to escape from Jose.

"Baby, are you sure that you and the girls are okay?" Stink questioned Bonni, his concern evident in his tone.

"We're fine, Rahsaan. It's you and Rah-Rah that I'm worried about," Bonni said, adding "How is he holding up, anyway?"

He's doing a whole lot better than I thought he would be," Stink announced truthfully, still surprised to find that Rah-Rah controlled a formidable force of heavily armed young men, who were actually holding their own against Jose's vast resources and never- ending manpower. "Where is Cross, baby? I need to speak with him."

'Shit!' Bonni thought. She hated to lie to her husband, but with no other option left to her, being that she couldn't rightly tell the truth, she blew into the phone and said, "Baby, we're receiving a bad connection…. I can't hear you. I'll try back later. I love you!" Bonni hung up.

Hearing the call go dead, before Stink could put his phone away, it began to vibrate in his hand. "What happened, baby?" He asked, thinking that Bonni had called back.

"He knows, Stink! He knows that I met with you and gave you the information on what they planned to do to Rah-Rah!" Melody blurted frantically.

"Slow down, ma." Stink walked out of the room that was filled with Blood soldiers in an attempt to process what Melody had just revealed to him. "Where are you, Melody?" he asked calmly.

"I'm at home."

"Has he hurt you?" Stink asked, hoping that no harm befell her.

"No, he hasn't hurt me but I'm scared, Stink!" Melody began to cry.

Sighing, Stink closed his eyes as he listened to the frightened sobs that echoed through the phone. "Melody, do you have any money and can you and your daughter make it to Virginia, or do you need me to come get you?"

"I… I have…money stashed in…a safety deposit box in Manhattan," Melody replied between sobs. "We can…we can…make it."

"Okay. You have to relax, Melody." Stink stated more calmly than he actually felt. "Leave everything behind. Grab your daughter, get in your car and go straight to the bank. When you reach the Jersey Turnpike, give me a call to let me know that you're safe."

Melody felt a sense of ease as she listened attentively to Stink's directions. Snatching up her purse and car keys, she ran down the stairs and stormed into the room where her daughter was playing, Melody said, "I'm leaving now, and I'll call you back within the hour. Thank you, Stink."

"No thanks are necessary, Melody. You have always held always held me down, and if there's ever anything that I can do to repay the favor, I will always be there for you." A part of Stink truly felt indebted to Melody for all that she had sacrificed in order to be with him only for him to leave her behind and go back to Bonni.

"And that's the exact reason why I will always love you," Melody said, ending their call.

Allowing his arm that held the phone to drop at his side, Stink couldn't understand the numbers that overcome him at the completion of their call. However, when Melody's words trailed off, it was as if he would never hear her voice again and he would forever be forced to remember her by what she had just expressed to him. Nevertheless, as he shook the thought off and headed back into the other room, he expected to hear from Melody again within the next hour as she had promised.

Chapter Thirty-Nine

Jose removed the headphones he was wearing and allowed them to drop onto the table with a loud thud, this instantly caused the men that mingled about to focus their attention onto him. He had heard the entire conversation that took place between Melody and Stink and he felt like a knife had been thrust into his heart. His shoulders slumped as the enormity of his findings crashed into his reality, and not even the presence of his men as they stood looking to him could stop the tears that freely flowed from his eyes. After all he had done for Melody and Stink, he felt absolutely betrayed. Although he felt it deep in his heart that his wife was cheating on him, he never thought it would be with the man that he had mentored. However, what pained Jose more was the fact that Melody had given herself to another man, desecrating their vows in the process. This proved that she cared very little about him and their marriage. The fact that she had divulged information to Stink that held dire consequences for him and his organization, further infuriated him. Such a level of betrayal was way beyond anything that Jose could ever possibly forgive. And even if he could ever muster the strength to forgive, the sound of Melody's voice reverberating in his mind, telling Stink that she would always be in love with him and was at that very moment on the way to meet him, destroyed everything.

"Melody is on her way to meet Stink at Bank of America's branch located in mid-town Manhattan," Jose stated to his head of security Javier. Jose was aware that Melody was in pursuit of the safety deposit box located in the bank's vault. This cash was money that she had been ciphering from him from years and he knew that as well. "Bring Melody to me and take my daughter to her nanny," he instructed Javier.

Javier, not fully understanding the intent of his Boss' statement of *'Bring her to me'* asked, "Patron,what if she doesn't want to come?"

Abruptly, Jose banged his fist onto the table and yelled, "I don't care what you have to do, just bring her to me alive! Now, do I make myself clear?!"

Javier bowed his head and nodded agreeably, then said, "You've made yourself very clear, Patron." Javier turned and headed toward the door in haste. As he exited, several of the men followed behind him.

As Jose watched the men exit the office, he looked over to the high-tech surveillance camera only to see his men rushing into twin black Caprice Classics that were parked just outside the buildings doors. Jose sat there in silence as he watched his men disperse, he then did something that he hadn't done in many years, he cradled his face in his palms and cried. He was deeply saddened by what Melody had done to their family, but he was even more saddened by what he now had to do to her.

"Mommy, who does all that money belong to?" Soana asked excitedly while pointing to the large stacks of bills that Melody sat on the table.

Melody's mind was working so fast she almost didn't catch her daughter's inquiry. "Umm... it's um mommy's," she responded halfheartedly.

"Why do you have so much money, Mommy?" Soana asked, then added, "Are we going shopping, Mommy? I like shopping"

Melody rubbed her daughter's head, momentarily thinking just how much her daughter resembled her father. However, as she quickly averted her attention back to the money on the table, the only man she longed for was Stink. Once she gathered the money, she gripped Soana's hand and made her way out of the room that housed her safety deposit box. As Melody moved through the large bank with over a quarter million dollars and her precious daughter at her side, she outwardly smiled at the notion that she was home-free. Against all odds, she was willing to do whatever it took to be with Stink *'if only for a while'* she thought to herself.

Melody slid her Chanel sunglasses over her eyes as she approached the bank's exit. Without any hindrance, she calmly exited the bank. Melody's smile was bright as the afternoon sun as she strutted toward her car. It wasn't until she saw a very familiar face coming toward her did her smile dissipate and quickly turned into a frown of horror. In a panic, she abruptly spun on her heels and went from whence she'd come. Without being prompted, Melody gripped her daughter's hand broke into a full sprint. Melody knew that she needed to get back into the bank to even have a chance at escaping. With the bank's entrance in view, Melody's world was shattered when out of nowhere another of Jose's men appeared and roughly grabbed her by the shoulders. At that moment, she knew that she was surrounded by Jose's men. Suddenly, Javier pulled Soana from her grasp and hand her to one of Jose's other men who appeared.

"Take your hands off of my daughter!" Melody yelled secretly hoping that her screams would attract the attention of the many people who passed. As Melody searched the sea of faces that passed, she began to pray that someone would stop and save her, but no one did. "Please give my daughter back. I will do anything you ask," Melody pleaded.

It was clear that her pleas fell on deaf ears when Javier instructed, "Take the girl away."

"Mommy! Mommy!" Soana yelled while struggling to get away from the man's grasp.
Without further delay, the man carried the child away kicking and screaming until they reached the awaiting car.

Melody looked on through disbelieving eyes. Her daughter had been ripped from her in broad daylight and no one did a thing. As the car smoothly disappeared through the mid-day traffic, she felt her heart drop in complete frantic, yet she knew that there was nothing she could do. She held on to the reassurance that Jose's men wouldn't harm a hair on their child's head. She knew that Jose would kill each of the men in the most heinous of ways if anyone of them harmed his Princess. That knowledge alone caused the flow of tears that cascaded down her cheeks to subside.

As if Javier was reading Melody's mind, he said, "No harm will come to your daughter, but you will have to come with us." He then led Melody to the matching Impala.

Melody allowed herself to be led to the car, yet when the door opened and she was set to get in, she yelled, "I'm not going anywhere with you! I want my daughter back!" This was her last effort to try and get someone to interfere with her abduction. "Let me go! Somebody help me!" She yelled in desperation while trying to free herself from Javier's grip.

Javier was usually a passionate man, but after witnessing the pain that she had caused his boss, he abandoned all passion when he reached back and delivered a crashing blow to Melody's chin, which instantly cut her protest short when she fell back into one of the other men's arms completely unconscious. Javier instructed the man to place Melody's comatose body in the rear of the car, then thought, *'I've done my job, now she's got to answer to Jose.'*

Chapter Forty

Crossed stopped the squeaking shopping cart that he pushed in the middle of the busy open air drug block and casually bent down to retrieve a bent up beer can. The role of a vagabond had become Cross with ease. He rose from retrieving the can and tossed it inside the cart. The cart already full of trash that he had gathered earlier raised none of the dealers' attention on the busy blocks. Although he had received a few awkward glances, no one inquired about his presence. Cross knew that was because of his slumped posture and disheveled state. He had been listening to the men for hours and as of yet he hadn't received the information he desired. He was just about ready to abandon his charade and resort back to his normal means of attaining the information that he needed, when suddenly a woman in much worse shape than he remembered appeared at the opposite end of the block. Initially, Cross couldn't put his finger on exactly who he was looking at, but after a brief bout with memory lapse, it hit him. He was looking at one the most sought-after woman that the city had ever seen.

Nikki used to be a beautiful woman at one point, but as he saw, her once lustrous mane was now just a covering of kinks. Her body had always been her strong suit, but now it was a distant memory as her clothes hung loosely from frame.

After a quick contemplation, Cross concluded that Nikki may have been able to assist him. Quickly, he left his cart and made a bee-line toward the woman as she crossed the street. "Nikki! Nikki!" He yelled instantly garnering her attention.

The sound of her name being called caused Nikki to stop in her tracks and turn toward the direction in which she heard it. She turned to see who was calling her. When she saw the ragged dressed Cross coming toward her, she frowned and turned away. Yet, before she was able to continue on her way, he called her again.

"Nigga, stop calling my name, I don't know you!" She responded full of attitude. With her hands poised on her hips, she gave him a look of pure disgust.

Cross found it hard to believe that even in her present state of disarray, she could even act as if she was in fact better than him.

Once he was within earshot, he said,"Nikki, it's me Cross. Let me speak to you for a minute."

Instantly, Nikki divulged a mouth full of broken and chipped teeth, which was proof that she was quite happy to see him, even if it was under such dire circumstances. "Damn, what happened to you, boo? Last time I saw you, you was that nigga"

Cross ignored her question and thought to himself, *'she's got some nerve questioning my situation'* Instead he said, "You trying to make a quick hundred bucks?"

"Does a bear shit in the woods?" She replied sarcastically. She then added," You damn right. I'm trying to make that money. Why, what's up?" Nikki didn't even wait for Cross to reply before continuing," But how you on deck to make any money?"

Cross smiled devilishly, then extracted a large wad of bills from his pocket and said," I'm looking for this young cat name B-Rock, you know him?"

Nikki couldn't pry her eyes off the fistful of cash that he held to answer the question, which prompted Cross to repeat," You know him or what?"

"Do I know him? Hells fucking yeah I know him. Know his momma too," she stated as she began to do a little dance, at the thought of the drugs she was about to purchase with the money that Cross held in his hand. "Shit, let me get that paper nigga and I'll take you to the nigga house."

Although Cross felt a tinge of pity for what was left of the woman and her integrity, he still chuckled at her '*crackhead*' performance. Quickly, he wiped the smile from his face and focused back to the task at hand." I got you mama, but first I need you to put me on dude's trail. You do that and I'll give you two hundred."

"Nigga, I'll put on his trail, his street, road whatever. In fact, this is one of his spots right here," she stated as she pointed to an old house across the street. Then just as Cross' mind began to replay the mental tape in his mind of the activity at the residence, she spoke again, "In fact, today just may be your lucky day because here he comes right now," she divulged as the sounds of loud music escaped the confines of three SUVs that bent the corner.

Cross quickly averted his attention in the direction of the music pouring from the SUVs. As the trucks passed them and parked in front of the house, Cross squinted in an attempt to get a better view of who may have been in the truck and how many of them there were. The task of seeing through the limo tint was a little difficult, but he still surmised how many men were inside the vehicles. As they exited, Cross scrutinized each man in search of what kind of artillery they were carrying.

"That's him right there!" Nikki announced a little louder than what was warranted, which caused nearby hustlers and junkies to turn in their direction.

"Bitch, quiet the fuck down!" Cross hissed in a tone laced with venom. He neither wanted nor needed any added attention. That was one of the reasons he was draped in bum's clothing.

The look of shock that registered on Nikki's face was enough for Cross to see that he had gotten through to her. Quickly, he turned in the direction in which the men were exiting the jeep and released a sigh of frustration. Due to Nikki's antics, he hadn't even gotten a look at the man known as B-Rock. Nonetheless, Nikki had given him a good lead that would surely lead him to Rah-Rah, which would lead him to Stink. Smoothly, Cross slid her the entire wad of money, then escaped through a nearby alley.

Although it took Cross longer than he expected, he finally figured out exactly which man was B-Rock. It took him nearly two days and drives that took him all over the Tidewater area, but he was confident that he had his man. It was not hard after witnessing how the other men fell over one another trying to cater to the slim brown skinned man that rode in the middle SUV. Cross kept a safe distance behind the trio of SUVs until the one that B-Rock rode in veered off from the rest, heading out into the city's suburbs. Once the traffic became sparse, Cross lagged behind even further, careful not to raise any suspicion. The last thing he wanted to do was alert the men to the fact that they were being followed. Suddenly, the turn signal on the SUV snapped Cross from his thoughts and caused him to slow the vehicle that he drove. From afar, Cross watched as the truck pulled into an *Applebee's* parking lot. Casually, Cross drove past the restaurant and pulled into a nearby service station. He quickly found a parking spot at the service station's that afforded him a clear view of the restaurant and the SUV that the men drove. After sitting there for a almost five minutes, a dark tinted Mercedes sedan pulled up and out stepped Rah-Rah, Stink and a strikingly beautiful female. Cross smiled a smile of victory for he was well on his way to doing what he had come to the U.S. to do.

Chapter Forty-One

Jose walked into the room like a zombie; his eyes were blank and his clothing was soaked with blood. He flopped down at the table in the middle of the room and wrapped his blood covered hand around a fifth of Jose Cuervo. Unscrewing the cork, he allowed it to fall onto the floor then turned the bottle toward his lips and drank from it greedily. And even though the warm liquid burned his throat, he felt nothing but numbness. At that moment he wanted nothing more than to escape the pain that ached in his chest, and the only immediate solace he could find was inside the bottle that he gulped.

"Patron," Javier announced as he slowly entered the room with a neatly wrapped towel draped across his arm, he added, "I thought you might need this."

Jose looked up and said, "Lay it on the table, I'll get it." Jose then turned his attention back to the bottle and the soothing affects that it caused.

Javier slowly backed out of the room in complete astonishment. He had never seen Jose like this in the two decades that he had known him. Jose had always been the prefect picture of strength and confidence, to see him now in such a vulnerable state, was mind-boggling to Javier. He cast one final glance at his wounded boss and friend then exited the room.

Before Javier was out of earshot, Jose instructed," Get the box Javier."

Javier didn't say a word; he simply followed his boss' demand.

Jose dropped the bottle on the table with a thud and reached for the towel. Smoothly, he wiped his face and hands then looked down to the crimson colored blood that covered the towel as if he was seeing it for the very first time. In a daze, he allowed the bloody towel to fall to his feet.

Suddenly, Javier reappeared carrying a large green and gold velvet covered box that resembled a small casket. "Patron, here is your request," Javier announced then sat the box on the floor.

Jose stumbled over the box. "This will work just fine," he stated more to himself than Javier. He then stepped back over to the table and took a large swig of the Tequila. "Javier, I want this wrapped up like a present," Jose instructed.

"A present?" Javier asked confused.

"Yes, have everything cleaned up and shipped to a very special friend," Jose explained.

Javier turned to go and process his boss' request when Jose's next request stopped him in his tracks.

"Bring a nice gold ribbon too, Javier," Jose said, then grabbed a pen and a piece of paper and flopped back down at the table. With shaking hands he scribbled something on the piece of paper then signed it. Jose took another swig from the bottle and began to reflect on the one incident that would forever change his life and the life of his daughter. There was only one person who Jose felt bore the responsibility of his plight and that was none other than Stink. Therefore, Jose was planning a surprise that would undoubtedly bring his ex-friend right to his door step, which was exactly where he wanted him.

_____

Chapter Forty-Two

"I like Tia," Stink commented to Rah-Rah as they quietly waited for Swoop's girl to arrive at the daycare.

Rah-Rah smiled at the mentioning of Tia. With his eyes focused on her as she sat on a nearby bench inconspicuously reading a book, he felt a rush of pride. Tia may have seem, to the naked eye, a beautiful young woman enjoying a leisurely read, but the truth was that she was packing two .45's and if anything proved to look fishy, she wouldn't hesitate unloading them both." Yeah, she's a soldier Pops," Rah-Rah stated with pride.

Stink couldn't help but think that he had found his first true love at about the same age. It wasn't hard for Stink to tell that his son truly loved the girl from the way he beamed in her presence. However much he wanted to mind his business, there were some things he wanted to get clear. So, he started by asking, "Do you love her, son?"

His father's words caught him off guard, yet the beaming smile that covered his face expressed all that words couldn't. Nonetheless, Rah-Rah chose to further reiterate his love by saying, "Sure I do, Pops." Rah-Rah continued to stare at his father because he knew that he hadn't asked the question without reason." Why you ask?"

Stink inwardly grinned at the way his son's instincts told him that there was more to the inquiry. "I can see how you fell in love with such a beautiful woman, she seems special. It's not every day that you find a young lady willing to hold you all the way down." Although his words were directed to his son, he could only see Melody in his mind. The thought of her has been weighing heavy on his mind for the last few days. Ever since she failed to contact him and not even answering her phone, he's been worried.

"Pop, you good?" Rah-Rah asked snapping Stink from his reverie.

"Yeah, I'm good, son, just thinking about something," Stink offered. He then shook his head in an attempt to erase the thoughts that played in his head.

Quickly, he jumped back to the original subject. "If you truly love her son, I suggest you separate her from what you do out here in these streets," Stink advised.

"I'm not sure of how I can do that because I've seen her in action and believe me, Pops, she gets down for hers," Rah-Rah said, then added, "I swear she loves this shit more than me."

"Damn," Stink replied, then thought that there was more to the dark skinned beauty than there was for the eye to see.

"Okay men, play time is over," Tia spoke into the unseen microphone that was attached to her shirt. "She's here," she divulged, referring to Swoop's girl Pam.

"Okay, you niggas heard her, let's look alive and be ready to roll on Tia's signal," Rah-Rah spoke into the walkie-talkie in his hand. He then sat up from his slouched position in the passenger side. Intently, he watched as Tia closed her novel, stood and pulled a pair of large frame *D&G* sunglasses over her eyes. Nonchalantly, she began to make her way toward the unsuspecting woman with confident strides.

Stink smiled at the way Tia approached Swoop's girlfriend in a no nonsense kind of way. He could only sit and watch her in action as Rah-Rah's words rang in his mind.

"Here goes nothing," Tia remarked more to herself than anyone else as she slid her hand inside her purse and gripped the cold steel of the .45's handle. With only a few feet separating her from her target, Tia scanned the area around her and felt a rush of confidence as she saw over 30 bloods inconspicuously placed around the scene. If she was somehow unable to sway Pam with the bitter truth, she was prepared to summon the gang members to assist in swaying her. Just as Tia was close enough to set off any one's personal alarm when their personal space is being infringed upon, she spoke, "Excuse me, Pam, but may I please speak to you for a moment."

With an evil glare etched into her features, Pam asked, "Do I know you?"

"No you don't, but I've…" Tia began.

"Well how about you began by telling me how you know me, then I'll decide whether I want to talk to you or not," Pam stated in a tone that was full of trepidation.

"That's fine," Tia stated calmly in an attempt to put the woman at ease. "First of all, my name is Tia and through a mutual friend I inquired about you."

"Why would you be doing that? And who is the mutual friend?" Pam fired off the questions without a break in between.

Tia exhaled loudly then began, "Look Boo, let's cut through the bullshit and lay it all on the table. You're involved with a nigga who has unresolved issues with some people who don't take too kindly to the bullshit that he's been doing, and even though you ain't done nothing to them personally, I've been sent to see just how deep your loyalties lie with Swoop."

Pam's heart skipped a beat at the realization that Swoop's enemies had approached her personally. The last thing she wanted was to have her life taken or the life of her daughters taken for something that Swoop did, especially when he cared nothing about neither of them. Slowly, she began back peddling as tears trickled down her cheeks. "I don't have anything to do with whatever he's done in these streets," Pam pleaded.

"But you do, Boo," Tia announced, moving toward her, then said, "The last thing I want to see is any harm come your way. I know you got two beautiful daughters," she concluded in a threatening tone.

Pam's voice was just above a whisper when she said, "Please, leave my daughters out of it." Abruptly, the floodgates of tears exploded from her eyes and began to pour down her cheeks again.

Tia shook her head agreeably, as she reached out to wipe the woman's tears. Deep in her heart, she felt genuine pain for the woman. The makeup covered bruises were unveiled with every tear, further caused Tia to feel sorrow for Pam. "Sweetheart, look at you. Whether you know it or not, there's something happening to your daughter every time they see those bruises on your face," Tia revealed earnestly. "Let me help you, Pam," Tia quickly added.

Pam knew that Tia's words were true and she knew exactly what kind of man Swoop was, yet she was still a little leery of entering into an agreement with a stranger. "Help me how? And what exactly do I have to do to receive this help?" Pam asked, hoping that maybe she could be rescued from Swoop's abusiveness.

Tia slid her hand out of her purse and produced a thick envelope and then handed it to Pam. "Look inside and you will find everything you need" she then stood back and watched as Pam fumble with the flap and peek inside.

"Oh my God!" Pam gasped as she eyed the neatly wrapped stacks inside the package.

"Now, do you believe that I can help you escape this situation?" Tia remarked as she noticedhat the tears running down Pam's cheeks went from being sad to glad.

"Tell me what I have to do and I'll do it," Pam vowed. She was prepared to do whatever it took to rid herself of Swoop, and thanks to the money that she received from Tia, she would be able to do just that. She would be able to now move herself and her daughters far away from 'Bad News.' For that alone, Pam felt extremely indebted to the woman standing in front of her, and whatever she asked of her she would definitely do. To cross Swoop would be the perfect payback for all the atrocious things that he did to her.

Tia wrapped her arm over Pam's shoulder and began to walk with her in the direction of the daycare. In very hushed tone, she began to tell Pam exactly what would be asked of her. Once she finished, Tia turned her attention toward the tinted vehicle that Rah-Rah and his father sat in and gave them a conspiratorial wink. It was just a token to let them know that she pulled it off.

Chapter Forty-Three

Restless and on the verge of starvation, Cross looked down to his watch and quickly concluded that after pulling an all-nighter that no useful information had come from his vigil. After scrutinizing his watch a second time, he figured that he had a little time to grab a bite to eat and a couple of hours sleep. Stretching his tired limbs and rubbing his eyes, Cross turned the key in the ignition and was about to place the gear shift in drive when something instantly caught his attention. In a flash, Cross had the high-tech binoculars to his eyes and was beaming in on the object of his attention. Through the lens of his binoculars, he watched as a black Lincoln Continental slowly drive up the street. However, what really peaked Cross' attention was the New York plates that the car donned. Upon closer inspection, Cross noticed that there were three Spanish men occupying the vehicle. To Cross, it seemed as if the men were searching each address as they drove slowly up the block. It became evidently clear that the men in the Lincoln had found whatever residence it was that they searched for when the car came to an abrupt stop. What really set off Cross's alert was the fact that Stink and Rah-Rah were laying their heads at that exact address.

When the car went to the end of the block and hastily made a U-turn, Cross' heart rate was near its maximum. "Please try and do some stupid shit!" he hissed to himself as he began to quickly gather all his tools for destruction.

Slowly the Lincoln crept pass Cross again as he sat poised and ready for war. This time Cross was able to get a better glimpse of the men and he quickly ascertained that they were professionals. Cross was quite surprised that these men had even found Stink and Rah-Rah's hideout. As their brake lights blared to life again, Cross grabbed one final piece of artillery and carefully cracked the passenger door. He disengaged the lock on the S.K-8 that he retrieved from the rear seat. Undetected, Cross escaped the confines of the car only to see the Lincoln pull to the side of the street where a young boy carrying a basketball appeared and approached the car. A short conversation ensued, yet from Cross' vantage point, it was impossible to get any inclination of what the conversation may have been about. However, once he witnessed a sly exchange of what looked to be a gift wrapped box and then the boy taking off toward the house in which Stink and Rah-Rah were staying. Then the car slowly crept away from the curb, leaving Cross with a grave dilemma and wasn't sure of how to deal with it. He wasn't sure whether to allow the boy to get the package near Skink and Rah-Rah or to follow the men that he knew that Jose had sent. Just when Cross was deciding what to do, he emerged from his spot only to witness Stink opening the door for the young boy with the box in hand.

"Shit!" Cross exclaimed to himself. As smooth as he had exited the car he slid back in. With his binoculars handy, he tried to see what was taking place.

Stink was scrutinizing the box closely, shaking it and holding it up to his ear to see if there was anything ticking inside. Cross felt a slight amount of pressure lifted from him when he saw that his friend was still very much intact.

Suddenly, Cross could see Stink sending the boy away while holding the neatly wrapped package in his arms. Stink then began to unravel the ribbons that held the box closed and meticulously remove the top. However, whatever was inside that box startled Stink tremendously. As if frightened, Stink jumped back and allowed the box to fall to the porch. Cross had no idea of what was in that box, but knowing his old friend, nothing ever rattled him easy, and from what he'd witnessed, his friend was rattled. At that very moment Cross realized he would have to do whatever necessary to keep the ones he loved safe, even if it meant giving his own life in the process.

Chapter Forty-Four

'Since you planned on taking my wife from me forever and the two of you were so very in love...' Stink read the letter that was attached to the box that contained Melody's decapitated head aloud as if he was in a daze. Rah-Rah and Tia Sat opposite of him listening intently. 'I felt that it was only right that I give you a piece of her to always remember her by.' Stink couldn't believe the viciousness that Jose had displayed with Melody.

Stink dropped his head in his palms and fought back tears. He couldn't get Melody's mangled neck and terror filled eyes out of his head. Deep down, he knew that he was responsible for her death.

Rah-Rah wiped Tia's tears away as her head rested on his chest. It was clear that this situation was weighing heavily on his father and Rah-Rah didn't quite know why. He had never heard of 'Melody', but it was clear that the woman held a special place in his father's heart. There were several questions that he wanted to ask his father, but that moment would have to wait. However, he wasn't about to let the fact that their hideout had been compromised without saying as much. "Pops, I'm sorry about your lady friend and all, but fo' real, we gotta get up out of here before it's our heads in that box." Rah-Rah concluded in a matter-of-fact tone. Before his father could answer, Rah-Rah added, "They know where we at Pops and I refuse to be a sitting duck any longer than I have to."

"Just give me a minute, son," Stink responded in a tone laced with emotion. With the powerful thrust of one fist crashing into the other, Stink vehemently vowed," That motherfucker is going to pay for doing her like that, man!"

Rah-Rah nodded agreeably, then said, "I know, Pops. I know, man. But right about now we have got to be up and out of here."

Stink exhaled deeply, then said, "You're right son. Let's be the fuck up outta here."

Seeing the look of pain and anguish that covered Tia's face, caused Rah-Rah to grip her in his arms and hug her tightly. Although she was a real 'trooper,' the sight of a decapitated head was very traumatic for her. With her in his arms, he couldn't help but think that it could have very well been her head instead of Melody's. This was something that he could not live with. He could hear his father telling him that this life was to be separated from those you love.

Chapter Forty-Five

"Where the fuck you think you're going!" Swoop Barked angrily, instantly causing those who sat around the table to look up from their food and drinks bewildered.

"I...I... was just going to take the girls down to my mother's house. I'm... not going... to be long," Pam stammered while trying to maintain eye contact with Swoop. She knew to look away from him while he talked, could possibly end in a beat-down.

Swoop, naturally a menacing figure, caused his chest to swell with every breath he breathed. "Yeah, Aight... you just hurry up and bring your ass back, 'cause me and my boys might need some more drinks and snacks." Swoop then reached into his pocket and produced a fifty dollar bill. In an act of defiance, Swoop balled the money up and said, "Bring us a 12 pack of Beck's beer and a box of Black &Mild Too." With that said, Swoop threw the money at Pam in a disrespectful manner and turned his attention back to his audience.

Pam stood there in a state of disgrace, until Swoop barked, "You ain't gone yet!"

On the verge of tears, Pam reached down and retrieved the money then turned and exited.

Swoop smiled to himself once Pam left the room. He absolutely loved the way in which she took his abuse. This filled him with a level of pride that was incomparable to anything that he had ever experienced. Unbeknownst to him, it was this same level of disrespect that had pushed Pam to betray him in the gravest fashion.

"Open the door," Tia ordered the man who had been ordered by the *'Bloods'* to act as a guard of sorts. The sight of Pam and her daughters bending the corner filled Tia with a great sense of achievement. She was doing something right and it felt good.

Stink on the other hand was feeling the exact opposite. The thought of another mother enduring any kind of hardship due to a man, infuriated him. The thought of Melody and the fate that she met was just something that he couldn't shake from his mind. No matter how he tried to rationalize it, he just couldn't think of anything but her. He felt as if he could've done so much more to protect her. His inability to protect her, coupled with the compassion that he felt for any woman in need, made the situation with Pam that much more personal. "Tia, if you don't mind I'd like to talk to her," Stink divulged, then shot his son a look that was asking for the same courtesy.

"It's fine with me," Tia replied

Rah-Rah nodded his head in agreement, signaling that he didn't have an issue with that either.

As Pam ushered the kids into the S.U.V., then slid in herself, Stink was the first to speak. "Did you have any problems getting out of the house?" he asked.

Pam looked to Stink with a confused expression. She then turned to Tia and without saying a word, asked, "Who's this strange man inquiring about my situation?"

Tia quickly gave her a wink, which ultimately set her at ease.

Pam looked around at those seated inside the large cabin of the Suburban and knew at once that these men were serious. "No, it wasn't much of a problem," she stated replaying the disrespect that she had endured at Swoop's hand just a few minutes before.

"That's good," Stink said, his sincerity evident in his tone. He then reached in his pocket and pulled out a business card. "We have some people who are going to take you and your daughters to the airport. If you have any problems please feel free to call me," Stink concluded.

Pam glanced down at the card momentarily, then focused her eyes onto Stink. "Thank you all so very much, I don't know how I'll ever be able to repay you all,"

Stink brushed the show of appreciation off as nothing, then said, "It's nothing. However, now is the chance to repay us."

Pam looked to him confused. She knew that there was a price behind what the people were doing for her; she just didn't know what it was.

"Now, please tell us exactly where everyone inside the house was situated when you left," Stink inquired

Pam wasn't sure if this was all that they wanted from her, but if it was then she would be more than glad to help.

"Yeah, I see you bitches!" Cross stated readjusting the focus on his binoculars. Chuckling to himself, Cross found it funny that he was watching the same men who were watching Stink. And the funny part about it was that they had no idea that they were being watched. Cross kept his attention fastened on to the same Lincoln that he had observed just the day before. What confused him more was why Stink and Rah- Rah were parked in front of one of the most notorious projects in the city at sunset. Though Cross had no answers for the many questions that ran through his mind, one thing was very clear; he would protect his best friend and Rah-Rah at all cost. The sight of the Spanish men squatting on Stink and Rah-Rah suddenly filled Cross with the rage that had been the driving force behind his violence for years. If they made any hasty movements, Cross would gladly emerge from the shadows and unleash a torrent of bullets in their direction. Cross had been trying to suppress his appetite for destruction, but the more he sat around, the more he wanted to act out. At the moment, Cross decided that his longtime friend would just have to be mad at him because he was about to let his appearance known.

"Okay, so that gives me a pretty good idea of how we need to proceed," Stink said, with his attention focused on Rah-Rah. "Can you think of anything else, son?" Stink asked.

"Nah, I think you covered everything, Pops," Rah-Rah replied as he slipped a clip into the high-powered assault rifle. "I'm ready to get this over with, Pops. Let's roll," he concluded.

In response, Stink lifted his own firearm from his lap and began to prepare for war. His taste for blood had risen and nothing was going to stop him from acquiring it. "Tia, I want you to accompany Pam and her kids to the airport," Stink instructed.

Immediately, Rah-Rah picked up on what his father was doing. Rah-Rah chimed in, "Yeah Tia, Make sure she gets on that plane safely." Before she was out of the door, he added, "Make sure you take Bear and Trooper with you to drop them off at the airport, too." Rah-Rah stood to leave and never looked back to see the angry glare that was plastered on Tia's face. Nevertheless, his father's words of wisdom were enough to let him know that he truly loved her and to intentionally place her in harm's way was a thing of the past.

Chapter Forty-Six

"Where the hell are you two going?" Cross blurted to himself, quickly bolting from the confines of his car. Two men were exiting a truck wearing hooded sweatshirts moving in a crouched manner toward the projects. Though, he couldn't see the men's faces, he was well aware that the two men were Stink and Rah-Rah .He surmised that he would know his best friend and nephew's build anywhere.

Cross instantly saw movement in the car that the Spanish men were in as soon as Stink and Rah-Rah's getaway car pulled away from the curb. Cross patiently waited to see what the men would do next while his blood rate began to soar with anticipation. He wondered whether the men would go after the S.U.V. that Stink and Rah-Rah had exited or would they seize the moment and go after Stink and Rah-Rah. There was no doubt that the men had been sent to kill Stink and Rah-Rah. Suddenly, the doors to the Lincoln swung open and out came three men with guns in hand. This caused a demonic smile to linger over Cross' face. "Oh, that's how you motherfuckers want to play?" he stated to himself as he quickly went into motion. With his assault rifle in tow, Cross exited the car in haste, leaving the car's door ajar. Although, he was a much heavier version of himself, he still moved with the agility of a young man.

The succession of men darting through the project left the property sparse. Cross witnessed nosy proprietors peeking through curtains and he knew that there was only a designated amount of time before the police were called.

With his back against the project buildings' rigid concrete wall, Cross watched as the men he hunted did the same. He was only a short distance from them, yet he chose to keep his presence unknown until just the right time. When the men began to make hand motions to one another he knew that they had located their targets. Unbeknownst to them, Cross had them within his scope's sight a day ago. Quickly, Cross darted across a small grassy area to get a better view of the men and what they saw. Once he positioned himself in a spot where he had an unobstructed view of all that there was to see, it was time to go to work.

The sight of Rah-Rah's lower half dangling from an upstairs window absolutely confused him. Then to see Stink Expertly crawl in behind him almost caused a light chuckle to escape him. He had no idea what they were up to, but it was clear that the men down below them were banking on an ambush.

Cross smiled and dropped to his knees like a war veteran and broke his assault rifle down with its tri-pod brace sticking into the ground. Positioning himself on his stomach, Cross was now prepared to inflict chaos.

"I'm gon' beat the hell out of her," Swoop swore as he paced back and forth inside his living room. Banging his fist in his palms, Swoop ignored the occasional glances he received from the Spanish men who played cards around the large table. Swoop tossed angry glances at the clock every time he walked past it. He was becoming angrier and angrier every passing moment. She had been gone over 45 minutes and all Swoop could think was that she was with another man. Swoop felt that Pam was his own piece of property, his personal slave and for her to be disobedient, infuriated him.

All Swoop could think about was how he was going to beat Pam when she returned. He had all but concluded to kill her when one of Pam's daughter's toys made a squeaking sound. Instantly, Swoop and the men turned their attention to the strange sound. Once their eyes focused in that direction, it was entirely too late. A reach for any of their guns would have been suicide, and silently these men were praying that the two partially masked black men only wanted cash and not blood. However, there was one man who knew that these men had come for blood.

Rah-Rah felt the cushiony toy under his shoe before it even made the sound. Once the tiny toy squeaked to life, he knew that their entrance wouldn't be as they planned it. The sight of the shocked four Spanish men staring in their direction was nothing compared to the crazed expression that covered Swoop's face. Rah-Rah could see the sweat budding up on the man's forehead. It was evident that his uncle was ready to make a move. Even the sight of his father holding a short stock Mini-14 couldn't deter what Swoop was about to try.

"It's ov-"Rah-Rah began before his uncle dove behind a couch, Miami Vice style and produced his gun. What happened next was absolutely pandemonium as shots began to fly from each side of the room. Swoop's act of bravery quickly caused the Spanish men to reach for their weapons.

Rah-Rah raised the M1 that he carried and ripped the four Spanish men to shreds. Meanwhile, Stink was stalking Swoop inside the small apartment. He had sidestepped a number of Swoop's shots and from the sounds of it, he ran low on ammunition.

"Got yo ass now, don't I, big boy?" Stink yelled out.

"Fuck you nigga!" Swoop yelled back.

Carefully, Stink stepped around the couch with his gun leveled. The sight of Swoop laying there with blood covering his right shoulder caused Stink to smile.

Rah-Rah appeared with a crazed look on his face. "Kill him, Pops."

Swoop began to chuckle, which gradually turned into a bellowing laugh. The fact that he had turned the city on its roof looking for his nephew, he somehow managed to walk right into his house. The fact that he was going to die anyway, Swoop decided to inflict a little pain of his own. "Only a bitch would get his father to do what he himself can't," Swoop stated through grimacing pain. He then added, "Oh, I forgot this nigga ain't even your daddy." Swoop's mocking laugh returned as the sight of pain transcended onto Rah-Rah's face.

Stink could see the hurt in his son's face as the painfully truth crashed into his reality. Stink wished that he had killed the man before he had the chance to hurt his son with the words. Stink never liked Swoop and when he began to pull the trigger, the sight of his shuddering body filled him with a small sense of relief. Once the final shot was fired, it was Stink and Rah-Rah who wore smiling faces, while Swoop's face was twisted with agony.

After Stink and Rah-Rah stood there and took pride in their work, they both made a move to the rear door. There were no words spoken as they exited the apartment and made their way back the way they'd come. Both of their minds were replaying what had just taken place, and although they ended Swoop's life, they still had unfinished business. They were engrossed in a war and it was nowhere near its end.

Once they rounded a corner, the three Spanish men that awaited them, appeared, catching both of them by surprise.

With their guns drawn, the leader of the three said, "Take their guns."

"Get the fuck off of me!" Rah-Rah hissed as the man closest to him relieved him of his weapon.

Stink kept a cold hard glare focused on his capture as the cold steel pressed against his temple caused him to anticipate death. Stink was in the midst of a brazen attempt to knock the gun from the man's hand when his head burst abruptly, sending brain matter all over Stink's face. After wiping the warm bloody goo from his eyes, Stink witnessed Rah-Rah overpowering the Spanish man who was in complete awe witnessing the detonation of his comrade's head. The third man was so shocked by the change of events, he dropped his gun and ran only to be lifted from his feet by the shooter that neither Stink nor Rah-Rah could see.

After taking the Spanish man's gun, Rah-Rah placed a lone shot into his forehead, leaving all three men dead. In unison, both Stink and Rah-Rah began to move in a way that would shield them from the shooter in the dark. Suddenly, the sight of a familiar face appeared from the darkness, causing both Stink and Rah-Rah to smile defiantly.

"I don't believe this shit!" Stink announced in awe.

Rah-rah couldn't even muster a word as his uncle and mentor approached.

"I thought I needed to come and save y'all asses," Cross stated jokingly. Instantly, Cross noticed the perplexed look covering Stink's face and what it represented caused him to add, "Bonni and the girls are safe as promised. Now, how about we carry this reunion someplace where there ain't a bunch of dead bodies thrown around?"

As the sirens in the distance began to appear near, all three men jogged off into the night.

"Thank you sweetheart," Cross said, taking the cold glass of champagne from Tia. He couldn't help but watch as her well-defined back side covered in fitting jean shorts, jiggled on her over to Rah-Rah where she plopped down onto his lap.

The mesmerized look that Cross had on his face as he eyed Tia's butt prompted Stink to say, "When you get finished staring at your nephew's woman's ass, please get back to the story."

Cross smiled bashfully, then said, "Oh…oh my bad, I was umm… thinking."

"Yeah, you was thinking alright," Stink tossed back.

Cross shook his head as if he was erasing a vision from his head, then continued with the story that he had begun before he became enthralled in Tia's physical attributes. "Anyway, I thought the two of you would need my help, so I put Bonni and the girls on a plane to Dubai and I came here as quick as I could," he explained.

"Do you think it was smart for you to do that? You know this nigga Jose play for keeps," Stink stated in a worried tone.

Cross couldn't help but note just how ungrateful his friend was. *'He could at least be grateful for me saving his ass'* Cross thought to himself before he responded. "Come on High, they're in Dubai under close watch of some people that owe me dearly."

This eased Stink's anxiety about the situation somewhat, but this only created even more of an urgency to get this war over with. And now that he had his ace, he was really ready. However, there was one more thing that bothered him, causing him to ask, "And you think it was smart for YOU to come to the U.S.?"

Cross exhaled deeply, then retorted with a sly chuckle, "You better think it was smart, 'cause I'd hate to see what that oye was about to do to y'all."

Stink opened his mouth to launch a retort but decided against it. Cross had saved them and it wouldn't be the last time. "You win Cross," Stink announced in defeat.

"I know I do! Now let's handle this B.I.!" Cross announced jubilantly, giving Rah-Rah and Tia a conspiratorial wink. Suddenly Cross became extremely serious as he focused on Stink, "Now, tell me what was in that box, it had to be serious."

Momentarily, Stink relived the scene of him opening the box and seeing Melody's head. Quickly shaking the scene from his mind, he somberly said, "Melody's head."

Chapter Forty-Seven

"I've got to say you've got a tight little operation going on around here, nephew," Cross commented as they drove through the gates of a compound located deep in Chesapeake. Eyeing the men as they strolled the grounds with assault rifles and German Sheppard s in tow, Cross had to admit Rah-Ra's organization was a lot stronger than he initially thought.

"Thanks Unc," Rah-Rah responded with a hint of pride in his tone.

Once they pulled in front of the house, a group of heavily armed men approached the car and opened the doors for them, as if they were royalty.

"Come on Unc, I want to introduce you to my man," Rah-Rah said exiting the car.

Crossed stepped out of the car behind his nephew and watched as Rah-Rah gave each man an intricate handshake. When Rah-Rah got to the last man in the crowd, he gave a brotherly hug. Cross could see that his nephew had formed a special bond with each of the men, but the one he gave the hug to seemed to be the one who he shared the closest bond with.

"Uncle Cross, this my man B-Rock," Rah-Rah announced leading the man that Cross already knew was his partner.

B-Rock firmly shook Cross' hand, then said, "Rah-Rah speaks very highly of you and I am glad to finally meet you."

"Nice to meet you too," Cross replied flatly, doing a visual surveillance of the huge grounds. Suddenly he asked B-Rock," What the hell y'all doing way the fuck out here?"

B-Rock chuckled, then said," How about I just show you *what* we doing out here."

"Bay, are you alright?" Bonni asked in a worried tone, and although he hadn't answered her yet, she had already heard the sadness in his voice.

Stink closed his eyes and allowed his wife's soothing voice to comfort him.

"Rahsaan! Talk to me!" Bonni snapped, then added inquisitively, "What's wrong, baby?"

"Things are crazy here, baby, that's all," Stink offered.

"What do you mean crazy, Rahsaan? Crazy like what? Is Rah-Rah okay?" Bonni fired off questions rapidly.

"Yes, baby, he's okay. Everything is fine with us, it just that…." Stink's voice trailed off.

"It's just what, Rahsaan? You're scaring me, bay," Bonni revealed.

Stink released a light chuckle, then said, "Nah, bay, it's just that I miss you all and I can't wait to see y'all."

Bonni wasn't fully convinced with her husband's attempt at getting her to back off, but like the good wife she was, she acted as if she did. "Baby, just know that I love you and that I am always going to be here for you. Know that," she concluded in a sweet tone exemplifying the gravest amount of sincerity.

"I know, baby. I know," Stink replied. Bonni's voice alone had filled him up with a newfound vigor.

"I love you, bay, and I just want you to come home. Until then, I'll be here." With that, Bonni ended the call.

"Whoa!" Cross exclaimed loudly as the contents of the dimly lit basement came into view. "You can't be fucking serious, son," Cross stated beyond belief as the surface to air missiles that donned the U.S. Army insignia on them came into view.

"What do you think? Think we got enough shit to go to war?" B-Rock asked proudly.

"Depends on who you're fighting," Cross retorted, and then went over to examine the artillery.

Suddenly Rah-Rah appeared and handed Cross a very high-tech machine gun and said, "This for you Unc."

Cross eyed the gun closely, then turned to B-Rock and said, "Now we've got enough firepower to go to war," then turned his attention back to Rah-Rah and asked, "Why don't you tell me now how all this shit kicked off."

"We took all this and upwards a few mill in product from Jose," Rah-Rah divulged.

"But why?" Cross asked confused.

"Mo money, mo power," Rah-Rah concluded triumphantly, then gave B-Rock a loud slapping handshake.

Cross wanted to dig further in the matter, but the show of solidarity from the pair only filled him with glee. Instead, Cross switched gears and began to survey the situation. "Now, your sisters and Bonni are safe in Dubai. And the only woman your Pops ever really loved has gotten fucking decapitated by this sick motherfucker," Cross stated more so to himself than Rah-Rah and his partner. Then, as if it was common knowledge, he said, "Melody gets her fucking head cut off because she told Stink about Jose's plans to kill you and your men." Once the words were out, Cross couldn't take them back. He glanced at Rah-Rah and could see the hurt on his face. "You didn't know, huh?"

Somberly, Rah-Rah shook his head *'no'*.

"Well, there's nothing either of us can do now to bring her back or change any of the other shit that's happened, so let's finish this war that you started," Cross stated.

"Yeah, you right Unc," Rah-Rah replied in a low tone. It was evident he was bothered by the fact he had caused the entire fiasco.

Playfully, Cross punched Rah-Rah in the arm and said, "Well, let's go through some of these boxes and go get these rice and beans eating bitches."

Chapter Forty-Eight

"Baby, I want to go," Tia whined as she sat with her arms crossed at the end of the bed watching Rah-Rah dress.

"Nope," Rah-Rah answered flatly.

Tia acted as if she was a spoiled child, sitting there with her lips poked out making sulking noises. "Why can't I go, babe?" She pressed on.

"Because I said so. Now stop asking, because I'm not going to change my mind," Rah-Rah concluded with a sense of finality in his voice. As he continued to get dressed, Tia's sniffling cries filled the room. When Rah-Rah turned to look at her, her tear streaked face touched him deeply. "Come here, babe," Rah-Rah said gently.

Tia did as she was asked and swayed her sexy body over to his and fell into his outstretched arms. While they embraced as if they were never going to see each other again, Tia felt a kaleidoscope of emotions run through her body. There was no doubt that she loved him more than she loved anything and she wanted nothing more than to be with him. "Why can't I go baby?" She inquired in her most sincere tone.

Rah-Rah didn't want to go all into the spiel that his father had laid on him, therefore he simply said, "Cause I love you."

Tia's floodgates opened up as her cries became shrieks and tears wet Rah-Rah's clothing.

"Tia, look at me baby," Rah-Rah said lifting her tear stained face to meet his gaze. "Tia, I need you to be strong for me. There's no way I can go up against these dudes if I'm out there worried about you," he explained.

Tia looked up to Rah-Rah and said, "Babe, with the exception of my brother, you are all I have in this world and if I lose you, I don't think I could make it."

"I know baby, just be strong for me, okay?" Rah-Rah concluded, then placed a soft kiss onto her forehead. He reluctantly pulled himself away from Tia and busied himself while gathering the remainder of his things. With his back to her, he delivered the next twist. After talking with my father and uncle, they have made arrangements for you to be taken care of while we're away. But, I've made some arrangements myself-"

"Arrangements! What do you mean arrangements?" Tia asked apprehensively.

Rah-Rah swung around and presented her with a ring that he had made arrangements for just that day. "Will you marry me?" he asked kneeling on one knee.

Tia's face showed absolute shock as she exclaimed, "Yes! Yes, I will marry you!" She then hopped into his arms and began to kiss him wildly.

Rah-Rah endured this momentarily, then he expertly maneuvered her to where she was staring into his face. "Tia, I love you, babe, and after this is over, I'm outta here and I want you to go with me."

Tia planted a wet kiss onto his lips and said, "Babe, I'd follow you to hell."

Rah-Rah beamed at the happiness Tia exuded, then said, "B-Rock and a couple of our men are on the way here to meet with you."

"For what?" She asked.

"To bring you 2 million dollars."

"What do I need with 2 million dollars?" Tia inquired.

"You're going to meet my mom and my sisters in Dubai," he answered flatly.

"Dubai? Where the hell is that?" Tia asked.

"You'll see in about 24 hours," he stated slyly.

"Damn I'm glad you finally finished your goodbyes," Cross joked. "Did you tell her you love her?" he added full sarcastic humor.

Both Rah-Rah and Tia laughed at Cross' attempt at comedy.

Suddenly, B-Rock entered the house followed by two men carrying briefcases. B-Rock walked over to Rah-Rah and performed their customary handshake. "You all set, Blood?" He asked Rah-Rah.

"Ready as I'll ever be. Did you get everything I asked for?"

"Ain't no question I did," B-Rock retorted, pointing toward the two suitcases that the men carried.

Rah-Rah turned to Tia and gave her a somber look. She knew at that point it was time to part with Rah-Rah. The look that she received back from Rah-Rah said everything that needed to be said. With his unspoken statement playing in her mind, Tia held her head high, stepped over to Rah- Rah and gave him a sensuous kiss on his lips, then sashayed her way over to where the men carrying the briefcases were as they relinquished the briefcases to her.

Before Rah-Rah could show his appreciation for the way in which his woman handled the situation, B-Rock began to mount his own argument for why he should be allowed to accompany his friend and partner. "Blood, you know I need to be there with you, man," he began before Rah-Rah held his hand up instantly silencing him.

"Listen, B-Rock, man, you have been realer to me than anybody I know and for that I'll always be grateful, but *fo' real,* after all of this, I am out, homie. I'm out!" Rah-Rah stated as if he was trying to convince himself.

B-Rock looked to him with a look that was even more painful than the one he had received from Tia just minutes before. "I guess this is where we say our *goodbyes,* huh?" B-Rock joked.

"Nah, don't say goodbye, say see you later," Rah-Rah corrected.

"I love you man," B-Rock stated, then turned and walked away.

Had Rah-Rah been able to see his friend's eyes he would have seen the tears that shed from them.

Chapter Forty-Nine

"So you're standing here telling me that the men we sent are all dead?" Jose asked in bewilderment. "How is this possible?!" Jose yelled inquisitively. He peered around at the men in disgust, only to be met with bowed heads.

The room was so quiet that you could hear a pin drop if Jose hadn't been so engrossed in tapping his own pen against the table, as he waited for an answer from anyone of them.

"Answer me!" Jose yelled, which caused each of the six men situated around the table to focus their attention onto him. With his hands gripping the table's edge, Jose asked, "Why are Stink and Rah-Rah still alive and our best men dead?"

It was silence until Hernandez spoke, "We're not sure, Patron, but something happened that neither of them were prepared for." It was Hernandez who was Jose's second in command besides the now deceased Javier.

"You're not sure. What do you mean you're not sure?" Jose asked leaning in close to Hernandez sitting at the table. "If none of you know and some of you are not *'sure'* about what happened, maybe I should just kill all of you.

Everyone at the table began to fidget nervously as the realization of what Jose said set in. Even Hernandez, a long time servant of Jose, was fearful for his life. He had no idea how to perceive the man that stood before him. At that moment, Jose was not the man that he had come to love and honor. With nothing else o offer his boss, Hernandez said, "Patron, if you would allow me to take a small force to handle this situation, I promise you that I will not fail."

Jose laughed aloud, then retorted, "What makes you any better than the men I've sent?"

Hernandez felt as if his boss had smacked him in the face with an iron pipe. Stunned, he looked around at the other faces that were at the table and thought that maybe Jose had a point. Each man at the table sported a defeated look, further confirming Jose's belief. "Patron, if you give me this chance, I promise that I will not come back without annihilating your enemies," Hernandez pressed on.

Jose's laughter suddenly subsided as he began to speak. "Hernandez, your offer seems sincere and maybe if I had more time, I would take you up on it, but there will be no need for you to go anywhere. After the failed attempt on Stink's life, he will most definitely be coming to us."

Each man at the table looked around to each other as of this was some sort of shock to them. Nonetheless, it was Jose who knew better than any of them, and he knew that Stink was coming and he was coming full force.

Chapter Fifty

"So this is the notorious New York City, huh?" Rah-Rah asked from the backseat of the S.U.V. He stared out of the dark tinted windows at all of the city's early morning glitz and glamour.

"That's right, nephew, welcome to Harlem, U.S.A!" Cross said in an excited tone. He hadn't seen the city which had raised him, in over thirteen years. Suddenly the thought of his mother and sister crossed his mind. He desperately wanted to see them, but such a move would be crazy.

Stink glanced at Cross and his exuberance about being in the city and could only smile. Even that moment brought back memories for him as he thought of the times they ran the city as wild, rich and reckless teenagers. Momentarily, Stink reminisced about the times that they came to the city for no other reason than to *'stunt'*. "Man, we had a hellava time up this motherfucker," Stink stated as he was speaking his thoughts.

"Son, you took the words right out of my mouth," Cross replied as he steered the S.U.V. onto the familiar block and pulled in front of a tall building. "There it is," Cross stated to no one in particular.

Rah-Rah, although ready for war, was not sure whether they had reached their destination, so he asked, "We're where?"

Stink could see the deep contemplation going on in his friend's mind as he stared up to the building in which his mother and sister still lived.

Meanwhile, Rah-Rah was in the backseat asking questions in rapid fire fashion. Stink attempted to answer them all, but that was nearly impossible.

"Yeah, this is where I lived before…before everything…" Cross was unable to finish as his emotions boiled up inside and threatened to overflow. Suddenly, Cross' sights were drawn to the tenement's door as an older woman exited followed by an older gentleman. The sight of his mother caused Cross to lose it momentarily as tears began to run down his cheeks. He desperately wanted to reveal himself to her, but he knew it would have been too risky.

Stink reached over and gave his friend a reassuring pat on his shoulder. He understood the pain and anguish that his friend endured and he also understood that there was nothing neither of them could do about it.

Stink's reassuring pat erased all signs of emotion in Cross. Stink had always been there and Cross appreciated him dearly for that. Just as he whipped the S.U.V. out into the early morning traffic in the direction of Jose's East Hampton estate, he silently vowed to do whatever possible to insure that Stink and Rah-Rah made it home safely.

Chapter Fifty-One

As they drove by Jose's estate, Stink was surprised to see that the grounds were deathly dark, yet the interior of the cavernous house was lit up as bright as day. He was also surprised that they hadn't accosted any of the many guards that he knew normally patrolled the grounds around the estate. Stink knew that all of this was some type of ploy to lure them onto the estate. However, at that moment he was prepared for just about anything. He tossed Cross a knowing smirk, then said to his son, "You ready, son?"

"Ready as I'll ever be, Pops," Rah-Rah shot back full of vigor.

Without another word, Stink began to prepare himself for war. With an array of weaponry and several tools and gadgets in their possession, Stink, Cross and Rah-Rah exited the vehicle and began to strategically converge on the house.

After a short trek, the trio found themselves within twenty yards of the main house. Cross peered over to Stink, who was braced against the base of a tree trunk, and chuckled. His friend was way too cautious in times like these, yet in this case it may have been warranted.

Suddenly, Stink darted across the grounds to a large veranda that was connected to the house. As he took a quick look back, he saw Cross on his heels. It was already agreed upon that Rah-Rah would not come into the house with them.

"Everything looks clear, Pops," Rah-Rah's voice chimed in over the earpiece they wore for communication.

Cross looked to Stink with a look of apprehension and said, "This shit don't seem right, High."

"Way to easy, huh?" Stink added, then checked the harness strapped to him that carried the array of ammunition. The Kevlar vest that he wore was light in comparison to the firearms that weighed it down. Stink shot Cross one final look before taking position in a low crouched manner toward the French doors that led into the house.

"No movement, Pops, but be careful because once y'all are inside there is nothing else I can do but wait," Rah-Rah said over the earpiece. As soon as he saw his father and uncle enter the house, Rah-Rah quickly went into motion. There was no way that he was going to allow them to go into the dragon's lair without him. Once he reached the veranda, he swung his sniper rifle in all directions, using it's infrared scope to see through the darkness. Suddenly, something came into view that caused a cold chill to cover his entire being. And even though he saw what he saw, he still couldn't stop himself from walking right into the trap that awaited him. Unable to do anything to thwart what was about to take place, all Rah-Rah could do was watch.

"Wait until he is all the way in the room before you kill him," Jose instructed Hernandez as the large wall of monitors displayed Cross creeping down a long hallway. Jose then turned his attention to another screen where Stink was shown moving in the same way. Chuckling to himself,

Jose said, "Looks like today is my lucky day. Two for the price of one. I like deals." With a demonic grin on his face, Jose just knew he had both men where he wanted them. However, what he didn't see was his daughter roaming the house, clutching her teddy bear.

Cross could only hear static in his earpiece, yet he could vaguely hear either Stink or Rah-Rah attempting to reach him. After toying with the device without any luck of changing the sound, he tossed all inhibitions out of the window and said, "Fuck it," and continued on his course. He peeked inside every room in the hall looking for any threats that might try and present themselves. After several doors were opened, Cross finally hit pay dirt when he slid a door open only to see Jose with his back to him and a long streak of cigar smoke floating to the ceiling. Cross knew he had his man, but he didn't think that maybe his man had him. In his haste to destroy Jose, he had walked right into a trap.

From the moment he heard Rah-Rah make the call of distress for Cross, Stink's heart rate rose to levels of cardiac arrest. All he wanted to do was save his friend. With reckless abandonment, he ran through Jose's house with only Rah-Rah's instructions to guide him. Although Stink wasn't a religious man, he said a silent prayer that God would help to spare his friend's life.

"Pops, it's the next door on the right, but be careful because one of his men is behind the door.

Just before he reached the door that Rah-Rah had directed him to, he heard a succession of gunshots coming from within the room. This only incited Stink to move faster to save his friend. Although it was something that he didn't want to face, but at that moment he knew that his friend was dead.

"They shot him, Pops," Rah-Rah's voice somberly stated over the headset.

Stink's hurried pace was instantly slowed by his son's word. "I know, son. I know," he stated on the verge of tears. Suddenly the familiar touch of cold steel against his skin brought him back to reality. However, at that moment life didn't have the same meaning as it did a few minutes before. "Go ahead and kill me, nigga, I'm already dead," Stink retorted to his captor.

"Stink, my friend I've been awaiting your arrival. You've never been one to disappoint now, have you?" Jose's voice stated in a cold and murderous way.

From Rah-Rah's vantage point, he could see that his father had been captured as well. Although his heart beat like thunder in his chest, he knew that he held the wild card to the whole situation, He turned to the little girl that sat on the bed, and said, "Come on, let's go and see your father."

"So Stink, my friend, this looks to be the end of the road for you. I've have always held a high amount of respect for you but now it is all gone," Jose stated as he walked Stink inside the room where Cross' dead body lay crumpled on the floor.

Stink could do nothing but look at his fallen comrade through disbelieving eyes. Once the realization set in that he too was about to die, he looked up to Jose and said, "Fuck you, bitch!"

Jose chuckled and began to raise his gun to Stink's temple when a soft knock on the door halted him. Jose motioned for Hernandez to answer the door while he kept a close watch on who it may have been.

Hernandez carefully made his way over to the door then slid it open with his gun leveled at whomever it may have been.

Once the door was opened, the vision of Rah-Rah lovingly holding Soana in his arm nearly knocked Jose to his knees.

"No! Not my baby, please!" Jose begged

"At least say hello to your daughter, Jose. She was on her way to the kitchen to get some milk and I was nice enough to take her. You should be happy," Rah-Rah stated sarcastically.

"Please don't hurt my baby. I'll do anything," Jose pleaded.

With a devilish smile, Rah-Rah pointed to Hernandez and said, "Okay, shoot this motherfucker then."

Without a second thought, Jose raised his gun and shot his long time aide in his head, instantly killing him.

"Good. Now drop the gun and move over there," Rah-Rah instructed.

Jose did as he was told, then said, "Please don't harm my baby. She's all I got."

Stink jumped from his seat and retrieved Jose's gun from the floor. With the look of a crazed madman, he said,

"She's all you had." He walked towards Jose to face him. "You really think you're gonna live to be a father to her?" Stink asked sarcastically. "I will give you all that I own, just give me the chance to raise my daughter," Jose begged. "It seems to me, you didn't care if her mother raised her, so why should you be so lucky?" Stink toyed with him. Before Jose had a chance to respond, Stink raised his gun and shot him right between his eyes.

Chapter Fifty-Two

"Can I get either of you ladies anything else," the waiter asked as he stood at the foot of the lounge chairs that Bonni and Tia were lying in.

"Nothing for me. You want something, Tia?" Bonni asked snapping Tia from her thoughts under the bright sun.

Tia shielded her eyes from the sun, then said, "Yes, I'll have another Mimosa."

"Be right up," the waiter announced, then disappeared .

Bonni sat there behind the tint of her D&G sunshades and looked at Tia. There was something that she really liked about the girl. She could understand why Rah-Rah liked the pretty girl so much and they all were in agreement that she would be a nice addition to the family. However, the worried look that Tia kept etched into her features had begun to weigh heavily on her as well.

"Is there anything that you want to talk about, Tia?" Bonni asked

"I just miss him, Mrs. Jones. I've never been away from him this long and it hurts," Tia revealed.

"It's okay baby, they'll be fine," Bonni reassured her.

"I know, but I jus… just…" Tia voice trailed off as something in the distance caught her attention.

Suddenly, Bonni's attention was drawn to what had Tia's attention. The sight before them caused each of them to release a loud squeal. Coming their way was Rah-Rah,

Stink along with a little girl that Bonni had never seen before. She was so happy to see her husband that the little girl was an afterthought. Jumping to her feet, Bonni rushed in their direction with Tia on her heels. Once she reached Stink, she hopped in his arms and hugged him tightly. After planting kisses all over him, she slid from his embrace and quickly noticed the sadness in his eyes. At once, she asked "Where's Cross?"

"He didn't make it back," He answered flatly.

Bonni fought back the tears that threatened to come, then asked, "Who is this pretty little girl?"

"This is Soana, Melody's daughter," he said looking closely to judge Bonni's reaction.

"And where's Melody?" She asked

Stink dropped his head in defeat and that was enough for Bonni to understand that she had met the same fate as Cross.

Once again, Bonni fought back tears. The realization of what happened to the child's mother deeply saddened her. "Give her to me," Bonni stated in a motherly tone.

As Stink watched his wife walk away with the little girl whispering words of reassurance in her ear, he knew that she would raise her as her own, just as she reared Rah-Rah as her own. With that in mind, Stink looked up into the puffy clouds and said a silent prayer for his friend Cross and then made his way over to where the rest of his family was.

Tia was sad that she didn't get a chance to give her brother a proper funeral, but his cremated body remained with her in yearn. He was killed when her house was ambushed. She never talked about it, because the soldier in her wouldn't allow it.

<u>THE END</u>

Sample Chapter

Coming March 2013

Sexual Exploits of a Nympho III

By
Richard Jeanty

Chapter 1

"Damn, baby, you're tearing my pussy up! I don't know what's gotten into you this early in the morning, but I'm loving it," Tina told Darren while one of her legs was up on the dresser as the rest of her body leaned forward to allow Darren's twelve-inch dick full penetration. Since Tina and Darren got married, he made it his business to keep his wife sexually satisfied. Her sexual appetite never decreased and Darren figured he had to man up in order to please her. Sweat poured down his muscular frame as he stroked Tina hard, hoping she would climax at any moment, so he could rest for an hour or so before they went at it again. "Give it to me, baby," she moaned to encourage her husband's diligence to make her cum. Her sweet moans energized him. He slowly pulled his dick all the way out to the tip of his shaft, so she could feel the full throttle of his longness thrusting back in. The circumference of her opening wrapped tight around the head of his dick as he slowly stroked her pussy into submission. Tina's round booty had become Darren's natural aphrodisiac. He would get hard at the site of her body stepping out of the shower, or whenever she came to bed wearing sexy lingerie to entice him. Tina was buck naked and exercising her pussy muscle to maximize the thrilling feeling of her husband's big cock inside her. Darren enjoyed the tightening of her pussy muscle even more as the pressure mounted and forced him to grab her ass tightly and poured all of his love inside her. There was hardly any room between Darren's pubic area and Tina's ass, as his entire twelve inch dick found her sugar wall. "I'm coming again, baby. Stay right there. Don't move," Tina ordered, as she grinded her way to another explosive nut. Darren simultaneously closed his eyes to allow his own explosion to come about, inside Tina's wet pussy. "I will never get tired of this pussy," he whispered, almost out of breath.

That was pretty much the routine for Tina and Darren whenever it rained on the weekends. Rainy Saturdays basically consisted of hot sex, breakfast in bed, hot sex, take-out, hot sex, a rented movie, hot sex and then sleep. Darren had learned to reserve his energy for the rainy weekends to satisfy Tina's voracious sexual appetite. Darren needed to conserve energy for work during the week. He also had to be focused in order to keep from making an accounting mistake on his clients' reports at work. Burns and Young hired the best and brightest and Darren was definitely one of the best CPA's that firm had seen. During the week, Tina made use of all the toys she kept in the top drawer on the nightstand. Monday night was her rabbit night. That rabbit went through more batteries than a portable radio. Tina would spread her legs wide open on the bed while lying on her back and her rabbit would be in her right hand, ready to taste her carrot.

One Monday night, Darren came home early to find his wife screaming at the top of her lungs while the speed control for the rabbit was on top speed. The pulsating vibration sent to her clit by the rabbit forced Tina's octaves to go up as high as an opera singer. If it was anybody else walking through that door, they would've panicked and looked for the biggest knife they could find before heading upstairs, because they would've thought someone was hurting Tina. However, Darren had gotten used to her screams. Tina could never contain her loud screams whenever she was experiencing what she called "an outer body experience" orgasm. Darren stood in the middle of the kitchen and smiled to himself before sneaking upstairs to watch Tina and the rabbit go to war with her clit. He had that devious look on his face as he stroked his penis in the buff while standing at the door watching his wife with her eyes closed pleasing herself like the next nut meant the world to her.   Darren had started taking off his clothes while making his way up the stairs. By the time he reached the doorway, he only left his tie on, a hard dick in his hands and the will to fuck his wife until she passed out.

Tina was pleasantly surprised when she opened her eyes to find a naked Darren, a wide grin and a hard 12-inch dick ready to satisfy her more. "Do you need any help with that nut?" Darren asked while he massaged the shaft of his dick with his hand. "I think my mouth might be more of service to that big dick of yours," Tina responded. Darren moved towards the bed as Tina lay on her stomach and reached for her favorite 12-inch bat. Darren's dick was rock hard and Tina's mouth was running like a faucet. She was especially happy because Darren always worked extra late on Mondays and he would come home tired to the point where he could only take a shower and go right to sleep. The head of Darren's penis almost filled Tina's mouth as she wrapped her tongue around it before it disappeared into the warmth of her throat. It was soothing enough for Darren to close his eyes to allow the stress of his day to disappear from the forefront of his mind into the limited cluttered space he had in his brain. "Aaaaah," he whispered as Tina's magical tongue soothed the head of his hard dick. With both hands on his hip, Darren stood there like a super hero, but he wasn't rescuing anybody, he was being rescued by his wife's tongue. Tina had conjured up enough tricks with her tongue to know exactly how to make her husband cum. She wrapped her tongue around his dick like she was tying a knot and Darren knew he had to step back to keep from cumming prematurely. "Not yet, baby. I wanna enjoy your tongue. Don't make me cum yet," he begged. Tina smiled to herself because of the effect she knew she had on her husband. She sashayed her tongue down to his nuts and continued to massage them slowly. Darren reached for a hand full of hair as his wife comforted his balls with her tongue.

Finally, Darren could wait no more. Tina's skin glistened under the dim light that cast a shadow against her beautiful round ass. Darren reached to caress it and lost control. He grabbed both cheeks with both hands as Tina took his long dick in her mouth. Darren had also discovered in the last few months that Tina would lose control every time he massaged her anus. He used his middle finger to run circles around her anus, gently. Tina couldn't contain herself. "Fuck me! I want you to fuck me, baby," she begged. She spun around to bring her ass towards the edge of the bed so Darren could penetrate her from behind. He slowly entered, teasing the outer lips of her pussy with his gigantic dick. She shivered. She understood that his thrusts always made her lose control, so she grabbed a hand full of sheets for comfort as he dug deeper into her pussy. His dick was heavenly, totally incomparable to the feeling she received from the rabbit. This was the ultimate for her, penetration, no, Darren's penetration. He glided in and out of her slowly while squeezing her ass cheeks just hard enough to excite her further. "Baby, your dick is so sweet. Give it to me," she lamented, almost regretting that she had to use her rabbit before he walked in. Darren never felt he was in competition with any of her sex toys. As a matter of fact, he started buying them for her. He wanted to keep her happy. The site of her round booty kept his blood flowing and he wanted to please her. He augmented the speed of his strokes because he knew and understood that she would soon command him to go faster. "You know how I like it, baby. Yes! Give it to me," she yelled. Darren obliged. He released his grip from her ass, so she could feel the sting of his smack that would soon come. "Yeah, smack my ass, baby. Smack it like I'm on punishment, daddy" she said after the first sting. Darren knew her threshold for pain, so he added a little more force to the next few smacks on her ass while he stroked her pussy hard. There has never been a time when Tina didn't cum while Darren was fucking her from behind, and this time would be no different. Darren leaned his body forward and dug himself deep inside Tina's pussy, allowing her to feel every inch of him until she started rocking to the rhythm of his strokes while screaming, "I'm there, baby. I'm there. I'm fucking cumming!" Darren was always proud of his work in the bedroom. It was his turn to gather up his protein to make the dash to the finish line. He wrapped his hands around Tina's waist and brought his strokes from his knees up to a comfortable distance until he forced a nut out of his body into Tina's canal. He collapsed on top of her and she knew there would be no second round, at least, not on that Monday night.

Life has been pretty easy since Darren and Tina got married. They decided to delay having children because they wanted to spend more time with each other before bringing them into the world. Darren also wanted to travel the world with his lovely wife. Though he worked long hours and spent way too much time at work, Darren had accumulated a significant amount of vacation time at work. His boss was always forcing him to go on vacation, but he refused. Darren had a goal and he never even revealed it to his wife. He worked so hard and saved his money because he wanted to open his own accounting firm. It was while he was in bed with Tina one night he decided to let her in on his plans to leave his job the upcoming year. He had earned stock option, a 401K plan and had earned enough vacation time that equaled three months of his salary, whenever he decided to cash it in. Darren thought long and hard about his decision, but he knew he had to go with his heart. The short long weekend trips to the Bahamas, Miami and the Virgin Islands had become routine in Darren and Tina's life, but it was time to see beyond the Caribbean. However, Darren needed to maintain his focus and decided that he would wait a little while longer before taking his wife to Paris, France, on her dream vacation.

Tina played the role of supporting wife and decided not to press the issue with her husband. Darren's happiness was the ultimate to her and she didn't feel complete unless her husband was happy in every aspect of his life. Besides, she also understood that Darren was a visionary and he was planning for their future.

Serosa becomes the subject to information that could financially ruin and possibly destroy the lives and careers of many prominent people involved in the government if this data is exposed. As this intricate plot thickens, speculations start mounting and a whirlwind of death, deceit, and betrayal finds its way into the ranks of a once impenetrable core of the government. Will Serosa fall victim to the genetic structure that indirectly binds her to her parents causing her to realize there s NO WAY OUT!

In Stores!!!

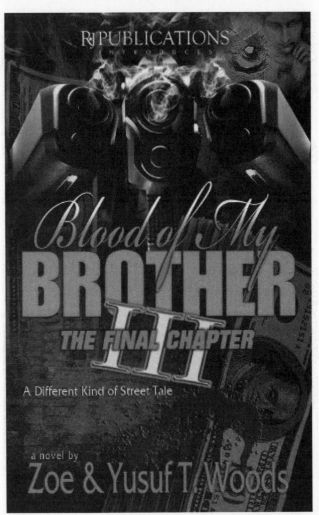

Retiring is no longer an option for Roc, who is now forced to restudy Philly's vicious streets through blood filled eyes. He realizes that his brother's killer is none other than his mentor, Mr. Holmes. With this knowledge, the strategic game of chess that began with the pushing of a pawn in the Blood of My Brother series, symbolizes one of love, loyalty, blood, mayhem, and death. In the end, the streets of Philadelphia will never be the same...

In Storess!!!

After Chasin' Satisfaction, Julius finds that satisfaction is not all that it's cracked up to be. It left nothing but death in its aftermath. Now living the glamorous life in Miami while putting the finishing touches on his hybrid condo hotel, he realizes with newfound success he's now become the hunted. Julian's success is threatened as someone from his past vows revenge on him.

In Stores!!!

It may not be Histeria Lane, but these desperate housewives are fed up with their neglecting husbands. Their sexual needs take precedence over the millions of dollars their husbands bring home every year to keep them happy in their affluent neighborhood. While their husbands claim to be hard at work, these wives are doing a little work of their own with the bedroom bandit. Is the bandit swift enough to evade these angry husbands?

In Stores!!

NEGLECTED SOULS

Motherhood and the trials of loving too hard and not enough frame this story...The realism of these characters will bring tears to your spirit as you discover the hero in the villain you never saw coming...

In Stores!!!

Jimmy and Nina continue to feel a void in their lives because they haven't a clue about their genealogical make-up. Jimmy falls victims to a life threatening illness and only the right organ donor can save his life. Will the donor be the bridge to reconnect Jimmy and Nina to their biological family? Will Nina be the strength for her brother in his time of need? Will they ever find out what really happened to their mother?

In Stores!!!

Betrayal, lust, lies, murder, deception, sex and tainted love frame this story... Julian Stevens lacks the ambition and freak ability that Miko looks for in a man, but she married him despite his flaws to spite an ex-boyfriend. When Miko least expects it, the old boyfriend shows up and ready to sweep her off her feet again. She wants to have her cake and eat it too. While Miko's doing her own thing, Julian is determined to become everything Miko ever wanted in a man and more, but will he go to extreme lengths to prove he's worthy of Miko's love? Julian Stevens soon finds out that he's capable of being more than he could ever imagine as he embarks on a journey that will change his life forever.

In Stores!!!

The police in New York and other major cities around the country are increasingly victimizing black men. The violence has escalated to deadly force, most of the time without justification. In this controversial book, noted author Richard Jeanty, tackles the problem of police brutality and the unfair treatment of Black men at the hands of police in New York City and the rest of the country.

In Stores!!!

Just when Darren thinks his relationship with Tina is flourishing, there is yet another hurdle on the road hindering their bliss. Tina saw a therapist for months to deal with her sexual addiction, but now Darren is wondering if she was ever treated completely. Darren has not been taking care of home and Tina's frustrated and agrees to a break-up with Darren. Will Darren lose Tina for good? Will Tina ever realize that Darren is the best man for her?

In Stores!!

Ronald Murphy was a player all his life until he and his best friend, Myles, met the women of their dreams during a brief vacation in South Beach, Florida. Sexual Jeopardy is story of trust, betrayal, forgiveness, friendship and hope.

In Stores!!!

Tina develops an insatiable sexual appetite very early in life. She only loves her boyfriend, Darren, but he's too far away in college to satisfy her sexual needs.

Tina decides to get buck wild away in college

Will her sexual trysts jeopardize the lives of the men in her life?

In Stores!!!

RICHARD JEANTY

Author of Rejected Sale, Writing Miss Right & Sexual Exploits of A Nympho

INTRODUCES

Me & Mrs. Jones

"A terrific debut effort from a great author"
Te Shaw E. Blue, best selling author of Harlem Girl Lost

A NOVEL BY

K.M. THOMPSON

Faith Jones, a woman in her mid-thirties, has given up on ever finding love again until she met her son's best friend, Darius. Faith Jones is walking a thin line of betrayal against her son for the love of Darius. Will Faith allow her emotions to outweigh her common sense?

In Stores!!!

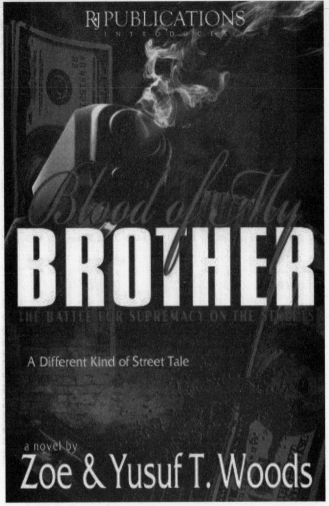

Roc was the man on the streets of Philadelphia, until his younger brother decided it was time to become his own man by wreaking havoc on Roc's crew without any regards for the blood relation they share. Drug, murder, mayhem and the pursuit of happiness can lead to deadly consequences. This story can only be told by a person who has lived it.

In Stores!!!

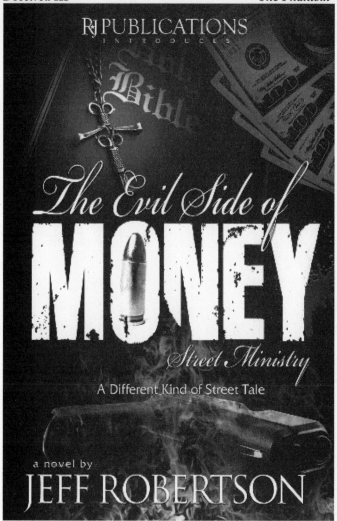

Violence, Intimidation and carnage are the order as Nathan and his brother set out to build the most powerful drug empires in Chicago. However, when God comes knocking, Nathan's conscience starts to surface. Will his haunted criminal past get the best of him?

In Stores!!

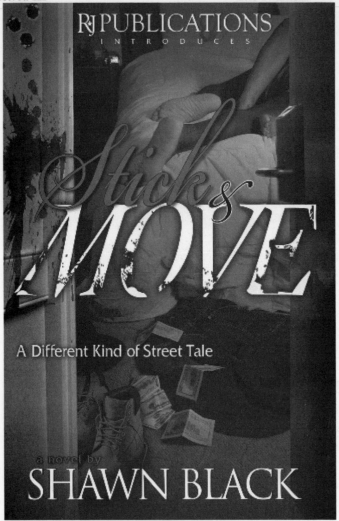

Yasmina witnessed the brutal murder of her parents at a young age at the hand of a drug dealer. This event stained her mind and upbringing as a result. Will Yamina's life come full circle with her past? Find out as Yasmina's crew, The Platinum Chicks, set out to make a name for themselves on the street.

In stores!!

Ashland's mother, Bianca, fights hard to suppress the truth from her daughter because she doesn't want her to marry Jordan, the grandson of an ex-lover she loathes. Ashland soon finds out how cruel and vengeful her mother can be, but what price will Bianca pay for redemption?

In stores!!

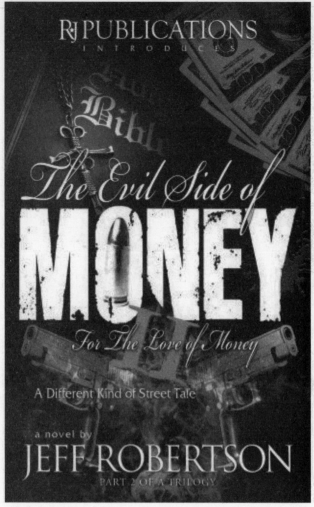

A beautigul woman from Bolivia threatens the existence of the drug empire that Nate and G have built. While Nate is head over heels for her, G can see right through her. As she brings on more conflict between the crew, G sets out to show Nate exactly who she is before she brings about their demise.

In Stores!!!

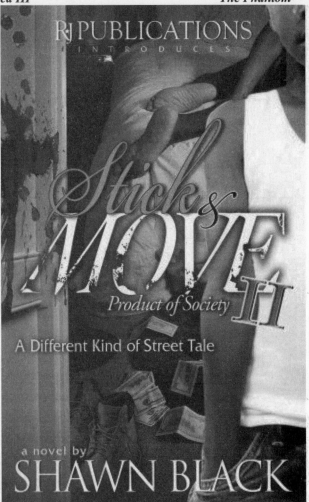

Scorcher and Yasmina's low key lifestyle was interrupted when they were taken down by the Feds, but their daughter, Serosa, was left to be raised by the foster care system. Will Serosa become a product of her environment or will she rise above it all? Her bloodline is undeniable, but will she be able to control it?

In Stores!!

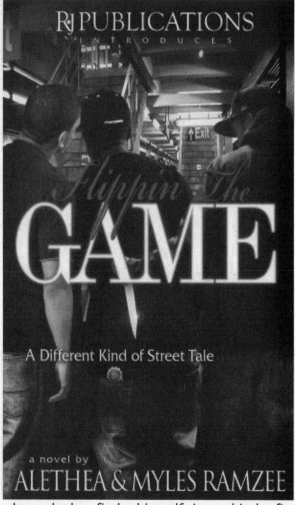

An ex-drug dealer finds himself in a bind after he's caught by the Feds. He has to decide which is more important, his family or his loyalty to the game. As he fights hard to make a decision, those who helped him to the top fear the worse from him. Will he get the chance to tell the govt. whole story, or will someone get to him before he becomes a snitch?

In Stores!!!

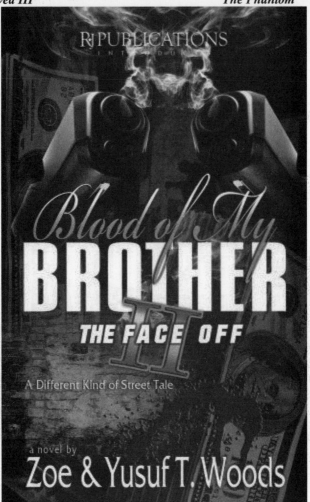

What will Roc do when he finds out the true identity of Solo? Will the blood shed come from his own brother Lil Mac? Will Roc and Solo take their beef to an explosive height on the street? Find out as Zoe and Yusuf bring the second installment to their hot street joint, Blood of My Brother.

In Stores!!!

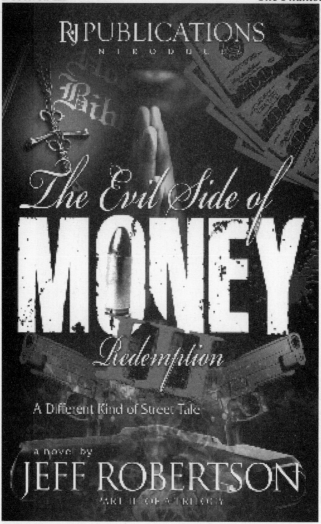

Forced to abandon the drug world for good, Nathan and G attempt to change their lives and move forward, but will their past come back to haunt them? This final installment will leave you speechless.

In Stores!!!

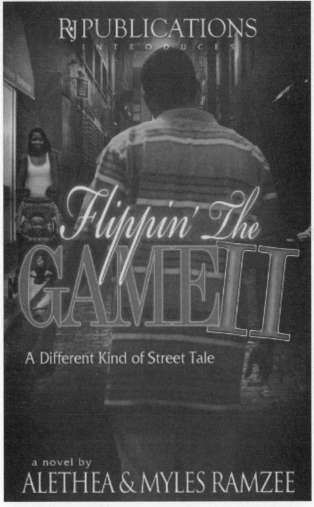

Nafiys Muhammad managed to beat the charges in court and was found innocent as a result. However, his criminal involvement is far from over. While Jerry Class Classon is feeling safe in the witness protection program, his family continues to endure even more pain. There will be many revelations as betrayal, sex scandal, corruption, and murder shape this story. No one will be left unscathed and everyone will pay the price for his/her involvement. Get ready for a rough ride as we revisit the Black Top Crew.

In Stores!!

Dave Richardson is enjoying success as his second book became a New York Times best-seller. He left the life of The Bedroom behind to settle with his family, but an obsessed fan has not had enough of Dave and she will go to great length to get a piece of him. How far will a woman go to get a man that doesn't belong to her?

In Stores!!!

Deon is at the mercy of a ruthless gang that kidnapped him. In a foreign land where he knows nothing about the culture, he has to use his survival instincts and his wit to outsmart his captors. Will the Hoodfellas show up in time to rescue Deon, or will Crazy D take over once again and fight an all out war by himself?

In Stores!!!

The drama continues as Deshun is hunted by Angela who still feels that ex-girlfriend Kayla is still trying to win his heart, though he brutally raped her. Angela will kill anyone who gets in her way, but is DeShun worth all the aggravation?

In Stores!!!

RICHARD JEANTY

Author of Neglected Souls and Neglected No More

Ignorant SOULS

THE FINAL EPISODE TO THE NEGLECTED SOULS SERIES

Buck Johnson was forced to make the best out of worst situation. He has witnessed the most cruel events in his life and it is those events who the man that he has become. Was the Johnson family ignorant souls through no fault of their own?

In Stores!!!

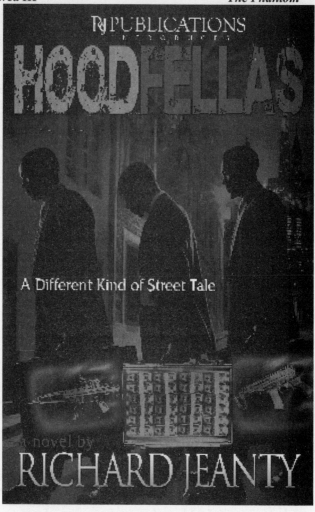

When an Ex-con finds himself destitute and in dire need of the basic necessities after he's released from prison, he turns to what he knows best, crime, but at what cost? Extortion, murder and mayhem drives him back to the top, but will he stay there?

In Stores !!!

RICHARD JEANTY

INTRODUCES

Insanely IN Love

WARNING
HIGHLY
ADDICTIVE
READING MATERIAL

A NOVEL BY
CEREKA COOK
Author of *Extreme Circumstances*

What happens when someone falls insanely in love? Stalking is just the beginning.

In Stores!!!

Pharaoh decides that his fate would not be settled in court by twelve jurors. His fate would be decided in blood, as he sets out to kill Tez, and those who snitched on him. Pharaoh s definition of Going All Out is either death or freedom. Prison is not an option. Will Pharoah impose his will on those snitches?

In Stores 10/30/2011

Kwame never thought he would come home to find his mother and sister strung out on drugs after his second tour of duty in Iraq. The Gulf war made him tougher, more tenacious, and most of all, turned him to a Navy Seal. Now a veteran, Kwame wanted to come back home to lead a normal life. However, Dirty cops and politicians alike refuse to clean the streets of Newark, New Jersey because the drug industry is big business that keeps their pockets fat. Kwame is determined to rid his neighborhood of all the bad elements, including the dirty cops, dirty politicians and the drug dealers. Will his one-man army be enough for the job?

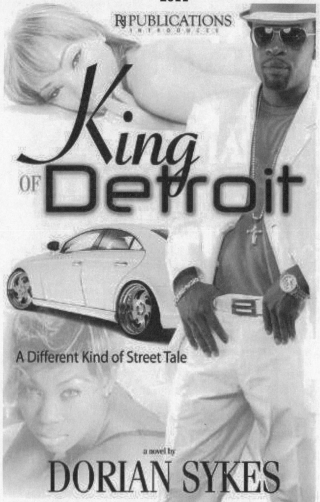

In Stores December 15, 2011

A Different Kind of Street Tale

a novel by

DORIAN SYKES

The blood-thirsty streets of Detroit have never seen a King like Corey Coach Townsend. The Legacy of Corey Coach Townsend, the Real King of Detroit, will live on forever. Coach was crowned King after avenging his father s murder, and after going to war with his best friend over the top spot. He always keeps his friends close. Coach s reign as king will forever be stained in the streets of Detroit, as the best who had ever done it, but how will he rise to the top? This is a story of betrayal, revenge and honor. There can only be one king!

In Stores February 15, 2012

PUBLICATIONS
BRINGING EXCITEMENT, FUN AND JOY TO READING

Use this coupon to order by mail

1. Neglected Souls, Richard Jeanty $14.95 Available
2. Neglected No More, Richard Jeanty $14.95 Available
3. Ignorant Souls, Richard Jeanty $15.00, Available
4. Sexual Exploits of Nympho, Richard Jeanty $14.95 Available
5. Meeting Ms. Right's Whip Appeal, Richard Jeanty $14.95 Available
6. Me and Mrs. Jones, K.M Thompson $14.95 Available
7. Chasin' Satisfaction, W.S Burkett $14.95 Available
8. Extreme Circumstances, Cereka Cook $14.95 Available
9. The Most Dangerous Gang In America, R. Jeanty $15.00 Available
10. Sexual Exploits of a Nympho II, Richard Jeanty $15.00 Available
11. Sexual Jeopardy, Richard Jeanty $14.95 Available
12. Too Many Secrets, Too Many Lies, Sonya Sparks $15.00 Available
13. Stick And Move, Shawn Black $15.00 Available
14. Evil Side Of Money, Jeff Robertson $15.00 Available
15. Evil Side Of Money II, Jeff Robertson $15.00 Available
16. Evil Side Of Money III, Jeff Robertson $15.00 Available
17. Flippin' The Game, Alethea and M. Ramzee, $15.00 Available
18. Flippin' The Game II, Alethea and M. Ramzee, $15.00 Available
19. Cater To Her, W.S Burkett $15.00 Available
20. Blood of My Brother I, Zoe & Yusuf Woods $15.00 Available
21. Blood of my Brother II, Zoe & Ysuf Woods $15.00 Available
22. Hoodfellas, Richard Jeanty $15.00 available
23. Hoodfellas II, Richard Jeanty, $15.00 03/30/2010
24. The Bedroom Bandit, Richard Jeanty $15.00 Available
25. Mr. Erotica, Richard Jeanty, $15.00, Sept 2010
26. Stick N Move II, Shawn Black $15.00 Available
27. Stick N Move III, Shawn Black $15.00 Available
28. Miami Noire, W.S. Burkett $15.00 Available
29. Insanely In Love, Cereka Cook $15.00 Available
30. Blood of My Brother III, Zoe & Yusuf Woods Available
31. Mr. Erotica
32. My Partner's Wife
33. Deceived I/ Deceived II
34. Going All Out I/ Going All Out II
35. Going All Out III 12/15/2012
36. Kwame 12/15/2011
37. King of Detroit / King of Detroi II 5/30/2013

Name_____

Address_____

City_____State_____Zip Code_____

Please send the novels that I have circled above.

Shipping and Handling: Free

Total Number of Books_____Total Amount Due_____

Buy 3 books and get 1 free. Send institution check or money order (no cash or CODs) to: RJ Publication: PO Box 300310, Jamaica, NY 11434

For info. call 718-471-2926, or www.rjpublications.com

Please allow 2-3 weeks for delivery.

Use this coupon to order by mail

1. Neglected Souls, Richard Jeanty $14.95 Available
2. Neglected No More, Richard Jeanty $14.95 Available
3. Ignorant Souls, Richard Jeanty $15.00, Available
4. Sexual Exploits of Nympho, Richard Jeanty $14.95 Available
5. Meeting Ms. Right's Whip Appeal, Richard Jeanty $14.95 Available
6. Me and Mrs. Jones, K.M Thompson $14.95 Available
7. Chasin' Satisfaction, W.S Burkett $14.95 Available
8. Extreme Circumstances, Cereka Cook $14.95 Available
9. The Most Dangerous Gang In America, R. Jeanty $15.00 Available
10. Sexual Exploits of a Nympho II, Richard Jeanty $15.00 Available
11. Sexual Jeopardy, Richard Jeanty $14.95 Available
12. Too Many Secrets, Too Many Lies, Sonya Sparks $15.00 Available
13. Stick And Move, Shawn Black $15.00 Available
14. Evil Side Of Money, Jeff Robertson $15.00 Available
15. Evil Side Of Money II, Jeff Robertson $15.00 Available
16. Evil Side Of Money III, Jeff Robertson $15.00 Available
17. Flippin' The Game, Alethea and M. Ramzee, $15.00 Available
18. Flippin' The Game II, Alethea and M. Ramzee, $15.00 Available
19. Cater To Her, W.S Burkett $15.00 Available
20. Blood of My Brother I, Zoe & Yusuf Woods $15.00 Available
21. Blood of my Brother II, Zoe & Ysuf Woods $15.00 Available
22. Hoodfellas, Richard Jeanty $15.00 available
23. Hoodfellas II, Richard Jeanty, $15.00 03/30/2010
24. The Bedroom Bandit, Richard Jeanty $15.00 Available
25. Mr. Erotica, Richard Jeanty, $15.00, Sept 2010
26. Stick N Move II, Shawn Black $15.00 Available
27. Stick N Move III, Shawn Black $15.00 Available
28. Miami Noire, W.S. Burkett $15.00 Available
29. Insanely In Love, Cereka Cook $15.00 Available
30. Blood of My Brother III, Zoe & Yusuf Woods Available
31. Mr. Erotica
32. My Partner's Wife
33. Deceived I/ Deceived II
34. Going All Out I/ Going All Out II
35. Going All Out III 12/15/2012
36. Kwame 12/15/2011
37. King of Detroit / King of Detroi II 5/30/2013

Name_____

Address_____

City_____State_____Zip Code_____

Please send the novels that I have circled above.

Shipping and Handling: Free

Total Number of Books_____Total Amount Due_____

Buy 3 books and get 1 free. Send institution check or money order (no cash or CODs) to: RJ Publication: PO Box 300310, Jamaica, NY 11434

For info. call 718-471-2926, or www.rjpublications.com

Please allow 2-3 weeks for delivery.